CODE ZERO

DAN ROY SERIES 8

MICK BOSE

CHAPTER 1

Dan Roy saw the muzzle flash seconds before the bullet found its target.

He did not think, he acted on pure impulse. He flung himself on the ground, and dived in the direction of a parked car. He needed cover.

A single shot, he assumed, from an elevation only meant one thing. Sniper. For any soldier on the ground, a horrible word. True, he was a retired soldier. For the last several years, he was a skilled black ops specialist, working for an ultra-secret organization called Intercept. But the reflexes had never left him. He kept his eyes peeled, and just as his six feet three, two hundred twenty-pound frame hit the concrete sidewalk, he saw a figure next to him crumple and fall. Less than six feet to his left. The victim looked like an old man. Dan kept himself pressed to the ground and watched as the old man's leg twitched, and his body shuddered. Then he was still.

Then the screaming began.

A pool of red liquid began appearing around the fallen figure. Pedestrians gathered around, unable to hide their curiosity. Many turned away, hand over mouth, shock on their faces. Dan had seen the round find its mark. Below the chin, aimed for the medulla oblongata of the brain. The only part of the body that caused flaccid paralysis. A professional hit. But he was not looking at the body anymore.

He was looking straight ahead, where he had seen the flash. A split second before the muzzle flash, sunlight had glinted off metal. The sniper was adjusting his aim. His target must have moved. That glint of sunlight had given him away.

The muzzle flash came from the opposite side, mid-level of a metal and glass office building. About the fifth floor, he guessed

Dan stood up, crossed the road, and walked quickly. Police sirens blared in the distance. He saw a woman standing on the sidewalk opposite, staring ahead with a blank expression on her face. Jet black hair, tied back in a ponytail. She wore a grey summer jacket, matched by grey pants. Her hazel green eyes were sharp, but attractive. She looked away as Dan caught her gaze.

She wasn't here by accident, Dan knew that. Momentarily, he stiffened. He didn't have a weapon on him, but he was willing to bet this woman did. There was pandemonium behind him, but this woman was quiet, observing. Like she was expecting it.

The building was half a block away, and as he got closer, he saw a tan coloured Ford sedan drive out leisurely from the subway parking lot.

One man driving. He wore a baseball cap and sunglasses, with a week`s worth of stubble on the face. The driver glanced at Dan, and their eyes met. For three seconds, the face stared at Dan. Dan looked back. He could not make out the features well, hidden as they were by the stubble, glasses and cap pulled low.

But for a second, a memory jolted in some dark recess of his brain. Like lightning over a desert night sky. Then it was gone. The car indicated and turned left, away from him.

The sedan was followed by a metallic blue Chevrolet, which turned in the opposite direction and went past Dan. Another solitary driver. Dark glasses again, but no cap. Short dark hair, heavy cheeks, Caucasian. He could not make out any other features as the car raced off. Dan broke into a run. He jumped up the stairs, and went through the revolving doors. There was a reception with a red carpet lobby. A security guard sat behind the desk. Dan ran past him and got into the elevator. "Hey!" said the guard, and scrambled to come around the desk. Surprise was in Dan`s favour. The guard got up to the elevator just as the gates shut. Dan got off at the fifth floor. There was no carpet on the landing. A long corridor led off to several rooms. Dan ran to the side that faced the street. He ran from window to window till he found the right one. Eight hundred yards away on the left, diagonally opposite, he could see the crowd gathering below. He looked at the bare floor. The killer would have taken any remaining shells. But there might be other signs. He knelt by the window, and touched the dust on the floor. He was at the right spot, because the dust had been disturbed.

"Freeze!" The scream came from behind him.

"Hands in the air!" Same voice, and he had not heard any other footsteps. He turned around slowly, hand locked behind his head. The guard was pointing a Glock 17 straight at him. Dan regarded him calmly. The guard was ten feet away.

Dan said, "There was a shooter here. Killed someone on the street." He jerked his head behind him. The guard licked his lips and looked nervous. Underneath his hat and uniform, he was just a kid. The Glock waved in the air like it was trying to catch a fly.

"Stand still," he barked, and shuffled to one side of Dan. He peered outside. He must have seen the knot of people, as he looked at Dan and his mouth fell open.

"How the hell did you know?"

Dan told him. The guard narrowed his eyes. "Who are you?"

"Call the cops," Dan said. "They will want to speak to both of us."

The guard gaped at him. Dan put his hands down. The guard looked uncertain. He was African-American, medium height, and looked barely out of school.

"What`s your name?" Dan asked.

"Leroy."

"Leroy, I am Dan Roy. Have you seen a tan Ford sedan or a blue Chevrolet in the parking lot today?"

Leroy thought. The Glock now faced the floor, but he did not take his eyes off Dan. "Why you wanna know?" he asked Dan.

"Because I just a saw man being killed in our capital city, in broad daylight. And I saw those two cars leave this parking lot straight after."

"Uh…no I haven't." He didn't seem to be lying, Dan thought.

"Put the gun away, Leroy," Dan said. "And come with me."

Dan ran down the stair well, and pushed his way out into the mild sunlight. Blue and white patrol cars had stopped traffic at both ends of the street. Uniforms shielded the public from the body on the ground. Two officers were putting yellow and black striped tape around the crime scene. A helicopter dissected the air overhead, the staccato beat of its rotors growing loud then fading. From the corner of his eye Dan saw two media vans arrive. A crew jumped out, and one went to the roof of the white van and opened up a small portable satellite dish.

Dan crossed the road, Leroy behind him. He jostled through the crowd and got to the front. A uniformed cop was ahead of him. Dan was about to call him when something got his attention. He saw the woman he had seen on the sidewalk opposite, staring at the dead man. Grey jacket. Hair pulled back in a ponytail, and a blue baseball cap. Her face was lifted up. From close up, her sharp features looked more attractive.

As Dan looked, their eyes met again. The woman turned her back and walked away. Dan was hemmed in by the crowd, but he turned and followed. He walked through the throng as fast as he could. He saw the woman turn the corner around a Starbuck`s and disappear.

Dan increased his pace. He passed by the posters on shop windows, welcoming the British Prime Minister for her upcoming trip to USA. A one week tour, with three cabinet members.

He stood for three seconds outside Starbuck's, and then saw her ahead of him, on the same side. Thirty metres away, roughly. He followed slowly. His mark did not seem to be in any rush. They headed up northwest on Pennsylvania South West. It was midday and traffic was growing on the avenue. Dan watched the woman cross the crowd outside Potomac Avenue Metro, stopping to let an old lady pass. Something about the way the woman walked bothered Dan. They had walked three blocks now. If she knew he was being followed, she gave no indication of it. That was the mark of a professional.

A pro always did routine, everyday things when she knew she had a tail. Hair prickled at the back of Dan`s neck.

As they got closer to Capitol Hill, the woman ducked inside a building that said Public Library. Dan walked slowly past the entrance of sliding glass doors. There were signs on a bulletin board outside for rental apartments, local book fairs, music gigs. Dan caught a flash of grey pants standing at the reception, with her back to him. Dan walked ten metres, then stopped at a newspaper stand, pretended to leaf through a magazine, then came back to the library. He could not see the woman at the reception anymore, and she had not walked out the library. Dan went in.

The library was a two story structure. White tables and red and yellow plastic chairs lay around the main foyer. Aisles of bookshelves lay behind the reception desk. Opposite the desk a flight of stairs wound up, next to an elevator. Dan walked past the reception to the bookshelves at the back. They were arranged alphabetically. He was standing at the first row of bookshelves when he felt a presence behind him. He turned around.

The woman was facing him, her hand resting lightly on a tell-tale bulge on her right hip. Her dark eyes appraised Dan with a cool gaze. She wore a white shirt beneath her grey jacket, the top two buttons undone. The tight grey pants were wrapped around a pair of toned legs.

"FBI", the woman said in a clear voice. She flashed her badge. "I am Special Agent Trisha Dunne." She fixed Dan with a dead stare. "You are wanted for questioning. You need to come with me."

CHAPTER 2

Riyadh
Saudi Arabia

Rashid Al-Falaj stared out the bulletproof black tinted windows of his Lincoln SUV as the 24 valve, 6 litre engine purred smoothly down the King Fahd Highway. The eight lane highway connected the city from north to south. As he watched the brightly lit skyscrapers on either side of the road that turned night into day, he wondered how the name of Riyadh was so apt. The word meant garden in Arabic. And a garden it certainly was. An opulent, exorbitant, shiny metal and glass garden in the desert.

They were driving past the main commercial hub, and in the mid distance he could see the green hued Kingdom Tower. Residential blocks surrounded the financial district, built in the grid format inspired by American cities, and designed by American architects.

Rashid leaned his head back on the seat. He had his usual two bodyguards with him, one at the front and the other beside him. But no one, not even the driver knew where they were headed. Rashid gave the driver manual directions. He had to be careful. Riyadh was the capital of the Saudi Kingdom, and its political, financial and military nexus. No member of his influential family knew he was here.

The Al-Falaj family were into oil field infrastructure. Rigs, cranes, hydraulic pumps, drills, they provided the whole lot. As the oil fields had boomed across the region, so had the Al-Falaj family business. Rashid personally knew several of King Abdullah`s direct cousins. His father, Farzad, knew the king himself. But his father was old now, and weak. Rashid`s inspiration in life had been his uncle. His father`s older brother. Khalid. That man, like Rashid, hated the Western world. Khalid, regarded the west as parasites feeding on his country`s natural resources. Like Khalid, Rashid had come to regard violence as the only way to rectify this. After Khalid died, no martyred, fighting for Al-Qaeda in Sudan, Rashid`s views had hardened.

Which put him at odds with his father, Farzad. The man who held all the power in the family. The man close to the royal family.

As Farzad`s only son, the money and power would one day fall to Rashid. He wanted that to happen. The Sheikh had shown the way. What a man could do with money from his family dynasty. To get it, Rashid knew he had to wait and bide his time. It was happening already. He was signing documents worth tens of millions of dollars. Much of it to hateful American contractors. He smiled as he signed the pages. One day, he would make them pay. Rashid had made his father invest heavily in the US real estate market following the financial crash of 2008. The more land and foreclosed houses Rashid made his father buy, the closer he got to his aims. In Rashid`s view, the stupid financial community made it easier for him, begging him to invest.

They only saw his money. His petrol dollars.

They never saw the hate. The rage. The burning rage.

How would they feel, his uncle Khalid used to say, if we went and occupied their country?

Are we not allowed to be patriots too? This is our revolution.

"Sir." The driver called, breaking into his thoughts.

"Yes?" Rashid asked, after a pause.

"We are approaching King Salman Air Base."

"Go past the base and head down south to Al-Nakheel," Rashid ordered.

"Very well, sir," the driver said. His body guards remained still. Compact Uzi sub machine guns rested on their laps, slung from shoulder straps. Their eyes were active, noticing the cars following them, and the road ahead.

Al-Nakheel was not a desirable part of Riyadh. In 2003, two terrorists were caught in a house arrest. Since then, the place had been gentrified. Still, it remained an area where petty crime and prostitution flourished, and where alcohol, which was illegal in the kingdom, was available easily.

The SUV turned down a succession of streets till it came to house inside a compound. The iron doors were opened by two security guards. Rashid waited till the doors were shut. Then he alighted from the SUV and walked towards the only entrance to the property, a bullet and bomb blast proof steel door. His bodyguard knocked on the door, and it opened. Rashid stepped inside with one of the bodyguards. The safe house was one of several Rashid owned in Riyadh. It was where he held meetings with the Islamist radicals who kept a low profile in Riyadh. Mainly, they came to him for money. To fund operations abroad.

And occasionally, as in now, they came in search of something more meaningful.

The sparse living room had brown carpet on the floor, and red curtains that hung from the windows. The windows had steel shutters, which were now lowered. The room was soundproof. The door clicked shut behind Rashid as he walked in. In the middle, on a table and three chairs, sat an old man. An old white man. He wore western clothes, a suit and tie. He even had a hat, which he clutched nervously in his hands. The man stood up slowly as Rashid approached him. "Salam walekum," the old man said.

Rashid nodded. "Walekum salam." He stretched his arm out, at once pleased that the man had shown the right manners. "Please have a seat."

Rashid looked at the man curiously. He had not expected a man of his years to have made the journey. A perilous journey, some would say. A forged passport, stopping at UK, taking the ferry across Gibraltar to North Africa, and then to Riyadh. The man`s clothes spoke of a bygone era. His suit was of dark blue twilled cotton, fashionable in Europe maybe three decades ago. The cuffs of his shirt were frayed. But his dark grey eyes were sharp. He caught Rashid looking at him.

"You are wondering what a man of my age is doing here," the man said in a clear voice. His accent was American.

Rashid remained impassive, but he could not help be impressed by the man`s powers of deduction.

"The thought had crossed my mind," Rashid said.

"I knew your uncle. Khalid. A good man."

"That is why you are here. The letters you sent had been written in my uncle`s hand."

"He spoke of you," the old man said. "He told me had a nephew who would one day be like him."

Rashid smiled. The old man was lying. Still, he could humour him. "Really?"

The old man shook his head. He looked rueful all of a sudden. "I am not lying. I have lived too long for that, and to waste your time."

Rashid sharpened his voice. "What are you here for then?"

The old man`s eye held Rashid`s. "Khalid and I had a Russian friend. I am here to tell you about him."

The old man began his story. Rashid listened, his attention suddenly hooked on what the old man had to say. When the old man had finished, Rashid got up and paced the room. He came to a stop in front of the man, who was watching him. "What do you want?"

"What does everyone want? Money, of course."

"You will tell me of the precise locations once the money has been transferred?"

"Yes."

Rashid thought for a moment. Abruptly, he motioned to one of his bodyguards. The man strode over, and poked the snout of his Uzi into the old man`s back. Rashid walked out of the room, and the old man followed. The Uzi remained buried in his back.

Rashid went down a flight of stairs. He followed it down three flights till he came to a basement. It was protected by a similar steel door. This section was made of three sea freight containers lain down next to each other. Each communicated with the other via a door. Rashid went to the last one, and switched on a bright overhead light. The roof of this container had been removed. A concrete ceiling was in place, more than twenty feet above ground. Above that, another twelve feet of concrete as foundation.

He watched as the old man came inside the room. He looked up, and stumbled a step backwards. The bodyguard muttered an oath, and pushed the old man straight. The old man`s face was drawn and white. His eyes were wide. He stared at Rashid, the earlier composure gone from his face.

The smell in the room was palpable. Urine and sweat. From a steel beam going across the ceiling, a man hung from a hook. His hands were tied above his head, and the rope was attached to the hook. His face was masked in blood, and he was naked apart from a loin cloth. Whip marks crisscrossed his body. Bruises and swellings adorned his limbs, signifying blunt trauma and broken bones.

Rashid motioned to the guard, and the steel beam lowered. The bodyguard pushed the old man forward. The man breathed heavily. They came up close to the body, a barely alive human being. Without a word, the guard reached inside the man`s mouth and thrust the jaw`s open. The old man gasped in fear and stumbled back again, only to feel the cold steel muzzle of the Uzi.

Dark congealed blood seeped out from the corners of the tortured man`s mouth. The old man stared in fear till he understood. He looked at Rashid, his breath hard, laboured. Rashid said, "This man was a traitor. He was working with the Saudi intelligence officers. He had infiltrated our organisation. Do you know what we did?"

The old man found his voice after a while. "You…you cut off his tongue."

"Yes," Rashid said. "I want you to remember this. Whatever happens, I do not tolerate traitors."

The old man was silent for a while. Then he said, "I understand."

CHAPTER 3

Knightsbridge
London, UK
One week later

The parade of Lamborghini`s and Ferrari's glinted in the street lights as they roared down Old Brompton Road. Traffic was light at this time of the night. Past 10pm. The age old cliché of London never sleeping has some truth to it. Pubs have lock downs, and night clubs go on till early hours of the morning. In the glitzy bars and cafes of London`s expensive western corner, the night was just beginning.

For the denizens of significantly higher echelons, the time of the night or day did not matter. That, mused, Rashid, as he tightened his grip on the embroidered leather steering of his Lamborghini Diablo, was just as well. Ostensibly, he was about to go into a party.

He kept his eyes on the rear-view mirror. His cousin, Syed, was following close behind in a red Ferrari Testarossa. They raced each other briefly, before Rashid slowed down. They could not afford to get stopped by police. Rashid parked the car smoothly, and opened the hatch door, stepping out into the cold night air. He nodded at Syed who approached him. No bodyguards today.

They turned and entered the private member`s night club. Frequented only by the wealthiest cream of London's elite, Rampton's had a waiting list of more than one year. Royalty and Hollywood glitterati made appearances here. So did Saudi playboys. The guards at the door politely let them enter. Rashid entered the dimly lit, plush interior and headed for the bar. He ordered coke with ice and lemon for himself and his cousin. They took their drinks and went upstairs to the private member`s room.

The two Arabs sat down and sipped at their drinks. The door was reinforced solid steel and grenade blast proof. There was one window in the medium sized room that looked down at a courtyard below. Two armed guards roamed the courtyard, helped by eyes on the roof of the buildings opposite. The glass on the window was bullet proof.

After two minutes, there was a discreet knock on the door. Syed got up and opened the door. A blond haired, dark suited Englishman entered. He shook Syed`s hand and then Rashid`s.

Rashid said, "Good evening, Mr..."

"Kuznevski."

They shook hands. The man worked for the military attache at the Russian Embassy in Kensington Palace Gardens. He decided to prod further.

"We are alone here, Mr Kuznevski. There are no bugs in this room. The MI5 or 6 would never be able to access this place."

Mr Kuznevski smiled. "You will forgive me for not underestimating the British secret service, especially on their

own turf. Even the Mossad respect their listening skills."
Rashid looked at the man closely. He had come highly
recommended, and it was showing. Rashid himself was
careful about these matters. He was paranoid about being
tailed, hence had arranged this meeting to look like friends
having a drink at a nightclub. His team had swept the room
for bugs, but Kuznevski was right, it wasn't worth taking the
risk.

Rashid said, "Very well. What do you suggest?"
Kuznevski said, "Shall we head down to my car?"
Rashid and Syed exchanged a glance.
"Do you mind if my cousin checks your car out first?"
Kuznevski was all smiles. "Of course not." He stood up.
In ten minutes, they were sat inside Syed`s Ferrari. If
Kuznevski was annoyed at having his Ford Mondeo turned
down, he did not show it. He explained his information to
Rashid, who listened carefully.

"Mr Kuznevski, or whatever your real name is, why should I
believe any of this?"
Kuznevski said, "You met the old man in Riyadh?"
"Yes."
"Then he would have told you. I have further proof."
Kuznevski pulled out a sheaf of papers from his coat pocket.
He handed them over to Rashid. They were satellite images.
Some of them had been magnified. The structures that
Kuznevski pointed out were clearly visible.
"So?" Rashid frowned.
Kuznevski pulled out a printed report. He handed it over to
Rashid. He read it slowly the nodded.
"So you think this will work?"
Kuznevski seemed slightly annoyed by the question. "Mr Al-
Falaj, I assure you, this has been a long time in the making.
This is guaranteed to work. Our main problem is an
operational one. We need to have men inside, and have
access."
"Access to America?"

"Yes."

Rashid smiled at the man. "Let me tell you something, Mr Kuznevski. If you have money, anyone can access America. My family is one of the biggest investors in real estate around Chicago, Atlanta and Dallas. We pumped $200 million into those markets last year alone. No one will stop me from going in and out of USA. I can arrange all our operational issues."

CHAPTER 3

FBI Field Office
DC

They sat in an interrogation chamber, with a rectangular, black tinted glass window on one wall. The walls were a drab gray, a color that seemed to suit the expressions on the faces of Trisha Dunne and a male agent, Mark Bellamy, as they faced Dan Roy. Dunne did the talking.

"Identify yourself," she said.

Dan took a closer look at her. Her hair was combed straight down and curled up just above the shoulders. Light green eyes, almost olive skinned, small nose and firm but nice lips. She sat with her back straight and her shoulders squared. FBI agent. A hot one. He noticed the shapely eyes moved rapidly from one end of his shoulders to another, and down his chest. Dan stayed relaxed in his uncomfortable chair. He told them his name.

Trisha repeated it, like she was expecting his name to spark a memory. "Dan Roy."

"Yes."

"What do you do?"

"Not much."

In the silence that ensued Dan stared back at Trisha. Her eyes were hard like early morning frost.

"Enough to get involved in a street shooting, I'm guessing,"

Trisha said.

"I didn't do anything."

"That depends. You crossed the road immediately after the event. That's when I saw you. You ran towards a building. The Langhorne Office block, as it happens, and went inside."

"If you say so."

Trisha leaned forward. "Mr. Roy, I don't know who you think you are. But we are the FBI, and this is our patch. By cooperating, you can help yourself. Do the reverse, and we can arrest you."

Dan raised an eyebrow. "On what charges?"

Bellamy intervened. "We looked into your file already. You have a military background. Special Ops, to be precise. Squadron B, SFDOD or Delta. Your operational info is redacted. We rang the DOD, but they couldn't provide clearance. In fact, they kicked it upstairs. We're still waiting to hear from them."

Dan said nothing. Trisha pursed her lips. "So how about you cut the crap, Mr Roy, and tell us what you were doing down here."

"Call me Dan."

"Ok, Dan. Now, answer the damn question."

Dan knew he had to play for time. He couldn't answer the question truthfully.

Trisha said, "What were you doing this morning at the corner of K Street and 13th South East?"

"I was heading down to the river for a stroll."

"We were looking at the CCTV camera footage," Trisha continued. "You were closest to the victim, and you dived just before the shot was fired. Why?"

Which meant they had their own cameras. It would be impossible to get hold of some sleepy official in the county hall to get the street camera film this quick, and get it analysed. Which opened up a whole new can of worms. The FBI was doing their own surveillance on this operation.

Dan kept his voice level. "What were you guys doing there?"

Trisha`s eyes glinted. "It's us who are asking the questions here, Mr Roy. I thought you got that already."

Dan held her eyes. Without taking his eyes away, he drawled slowly, "I saw the sun glint on the barrel, and then the muzzle flash as the shot fired. You ever faced sniper fire, Miss Dunne?"

Bellamy leaned forward. "One could say, you were almost expecting that shot to be fired, Mr Roy."

Dan swivelled his eyes at him. "As you had your own camera's there, I think it's actually you who was expecting the man to be shot."

Trisha and Bellamy exchanged a glance. She asked, "Who told you we had our own cameras there?"

Dan explained his reasoning. Both of them listened without changing expression.

Trisha said, "You ever worked in law enforcement, Dan?"

"No," Dan said shortly. But I know how you guys work, he thought to himself.

Trisha said, "The way you took cover, it seemed you were expecting the shot to come."

"We've been through this already, right?"

Trisha asked "You were not there to meet the victim?"

"No. I was not." From their expression he could tell they didn't believe him.

"Tell us why you went into the Langhorne building."

"That's where the sniper fired from."

Trisha said, "You saw a muzzle flash and learnt the location from just that?"

"In combat, a muzzle flash is what you look for to locate the enemy. I'm used to it. But no, it wasn't just that. The sniper adjusted his aim. The barrel moved and the sun glinted on it. That's what alerted me first, and I looked up."

He was right next to me. I could have helped him. But it happened too quickly.

Trisha asked, "What did you find when you went up there?"

"Pretty sure I was at the right window on the fifth floor. There was some gun powder residue on the sill. The office block is still under renovation, and the dust on the floor by the window had boot prints."

"Anything else?"

"I saw two cars leave the building straight after."

"Two cars?"

"A Ford sedan and a blue Chevrolet."

Dan watched as Trisha wrote something down.

"So?" she asked.

"So what?"

"So why are the cars important?"

"I reckon one was a decoy getaway car, the other one the real thing."

"Do you?"

"Yes. There is rear access to the building, but not for a car. The shooter stowed his gun and clothes in one car, and jumped in the other. They drove off in opposite directions."

"Did you get their registration plates?"

"Only of the Ford. They turned in opposite directions. I could not look both ways."

Trisha said, "Did you recognize any of the drivers?"

Dan kept his face impassive. Trisha was a skilled interrogator. She was fishing, but it was in the right spot. For now, a blind spot in Dan's mind. It was frustrating as hell to think he almost knew one of the faces. The driver in the tan Ford Sedan. But for the life of him, he couldn't be sure.

"No, I didn't," he said out loud. He looked at Bellamy, then Trisha. "Am I free to go now?"

Trisha stared at him for a while without speaking. Then she said, "Give me the license plate of the Chevrolet."

Ten minutes later, Dan was out on the street. He walked down three blocks, then went inside a Starbucks. He took out his cell and rang the number.

"It happened. We need to meet."

The voice on the other end said, "I'm sending you a link. Click on it to get a GPS location. Don't worry, the link is nontraceable. See you in half an hour."

CHAPTER 3

The park at the intersection of Fourteenth and Tenth was a less than an acre. Large enough for two men to sit on a park bench and without attracting too much attention. Dan was waiting for five minutes before he saw Jim McBride, his old handler from Intercept. Dan had quit Intercept two years ago, tired of their games. Officially, he was retired. Unofficially, he helped McBride out behind the scenes.
Dan watched McBride turn the corner of the enclosed kiddies playground. He wore his trademark black Fedora hat and black trench coat. Without a glance in Dan's direction, McBride sat down next to him. His right hand went inside the coat pocket and produced a cylindrical machine that looked like a flashlight. He pressed a button and a hum emanated from the top. He put the machine upright between them. Dan looked at the low frequency sound diffuser. Designed to hide their voices in case there was a listening bug nearby.
He said, "I thought this place was clean. It's a park."
McBride grunted. "Not like you to trust a location."
Dan shrugged. "You picked it. Anyway, you heard what happened?"
"I didn't have eyes. But heard it on the radio."
Dan explained to McBride. The old man said, "The Feds picked you up? Why?"
"I saw the female agent when I crossed the road. She tracked me later. More to the point, what the hell were the Feds doing there?"
"Damn," McBride said softly.
"You said he had information. Something big is about to happen, right?"
"Yes. But that's all he told me. Maybe he told the Feds as well, hence they followed him."
Dan nodded. "That makes sense. The Feds played kept their

cards close to their chests. But I got the feeling they knew nothing about this guy."

McBride was staring straight ahead. He swore again softly, under his breath.

Dan said, "You need to give me something more. Who was this guy?"

"Victor Kowalski. Don't know if that's his real name. He was an asset for the CIA. Provided information in exchange of us helping him to escape Moscow, and rights to settle here. Long time ago now, in the later years of the cold war."

Dan frowned. "A sleeper agent?"

"Not exactly. Most of the information he had on the GRU and KGB was old stuff. In this day and age, I doubt he would be of much help."

"But he knew something important enough to silence him." Dan narrowed his eyes. "Wait. He was obviously tracked, right?"

"Yes."

"How did they know he was about to speak to me? Or to the Feds?"

"I don't know."

"The sniper had a reason to take him out at that moment. He knew Kowalksi was going to make contact. With me, for sure, and if the FBI had surveillance on him, maybe with them as well."

McBride turned to Dan. "Are you saying there's a leak?"

Dan was staring at the green grass a few feet away. A deep frown crossed his face. "Or maybe the bullet was meant for me as well."

He met McBride's eyes, and he saw understanding in them. McBride said, "This has nothing to do with me, Dan."

"How did Kowalski contact you?"

"Through a friend in the Pentagon. A retired General."

"Let me guess. A general who works for Intercept as well?"

"He used to, yes. Kowalski was a ranking Colonel in the GRU. He had information we could get nowhere else. He became friends with this general. They lost touch till he rang a week ago."

"I wonder why."

McBride spread his hands. "Now, we need to find out." He softened his voice. "I wouldn't deliberately put you in harm's way, son."

"Is that why you didn't go to meet him yourself? To stay out of harm's way?" Dan's steely eyes held McBride captive. The old man stared back, unflinching.

"Go ahead and believe what you want," McBride said softly. "But this is bigger than you or me now. We need to find out fast what Kowalski knew."

Dan ran a hand through his hair. "I don't trust Intercept. You know that."

"I do. And for the record, I'm worried too."

His tone made Dan look back at the old man. McBride said, "You are right. There is a leak somewhere. Or they wouldn't know when to take him out. But you?" McBride shook his head. "I can't see why Intercept wants you dead."

Dan shrugged. "I know too much. Stuff the US Government will never admit to. You know that better than me."

"You're not the only one, Dan. There are three to four hundred special ops men and women who take part in deniable missions."

Dan said, "The first bullet missed. The second hit target. I'm thinking the sniper didn't miss deliberately."

McBride furrowed his brows. "I don't know Dan. It's something you'll have to figure out. But Kowalski did say something that you should know."

"What's that?"

"This thing he wanted to talk about? He said it will start a war."

CHAPTER

Valona stared in disbelief at the TV screen. A helicopter showed the view from above, and the camera zoomed down to street level. Valona could hear the bursts of speech from the reporter as her voice rose above the din of the helicopter's rotors.

"…elderly gentleman…gunshot wound…head…dead on arrival…audacious-

The rest of the words blanked out for her. She sat down heavily on the sofa. The remote fell from her hands to the floor. A numbness was growing inside her chest, spreading into her limbs. She closed her eyes to stop the dizziness threatening to overcome her.

Victor, her father's last words came back to her, his voice swimming across a million miles.

"You need to escape, Valona. They're coming after me, and they'll kill you too. Especially you. I have to meet someone today in DC. If anything happens to me, you'll know."

She gripped her forehead and thought about what her father had told her about the research. The findings she had made. When Victor had found out he promised her not to publish them. But somehow *they* knew.

Valona didn't know who they were. But her father's voice spoke in her memory again.

"*This country is no longer safe for us. They're coming to kill me. I'm sorry. I let you down.*"

She had listened wide eyed, till tears prickled at the back of her eyes. Her father seemed broken as he uttered the words. He never clarified what was happening, or why. His head hung over his chest and he was unable to meet her eyes. Alina, her mother's illness, had been soul destroying for both of them. Her death had taken a toll, but this was something new.

"Who are they Papa? Why are they after you?"
Victor never told her. "The less you know, the better. But your research puts you at risk, honey. Promise me you'll never publish that data." He held her hands and stared at her with dull grey eyes. Valona would never forget the haunted look on his face.

The TV reporter's voice filtered back into her consciousness. A bystander was speaking, pointing to the street. The camera panned back and Valona caught her breath. She recognized the bar where her father used to eat sometimes. A solitary tear escaped her eye and rolled down her cheek. The dead man was her father. She couldn't bear to look at the zoomed image on the inset of the screen. The head was practically obliterated by the gun shot.

Valona stood, feeling sick. She ran to the bathroom. She heaved on the sink, but nothing came out but a trickle of bile. She glanced at herself in the mirror. Her eyes were red, hair messed up. She tied it back in a pony tail. She heard a car door slam. From the bathroom window on the first floor of the motel, she could see the parking lot. She looked down.

A black SUV had just pulled up. Two men came out. They wore black suits and black sunglasses. They jerked their heads around, observing. Then they looked up, staring at the windows of the motel. Valona shrank back, hitting the sink.

They're coming after me, and they'll kill you too.

Nausea rose up inside her like a tidal wave. She swallowed and ran out the bathroom, heart hammering against her ribs. She needed to get out of the motel. She stuffed the few clothes and make up stuff she had inside her back pack and slung it on her back. She turned the TV off and left the room, shutting the door, but not locking it. The hallway had windows on one side and room doors on the other. Valona moved quickly. She avoided the elevator and took the stairs.

Before she opened the door to the reception lobby, she glanced through the glass panel. One of the men was speaking to the motel owner, while the other was walking around. He looked towards Valona and she ducked. She had used a fake name, but did these men have her photo? After all, her driving license and social security card were easily traced online.

When she looked up, her worst fears were confirmed. One of the men was walking purposefully towards the elevator door, and the other was striding straight for her.

She was trapped.

CHAPTER

Valona turned swiftly and ran up the stairs as fast as her feet would carry her. She was wearing sneakers, thankfully. She ran into the corridor and almost collided with a couple coming out of a room. She mumbled an apology and ran to her room. Behind her, she heard the elevator ping as it arrived on her floor. They knew her room number.

Valona pressed the card against the doorknob and the door buzzed open. Her mouth was open, chest heaving with panic. She looked around wildly. Her eyes fell on the bathroom door.

There was a loud knock on the main door.

Valona didn't wait. She went into the bathroom and locked the door. She stood on the toilet and opened the window. She unhooked the bag from her shoulders and peered out. The fall was about twenty feet, but luckily, her window was above a row of large square dumpsters.

The knock on the door came again, louder. A voice said her name. A split second later there was a crashing sound as the door was kicked open. Breath fluttering in her chest, Valona chucked her bag out the window. She grabbed the window sill and pushed her head and shoulders through. It was just wide enough. Valona was no gymnast. Panic engulfed her as she looked at the drop down to the dumpsters. But she was still head first. If she dropped like this chances were high she wasn't getting up anytime soon. Scrambling, she managed to bend her right knee, then dangle her right foot over the window sill. She was straddling the window now, desperately trying to maintain balance.

The bathroom handle turned. A voice said something, then the lock flew off the door as a suppressed weapon fired. A shoe kicked the door, and seconds later, a man was in the bathroom. For a brief second, their eyes met. Valona saw a Caucasian man, medium height, broad shouldered. A scar ran from his left lip towards the ear. He snarled and moved the same time she did.

Valona swung her other leg out the window. She screamed as her fingers held on to the window sill, but the rest of her body dangled in the air. A warm hand covered hers just as she let go. She felt the man's nails scraping her hand, then she was falling. She bent her knees for the impact, and it happened faster than she thought. She landed on the dumpster with a loud bang, the lid bending on impact. Pain shot up her feet like a lighting bolt. She screamed in agony, then rolled over to the ground. Her eyes were misty, head spinning. On the ground she could make out an object. She blinked; it was her bag. Grunting, gritting her teeth, she moved. She had to, staying still was not an option.

Clutching her back pack, she got to her feet. The pain was unbearable. She leaned against the dumpster, sweat running down her face.

What now? She had seconds in which to make an escape plan. The men would be on her in a flash. She glanced at the dumpster's lid. She took her phone out and set the alarm to ringing. She lifted the lid and chucked the phone inside. The sound was muffled, but still audible.

Valona grit her teeth and dragged her heavy legs to the cars. She collapsed against a pick up truck, shielded from the dumpsters. Running feet appeared in the forecourt. She tracked them to the dumpster. She heard them speak. Crouching, she poked her head out the side of the pick up.

One of them was in the process of lifting the dumpster lid, while the other was taking out his weapon. Valona glanced inside the pick up. The back had steel poles, some building tools and a tarpaulin. The driver's cabin was empty. Valona chucked her back pack in the back. She lifted herself into the truck as fast as she could. Lying flat, she pulled on the tarpaulin. After two tugs, it came loose. She covered herself with it the best she could taking care to tuck her feet inside. It smelt of sweat, diesel oil and another pungent smell like animal waste that made her gag.

She breathed softly, trying to stay still. The dumpster lid came down with a crash, then another. A voice shouted, swearing.

Then another. "She couldn't have gone far. Has to be around here. You head down to the road…"

Valona couldn't hear the rest, but she heard the man run down. Measured footsteps approached towards her. Her heart hammered against her ribs so loud she swore it could be heart. Sweat trickled down her head, burning her eyes with salt, but she dared not move. She clenched her teeth and dug nails into her palms.
The footsteps came closer, then stopped next to the truck. A weight leaned against the side. Her pulse surged, panic crawling like ants into her fingertips. She could hear him breathe. Any minute now…what could she do? It was too late to make a run for it. She cursed herself for not running away already. At least she could have flagged down a car on the road.

The weight shifted. She heard the man walking around. The foot steps faded. Two voices were speaking, it was the two men. She strained to hear.

"…into a car…driven off…"

Valona couldn't hear any more. Doors slammed and an engine revved. A car moved down the parking lot. She was about to poke her head out when she felt the truck lurch. Someone was getting inside the cabin. The door slammed and the pick up's engine came to life. Valona sighed in relief. A mixture of adrenaline and sudden joy leapt up inside her.

Yes, I made it!

The truck moved down the slope and exited the parking lot. It turned right and picked up speed. Valona lifted her head up slowly, pushing the tarp away. Wind whistled over her head. She was in rural Virginia, and had stopped at the interstate. She was going back the way she had come, up towards DC. A direction she didn't want to go in but now she had no choice, till the next stop. She debated whether to get the driver's attention. But before she could make her mind up, the truck decelerated.

It turned down a ramp, then took a left and bounced down a dirt road. It stopped in a field. Valona had moved out from under the tarpaulin. She figured this man was a farmer, and expected to see a farmyard up ahead.

The cabin door opened, and a man in a black suit stepped out. He took his black sunglasses off. Valona felt like she had been slapped. Her head reeled as if from a physical blow. The man had a scar running from the corner of his left lip towards his left ear, making a line across his lower cheek. It looked ghastly.

Nick Carlyle smiled at her. "Valona Kowalski. You are one hard woman to track down."

CHAPTER

Valona stared at the man with the disfiguring scar etched across his left cheek. Nick Carlyle grinned and on his face it had the hideous effect of making the scar stretch wider. "Thought you got away, huh?", his voice was raspy, like he needed to clear his throat. Valona saw the passenger door open and the other man step out. WIthout a word he came around to the rear of the pick up and lowered the tail gate. Valona looked around wildly. Her eyes fell on a hammer by her feet.

"Don't," Carlyle said in that dry, croaking voice. Valona looked up to see him pointing a gun at her. The man behind her grabbed her arm and pulled her back. He used plastic handcuffs, then put a black bag over her eyes. The coarse material scratched against her face. She heard another car roll up. She was directed to it and the vehicle set off. Valona could make out that she was in the back seat, between two men. No one said anything. She felt the dirt road beneath the wheel give way to the smoothness of the highway, and the swish of cars going past them.

"Who are you?" She asked. Silence greeted her.

"Did you kill my father? Answer me!" She raised her voice, anger suddenly burning inside her. She didn't know which one scar face was, but she figured he was the lighter man sitting to her left. She turned her face to him, seeing nothing but a black veil.

"Coward," she hissed. "The least you can do is speak the truth." She didn't avert her face. The car rolled on.

The raspy voice spoke from her left. "Yes I did. Happy now?"

Valona seethed for a few seconds, jaws clenched tight. She remembered how they had come to America, all those years ago, when she was barely ten years old. How hard her father had worked to give her a decent life. Rage and grief boiled up inside her and with a roar, the steam released. She flung herself at him, head butting she thought the face would be. She hit nothing, but felt an iron cast hand grab the back of her neck and force her head into the seat. Nose and mouth pressed against the upholstery, she couldn't breathe. The force on her neck increased and she grunted.

"Next time, it's going to hurt. Got that?" The raspy voice said. "Got it?"

Valona felt her lungs would burst. She nodded her head quickly. The pressure released and she was hauled back up. Through the mask she panted, sweat pouring down her face. "Fuck you," she said.

The car bounced over a ramp and went round a bend. Soon, she was pulled out of the car. She felt a breeze, all it did was push the mask closer against her face. Car doors slammed around her and multiple voices spoke in English. Valona was fluent in Russian. Although she was a scientist, languages came easily to her. She learnt Spanish in school and could speak very basic Italian. She strained hard to pick up words. All she heard was English, in an American accent. The air smelt fresh and she detected the odour of mown hay. She could be in a farmyard. How long had they travelled? An hour or two, she figured. They were inside rural Virginia still.

She was led in through a set of doors, then up a flight of stairs. Her flats made a soft sound against the floor. A door opened and hands guided her into a chair. She heard a few footsteps move away from her, then whispered voices. The the door clicked shut.

Someone approached her, and the mask was slowly lifted. Valona blinked in the sudden light.

A man in a white coat was peering down at her. His hair was sparse, but as white as his coat. Bushy eyebrows twitched above a pair of dark, glinting eyes. He smiled without mirth.

"Dr Kowalski, I presume?" He asked. Valona glanced at the label on his white coat. There was no name on it. She kept her silence, staring back at the man.

"My name is Dr Stainforth, and I am the head doctor at this clinic. I understand you are suffering with retrograde amnesia."

Valona frowned. "Who told you that?"

Dr Stainforth said, "I understand you cannot recall the details of your recent research."

Breath froze inside her chest. Speaking was an effort but she managed eventually. "And who told you that?"

"The men who brought you here. Believe it or not, they are your friends. They are trying to save you from doing great harm."

Valona almost laughed. "Yeah sure. Only friends shoot their way into my room and then abduct me."

The doctor's face lost the smile, and the grandfatherly look of mild concern. "That is exactly what a lot of amnesics say, Valona." He used her first name, and it made her blink.

He continued. "Because their memory has gone, they don't understand the significance of their actions."

She said, "I can remember that you just asked me about some research." She was careful not to say the word my. Her research was what this all about, like her father had warmed her. She fought to suppress the rising tide of panic. Her hands were still tied, and it hurt. She was a prisoner here, at the mercy of this weird doctor.

"Yes of course. You can remember everything after the event, but not before. Victims of a car crash. Or a great traumatic event, which could lead to prolonged grief or fear, forget their lives before the event. That's why you cannot remember your research.

"And that's what they…my friends as you call them, told you?"

Dr Stainforth straightened. He walked to the end of the room and stopped next to a gurney. He bent over a tray and picked up a syringe.

"You work for the Environment Protection Agency, and your research is in electromagnetic radiation. Do you remember that much?"

Valona stared at him, as he continued to fill the syringe from a vial of colourless liquid. The research that her father had warned her not to publish. She blinked rapidly, wondering what to do. She needed to get out of this place and contact the police, FBI, whatever.
Something her father had said floated into her mind.

They are extremely well connected. I'm talking about the highest reaches of government and law enforcement. Don't underestimate them.

Dr Stainforth turned around and approached her with the syringe in his hand. The cover was removed and the needle was upright.
"Do you remember, Valona?"
She gulped and nodded. "The EPA. That's where I worked."
He narrowed his eyes. "What else?"

CHAPTER

Valona knew she had to play for time. She closed her eyes, her face a mask of concentration. She thought furiously. Her father had warned about how high his killers influence reached. Did that mean she couldn't trust the FBI? She knew her father had contact with people who worked in the government. As to who these shady, grey faced men were, she had no idea.

She opened her eyes when she felt Dr Stainforth standing close to her.
He cleared his throat. "Well, do you remember anything else?"

Valona's eyes fell on the glistening tip of the needle. The doctor's gloved thumb rested on the plunger. She looked from the needle to his dark eyes. They bored into hers with an intensity that made her shiver like she was immersed in a tub of ice water.

At the same time, a thought occurred to her.

I have to be untied for him to inject me.

Valona shook her head. "No." Behind her back, she started pumping her fingers to restore circulation in them.

Dr Stainforth sighed. "Very well. In which case I have to inject you with a medicine that is going to help you remember. It will relax you and you might feel sleepy. Don't fight it. When you feel like answering something just go ahead and do it."

"Is it Scopolamine?"

The doctor smiled. "Scopolamine is an old-fashioned drug. There are many new truth serums now. We call DS-10. It has been tried on humans before, so don't worry. I wouldn't be giving you anything harmful."

I bet you won't.

Dr Stainforth put the needle down on a mobile tray next to him. He came behind Valona and she shifted forward in the chair. She felt the sharp clip of scissors as they cut through the plastic ties. Her fingers were warm now. As soon as her hands were free, she lunged forward. She picked up the syringe with one hand and kicked the chair back with her right foot.

The doctor was surprised by the sudden movement. He stumbled backwards and fell to the floor. In a flash, Valona was on him, the needle inches away from his face. Her chest was heaving with exertion, and sweat beaded on her forehead. She held him down with one hand on his neck.

"If you move I'll push this into your eye. Understood?," she hissed.

"Yes."
"Good." Valona felt unreal that she was doing this. She wasn't a daredevil. She had held a gun and been to the firing range a few times, but it was for self defense, at her father's insistence. She had never fired on anyone. Now, she was threatening to kill a person.

She swallowed and got a grip on herself. This was the card life had dealt her. She had no other option.

"Dr Stainforth, who are those men?"

The old man's eyes flickered from side to side. He licked his dry lips and spoke with an effort. "I honestly don't know." Valona clenched her teeth and pushed the needle closer to his right eye.

"I'll count till three. Then it's all over for you. One, two-

"OK, OK!" he croaked. "They said they work for a division of the FBI. Exactly what, I don't know. They told me you are a traitor, a scientist who is selling secrets to the Russians and Chinese. I needed to get information out of you."

"What else?" She increased the pressure on her right hand, throttling his neck. The effort was making her pulse surge, and her eyes shook. She blinked and focused.

"Nothing else. I don't know."

"What sort of a place is this? Call yourself a doctor and you torture people?"

For the first time, anger replaced fear in his eyes. "Who told you we torture people? This is a research facility…" He was going to say something else, but clammed up.

Valona grit her teeth and shook him by the collar. "Go on. What sort of facility? Who uses this place?"

Dr Stainforth had gone quiet, his face white as a sheet. "Look, I can't answer any more. They'll kill me if I do."

Valona stared at him for a few seconds then said, "Turn around. Face down on the floor."

She patted him down, and found a wallet, Iphone and a keyring in his pant pockets.

She put a knee on his back and looked up at the counter in front. Syringes, scissors and other clinical instruments were laid out neatly, labelled. She saw a crepe bandage roll and pulled it out.

"Don't move," she said. With the crepe bandage she tied his hands, then his legs the best she could.

Dr Stainforth mumbled, "You're making a mistake. They'll come after you."

"They're after me already."

She looked in the drawers till she found adhesive tape for dressings. She cut a strip and plastered it over his lips. He struggled but she managed to hold him down.

Panting with exertion, she stood. Her fingers felt the keyring in her pocket. The clinical room had a gurney at the end, and cupboards on the walls. Her eyes fell on a locker safe. She tried the keys till one turned and the small door opened. There was a gun inside. She took it out, hefting it in her hand. It was a Glock. She took out the weapon, racked the slide and checked the barrel. She slid the magazine out to make sure it was full.

Then she wondered what to do with the weapon. Would she have the guts to shoot someone, even in self defense? She closed her eyes for a second, then put the weapon on her back beltline. She made sure the doctor's wallet was in her pocket. She dismantled his phone and stomped on the SIM card with her shoes. She took one last look at the prone form of Dr Stainforth, then opened the door a crack to look outside.

CHAPTER 4

Dan took the metro back to his apartment. He chewed over his conversation with McBride.

Killing someone in DC like this was audacious. The sniper team was well resourced. Dan had to track Kowalski's house down fast, but his searches on the internet had shown nothing. McBride's address for Kowalski was further down south in Virginia, not in DC.

Dan's stop came and he jogged up the stairs and walked out into the habitual traffic smog that DC`s roads created at office times. The cars were at standstill as usual, even after the lights changed. The good thing about DC was the public transport system. The buses and metro made it easy to move around. Dan got to his apartment and checked his answerphone. He looked at the newspaper that had been stuffed in through the letterbox. More news about how the city was getting prepared for the UK Prime Minister`s visit. Her smiling face was on the front page.

He changed into his running gear, locked the door, and set off for his six mile run. He packed a ten kilo bag on his back as well to provide resistance. He ran in a north-westerly direction, heading for the Dumbarton Oaks Park. He had not run a proper length in a while, and he was in the stride of it soon, feeling the rhythm in his muscles.

It was past 1800 hours when he came back. The sky was darkening.

He stripped, showered and changed. He packed the same small backpack with a flashlight, black leather gloves, glass cutters and a length of nylons rope. The NiteGlo flash light`s handle was sturdy enough to be a weapon if needed. His real weapon was in his back belt. An eleven inch long curved knife called the kukri. Gurkhas used it as a ceremonial knife, but also in battle and for general use. Dan patted the black leather scabbard in which the knife was held, and made for the door.

Streetlights were coming on as he arrived at the cross of K Street and 13th South East. The commuters had gone, and a few tourists were walking up from the river. He crossed the street, and approached the cordoned off area from the opposite side. The shooting had happened in front of an electronics shop, and it was shut. On either side he saw the closed doors of other shops. At the corner of the intersection, there was a coffee shop that was still open, and next to it, a bar. Dan walked in that direction.

The bar was empty. He walked up to the counter.

A small Hispanic gentleman in a white apron turned around and lifted one finger.

"One second, *por favor*."

Dan nodded at him. He looked around the bar. A blue and red neon sign played at the glass front. He got off his stool and walked to it. From the windows, he had a good view of the yellow strip cordoned area. It was dark now mostly, but the place was lit up by the yellow glow of a streetlamp above.

Dan walked back to the counter. The Hispanic man appeared, rubbing his hands on his apron.

"*Lo Siento*," he said. "How can I help?"

Dan indicated outwards with his head. "Shame what happened today."

A look of sadness came over the man`s face. He shook his head. "Yes, a real shame. He was a nice old man."

"You knew him?"

"Yes, he came here often. Liked the coffee here, he said." He raised his eyebrows. "You want anything?"

Dan was starving. He looked at the menu on the white board above. "I`ll have a steak sandwich, medium rare. That Argentinian beef. And a beer."

"Coming up." Dan went and took a seat by the window. After he had finished his food, he went back to the counter and paid.

"Steak was good," Dan said.

The man smiled, showing yellow teeth. "Thanks. You from around here?"

"Live up in Dupont. Was walking down here this morning when this happened."

"Ah so you were there."

"Yes. Did you see the old man this morning?" Dan asked.

"Uh-huh. He came in here for his coffee."

"What was his name?"

"Called himself Victor. Victor Kowalski. Lived close by, on 17th South East. Came here almost every day. Still can't believe what happened." The man shook his head again.

"Was he always on his own?"

"Yes. He was retired, no family. He read the newspaper, drank his coffee and off he went. Never said much, to be honest. Seemed like a loner. I heard recently that his wife died. Never knew he had a wife."

"Heard from who?"

"A neighbor. His wife was sick. He saw the ambulance turn up a few times in front of his house. I still can`t figure out who would want to kill an old man."

Dan shrugged. "Maybe he was mistaken for someone else." He paused for a second, then asked casually. "Did you know what number he lived at?"

The man frowned at Dan. "Are you a cop?"

"No," said Dan, hoping the honesty showed on his face. "Just wondering, that`s all."

"We used to do home delivery for his food sometimes. Lived at number 1622."

"Thank you."

17th South East was not far. Dan walked up to the street in ten minutes, stopping often and looking around him. No one followed him. The houses on the street were interesting. They were set back from the road, virtually all of them accessed by steps that rose up a small embankment. They were terraced Georgian houses, and they reminded him of some houses on the residential streets of London.

1622 was a brown coloured brick house between a yellow and a light grey one. All of them looked the same. The lights were off. Dan spent some time looking at the block of apartment opposite. He stared at the window facing 1622, till he was satisfied it was dark, and the curtains were drawn.

Dan went up the steps, looking around him carefully. The front garden was narrow, long and overgrown. Weed plants rose above the fence. He walked to the front door. Yellow and black police tape was stuck across it. The one window on the ground floor, and two above were both dark. Light spilled from the front porches of the two houses on either side. Dan was wearing a black denim jacket and dark brown pants, with black sneakers. He merged into the background. He took out a skeleton key and put it in the keyhole. He could not see any alarms. After some jiggling with the skeleton, the lock clicked open.

Dan opened the door a crack. It creaked in protest. Visibility was zero behind the door. He opened it enough to let his broad frame through, then he shut the door behind him. He was crouched low, and he moved away from the door on all fours, and lay down flat on the floor. He could not hear a sound. All the lights had been turned off. The house smelled dank, musty. There was another smell, of antiseptic and a hospital ward. Someone had died here, slowly, over many years.

As his eyes got used to the dark, he could make out shapes.

The bannisters of the staircase was in front of him. He could see doors leading off the hallways. Dan got up, and crept up to the first stair. He took out his flashlight, and put his gloves on. He turned the flashlight downward. The circular white beam cut a swathe into the blackness. Motes of dust floated in the beam. He turned the light above. Old wall paper, and some damp on the ceilings. He went up the staircase slowly, the stairs creaking. He stopped at the landing. Three doors led off it, and the first one was a bathroom. He walked down till he came to the room that faced the front garden.

It used to be a bedroom. The old bed, stripped of its mattress, stood bare boned like an old skeleton. There was a dressing table with a mirror to one side. There were two more pictures of a younger woman on the table top. One was old and faded, the colours barely holding. It was of a little girl in the arms of her mother. The other was recent. A college graduation. A happy beaming, all American face. Obviously of the little girl in the old photo who had now grown into a woman. Dan took out his cell phone and snapped photos. He looked closely at the woman in the old photo. The face meant nothing to him. There was an ensuite bathroom as well. He put his hand on the door handle, opened it, and froze.

A sound, above him. Like a footstep. It had been very faint, but his senses were working overtime. There was a loft space above him. He stood very still, then heard the sound again. All of a sudden, the steps speeded up. Someone ran for the front, and he heard a window above him open and shut. Dan shone his flashlight up. Behind him he could see the hatch door on the ceiling, for the loft ladder. He was about to reach for it, when he heard a scraping sound at the front. A figure appeared at the window. It stopped for a second, looked at Dan, then sailed down again. Dan turned and ran down the stairs. He opened the door and ducked underneath the police tape.

As he ran out into the front garden, he heard the engine of a car start up in the street. With a screech of tyres, an SUV parked on the kerb took off. Dan ran to the road, and taking his cell phone out, took a couple of photos of the retreating back of the SUV.

He hurried back inside the house. He checked in all the rooms downstairs, and all the rooms upstairs. Clean as a whistle. The FBI had taken everything away, as he had expected. The loft would have been the only place of interest. He opened the hatch, lowered the ladder and climbed up. A few old chairs lay on their sides. An old TV from the eighties. He kicked it to one side. Nothing but dust, and the scurry of mice in the corners. Dan came down, shut the loft hatch and went out the front door.

CHAPTER 6

Dan jerked awake, right hand under his pillow, fingers curling around the butt of his Sig Sauer P226. Dull light gleamed from the side of the curtains. He looked around the bedroom quickly, but he was alone. He relaxed and his head fell back on the pillow. But the gun remained in his hand. Something had woken him up and he couldn't figure it out. The red dials of the digital clock said 06.15. He lay still for a while, mind churning over the events of the last two days.

The young woman's face on the photo in Kowalski's bedroom came back to his mind. He needed to find her, quickly. Another face came to his mind. The driver of that tan sedan. Where had Dan seen that face before?

After a while of churning through his memories, Dan decided to get up. He did his exercise schedule of push ups and free weights. He took the trash out, and his eyes fell on a new car he hadn't seen the night before. A grey Chrysler, parked under a tree.

Dan came out of his first floor apartment on the street off Dupont Circle and for the second time that morning, noticed the car parked opposite. A grey Chrysler sedan. A long front lawn lay in front of the apartment complex, and the car was parked on the opposite of the road, underneath the shade of a weeping willow tree. It was partially hidden from sight. He had only noticed it in the morning as it was his job to keep an eye on cars parked for long periods. It had disappeared after a couple of hours. Now it was back in the same place. Dan kept walking.

He got off the Federal Station SW Metro and walked down 401 E Street till he came to the coroner's office. He pressed the buzzer and the door opened. A shapely young brunette sat the reception desk. She moved a long finger away from the buzzer as Dan came up the stairs.

"Can I help you?" she asked. Her eyes swept over Dan, lingering over his shoulders and arms.

"I wonder if you may. A friend of mine has passed away. He was elderly, and he did not have any children. I just wanted to know if he was here."

"Sure thing. What`s his name?"

"Victor Kowalski."

"Gimme a second."

"Yes he is here." She frowned. "There`s a block on his details." Dan came closer to the counter. "What do you mean?"

She punched a few more keys and then shook her head. "Not seen this before. There`s a tab that says Closed for Examination. As far as I know, that`s not a tab the Coroner uses. Must be something new."

"You can`t access any of his details?"

"Nope. Just his name, and the date he was brought here, that`s all." She scrolled up and down the page. "Oh hang on."

Dan waited. The girl pressed her face closer to the screen, and then relaxed her face. "It seems his wife was here too. She died a month ago."

"The coroner would have examined her by now. Is there anything on her report?"

The girl raised her eyes to look at Dan. "Are you the next of kin?"

Dan shrugged. "Friend of the family." He knew what she was going to say next.

"Sorry, can`t release the coroner`s report unless you can prove NOK status."

Dan nodded. "Sure, no problem. Just a shame, how they both died so quickly."

The girl pursed her lips and her eyes went back to the screen. "Yeah. It seems she came here from the Riverside Memorial Hospital. We get a lot of our patients from there. But it doesn't say where he came from." She glanced up at Dan. "Do you know which hospital Mr Kowalski came from?"

Dan shook his head slowly. "You don't have that information there?"

"Nope. Nothing on him, really."

"Which ward in the Riverside Memorial Hospital was the wife a patient?"

The girl read the name off the screen. "C4 ward."

Dan thanked the girl and went down the stairs, out on the street.

Riverside Memorial Hospital was a few stops down due west on the Metro, closer to the Potomac South west riverfront. As Dan got off and walked down to towards the shining white and glass hospital building, he realized Pentagon was diagonally across the river. He asked the receptionist and took the elevator to C4 ward.

He pressed the door buzzer and waited. A woman's face appeared at the window panel of the door. She looked at Dan impassively for a few second then opened the door.

"Can I help you?" The nurse was in a blue uniform. She was in her fifties, Dan guessed.

"Do you remember a lady called Alina Kowalski, who died here on 14th September?"

The nurse frowned and thought for a while. Then her face cleared. "Yes. Yes, I do. She was quite sick, poor woman." She looked at Dan quizzically. "Who are you?"

Dan felt bad about lying. But he had no other choice. "I knew her husband. He died yesterday. I never got a chance to come and see her when she was sick." He passed a hand over his head. "Guess I just wanted to know if she died in peace, that`s all."

The nurse, whose badge identified her as Trudy Bradshaw, nodded. "Yes, she did. Are you not in touch with the family?"

"Yes I-

Dan was cut off by Trudy's bleep sounding. She reached for her pocket and glanced at it.

"Excuse me, would you like to sit down while I answer this?"

"Sure, no problem."

"The waiting room is here," she pointed Dan in the direction of a closed door. There was a light on inside. Trudy hurried off towards the end of the corridors. Dan looked around him. The patient rooms were all shut and he was alone. He followed Trudy. At the end of the corridor there was a long counter with the nurses station. Trudy went around it, opened a door and disappeared into a stairwell. The nurses station was empty. A red light was blinking silently on a board in front of Dan, with the number 21 on it. Dan crossed the counter, and pressed on the handle of the nurses station door. It gave way. It was dark inside, and he fumbled on the wall for a switch. A white light came to life. He saw a desk, with a chair and desktop computer. The screen was on. Dan closed off the light and shut the door. He sat down quietly on the chair and pointed to the mouse on the toolbar to recent files, and clicked. He went to the admission folder. It was an excel spreadsheet, and when he searched for Alina Kowalski, her name came up in a new tab.

He heard the sound of footsteps. He looked towards the door, and through the glass panel saw a shadow pass across it. Dan glanced back at the screen. Victor's name was there, but so was another name under next of kin. Antonia Kowalski. In brackets it said daughter. There were no other contact details. Dan was out of time. The door handle turned. Dan slid off his seat and crouched behind the desk. The light came on. Dan could hear the respirations of a single person, he guessed, at the door. The person stepped inside the room. A pair of stockinged feet, with black flat shoes. His eyes caught the hem of the blue uniform. It was Trudy. She leaned over the desk. Dan caught his breath, willing himself to be still as a statue. If Trudy moved her head a fraction to the left, she would see him. Dan had managed to close the excel file before he ducked, but the screen was still active. Maybe that was all Trudy was inspecting.

He heard her straighten and prepared himself. If she took another step, she would see him against the wall, knees curled into his chin. But she didn't. She turned on her heels and left the room. Dan didn't breathe till he heard the door handle click shut.

He got up quickly, and checked the screen again. Under Antonia Kowalski there was no address or cell number. He closed the screen down. He opened the door a fraction, but couldn't see Trudy anywhere. He slid out fast, and leaned with his back to the wall. He walked around the counter, but Trudy was nowhere to be seen. Dan walked quickly to the end of the corridor, pressed the red door release, and left.

A drizzle had started when he came outside. He looked above, at the dark bellied clouds reaching out arms over the high rise buildings. He wondered who Alina and Victor Kowalski had been. What lives they had led, what secrets they had gathered. There had to be some. No one died the way Victor had without a reason. But the daughter was the real revelation. A persistent doubt was gnawing away in Dan's mind. Both Alina and Victor were dead. Had Alina been a spy as well? Regardless, Dan had to assume the daughter's life was in danger. If she wasn't dead already.

He turned his eyes to the street.
He saw it after a bus had moved out of the way. At the far corner opposite the hospital a black Chevrolet SUV was parked. Streetlight fell in through the windscreen, and he could make out two men in jackets at the front seat.
Dan turned away as if he had not seen the car, and started walking towards the metro.

*****

Trisha sighed as she sat down at her desk and looked at the report folders she had to work through. The Kowalski case was priority now, and the coroner's report had just come through. As she opened it, her desk phone rang. She lifted it and spoke to her boss, Diego Martinez, the Assistant Deputy Director of the DC branch.
She filled him in on the case details, then asked her question.
"Did you get the information I wanted?"
Her boss paused before replying. "On that civilian you questioned?"
"Yes."
"I rang the DOD. They haven't got back to me as yet. Which means that either they won't tell us and I need to take this higher, or simple bureaucracy. You know how the Pentagon is."
"They might say the same thing about us."

"No shit. Is this Dan Roy a suspect? From what I can see, he's a goddamn war hero."

"He was there, Diego. The victim was six feet away. Then he ran to the building from where the shot came."

Diego was silent. Trisha said, "He's hiding something. I can feel it."

"Then bring him in."

"We arrest him he calls a lawyer then clams up."

"Then what do you propose?" Diego asked, impatience creeping into his voice.

"Interrogate him again. I doubt he'll crack, but he might cooperate."

"Cooperate?"

"If he knows something about why Kowalski was killed, then it's worth it."

Trisha heard Diego breathing softly. "OK," he said eventually. "We got heat on this from the Director, and the DNI and Homeland want to make sure its not terrorist related. You got anything on that yet?"

"No, but I am working on it. Ballistics have shown the round was from a SCAR-H sniper rifle, US made."

"Terrorists can get hold of domestic weapons easily. That doesn't rule anything out."

"No, sir it does not. We need everything we got on this right?"

"Right."

"So will you press DOD once again? Maybe play the DNI's office into it? That way they can't keep palming you off."

"You want my job, Trisha?"

Trisha grinned against the phone receiver. "Nope. Just want to do my own."

"Then get me some answers I can feed upstairs."

CHAPTER 7

They had followed Dan all day. When he had taken the Orange line from the Foggy Bottom GWU Metro station in the evening, he made sure he didn't have a tail. But he was not sure about the morning. Which meant they had watched him go to the coroner`s office. Then to the hospital.

Who were they? The FBI maybe. But there was a darker possibility. He had been spotted the night he went to Kowalski`s house. Someone had been in the loft. Dan increased his pace. He could see the Metro station in the distance. There was a park to his left, the interior shrouded in darkness, but the gates still open. He walked in casually. Trees loomed over him in either direction. He could barely read a sign in white that said Duck Pond Ahead. A straight road led into the park. It was dark, wet and silent. Not a soul stirred inside. Dan picked a tree and faded behind its shadow quickly. From his angle, he could see the streetlamp lit road. Pedestrian passed by hurriedly, some sporting umbrellas, some braving the light early autumn drizzle. He saw them within a few seconds. Two tall men, dressed entirely in black. They stopped at the park entrance. They did not confer between themselves. One of them leaned against the railings, while the other slipped inside the gates. He reached inside his shoulder holster and took his gun out. He held it in both hands, elbow extended but pointing down.

Whoever these guys were, they were not FBI. Dan reached behind his back, and pulled out the kukri from its scabbard. It would not be much use if bullets started flying. But hand to hand combat, or a knife fight would be a different matter. There was no way he would lose either of those.

Dan crouched low and stepped back against the trees. The main was diagonally ahead of him, twenty meters away. Dan`s foot caught on something, and he slipped backwards. His back landed against a tree trunk, and he rolled off it, falling on his knees. The damage was done. The gun man lifted his head up sharply, the gun pointing in Dan`s direction.

Dan ran, dodging the trees.

Thwack!

The sound of a suppressed round hitting bark above his head made him dive to the ground. He could not stay here. He stayed low, weaving between the foliage and the trees, hoping the light was dark enough not to allow visibility. He could not see much except dark shapes. Bullets kept slamming into trees and shrubs around him. There was a let up, and a sound, with a curse. Dan did not look backwards. The man might have fallen. But his friend might have joined him now.

Dan ran fast, and came upon a clearing. The night breeze was cool upon his face. He had found the duck pond. Dan scrambled to the side, and eased himself into the water, careful not to make a splash. It was freezing. The pond was shallow and full of moss. Dan waded in, poking just his nose and eyes above water. He saw a bunch of reeds and moved closer to it for cover. His sense were on fire. The wet ground around the pond masked footsteps, but he could still hear faint sounds. One pair approaching. He could see the silhouette. Gun arm raised, treading slow. Dan waited. The reeds were close to the bank, and the shadow moved closer, till it was directly above him. Silently, Dan submerged himself. Amniotic darkness enveloped him. He could not see anything. But sounds are multiplied under water. He heard the ripples as something came into the water. Staying below, Dan turned slightly. A slim dark shape in front of him, like a human leg. The man was standing with one foot in the water, scanning around him.

Dan waited. The man turned away to go. Dan broke water slowly. He raised his head. His feet were planted firmly on the mud. He rose up behind the man, weed and moss draped around his shoulders. He lifted the kukri up, and his left arm reached out to encircle the gun hand. But the man had sensed something. He turned as fast as he could. Dan was faster. He hooked his right arm against the man`s waist, jerking him close. The kukri rose up like a scythe, and buried itself in the man`s neck. It sliced upwards through the soft anterior triangle of the neck, cutting the jugular vein and the carotid artery. It smashed into the floor of skull, breaking the soft bones with a snap.

The man had the gun in his right hand. He could fire, but Dan was pressed so close the round would have to go through his own body. He did fire, as Dan had imagined, over his shoulder. But Dan`s head was ducked behind him, and the suppressed round flew harmlessly over him. Dan pushed the kukri in deeper, feeling warm blood pour down his arm. The dying man buckled and thrashed against him, but Dan held him tight and lowered him gently into the dark water.

He chucked his kukri into the shallow water next to him and caught the gun hand as quickly as he could. He did not want the chamber to get wet. He pulled the gun off the dead man`s hand. It felt familiar, the heavier weight of a Colt M1911, rather than a lighter Glock. The handle was wet. He picked up the kukri, stuck it back in the scabbard and looked around him. Darkness. The predicted support for his enemy had not arrived. But the man outside would soon start to worry about his friend. Dan did not want to face him with a wet handgun. If the chamber was not waterproof, the damn thing could blow up in his face. Unless of course, these guys had Sigs with waterproof chambers. Which meant a particular type of operative. The ex-Delta type. The Black Ops type. The type he was hoping they would not be.

Dan checked the gun`s barrel quickly. Not clogged with dirt or mud. He could not dry the gun, he was too wet. Dan cursed, and got out of the water, careful not to slip. He gripped the gun tightly, the familiar shape giving him some comfort.

The duck pond was a circle. Dan pressed himself against one of the trees at the edge, and looked back the way he had come. More than fifty metres away. Darkness shrouded the entrance, but in the distance he could see the dull glow of the streetlights.

Movement. Three o clock. Gentle rustle of leaves. A dark shape, barely above ground. Could be an animal. But he could not take any chances. And if Dan had seen him, chances were…

Thwack!

Splinters of sodden bark flew into his face. He dived into the ground and crawled away as fast as he could. He crouched behind a tree and saw the black shape moving, coming straight for him. Before the shape could duck, Dan fired. He braced himself for the gun not working, but it did. The Sig recoiled against his palm, and the suppressed round flew out of the barrel. Dan heard a grunt up ahead and then a heavy sound as a body hit the ground. He didn't move.

Bullets flayed the trees around him; wild shots. Dan crawled along the ground, out to the duck pond again. Outside the cover of the trees, he spread-eagled himself on the wet ground. He could see the man now. Clutching his shoulder, gun arm raised, behind a tree. Dan aimed, and fired at the head. A squelching sound as the round hit the back of the neck, and the figure fell forwards.

Dan stayed on the ground and did a 360 degree sitrep. Nothing from behind the duck pond, and nothing ahead. He waited. After two minutes, he got up and ran forward. It was silent. He frisked the dead body quickly. He did not find anything apart from a twenty dollar bill and some loose change. No cell phones. No wallets. No tags on the neck. He wanted to check for tattoos, but it was dark, and he did not have his flashlight. Lightly he touched below the chin. A beard.

He ran back to the duck pond and pulled the other body out. He searched, without expecting to find anything. Expectation fulfilled, he took both men`s weapons, stuck them in his front belt, and walked out to the entrance.

CHAPTER 8

Dan was soaking wet. The drizzle had stopped, and the commuter rush was less. But he could not board a metro train or a bus looking like this. He decided to walk. It was 2000 hours, and it took was 2130 by the time had walked the ten miles back to his home in Dupont. He stripped, showered and got changed. Then he sat down to examine the guns. They were both Colt M1911's. Both had waterproof chambers. He looked at the serial numbers. They were intact, but there was two of them, on each side of the barrel. One of the serial numbers started with UU. Dan knew enough about Colts to know that meant the gun had been assembled in the USA. But on the other side the serial number started with DE, and had two digits less. The grip was black polymer, and the steel case was finished entirely in black. He noted the picatinny rail below the gun barrel. Designed for extra attachments. This was not a civilian or even law enforcement weapon. This was military issue. He slipped out the magazine. Twelve rounds in them, with seven left. He recognized the rounds. 0.45 ACP. A nice, heavy round that he preferred. It had stopping power, unlike the 9mm. A deep sense of unease was spreading through his limbs.

Gangsters would not have guns like these.

Dan tossed the guns on the bed and thought to himself. He got up and turned off all the lights in the small apartment. There was one advantage of being in a basement. Access was difficult. The two apartments above him were occupied. There was one main door that led to outside. Then a hallway, and a door before the staircase that led down to his subterranean abode. In the kitchen, he made himself a quick chicken curry and boiled some rice.

After dinner, Dan lay down on his bed. Whoever had killed Kowalski now wanted him dead. Why? What did the old man know?

With his belly full, Dan began dozing to sleep. Tomorrow he needed to get answers.

*****

Morning's rays filtered through the curtains and woke Dan up.

He went into the kitchen, and put some beans in the coffee machine and turned it on. The aroma of fresh coffee helped him to wake up. He warmed up the milk and drank the coffee, inhaling deeply. He toasted eggs, fried some bacon rashers, and poached two eggs, keeping them runny. He cut the toasts into strips, and dipped the bread into the eggs. He washed it down with more coffee. He was about to get changed when he heard the intercom in the front door buzz.

He went to the door and peered at the video screen. A woman and a man, looking up at the camera because they knew exactly where it was. Special Agents Trisha Dunne and Mark Bellamy. Dan thought fast. He did not know how deep the FBI were in this. But they must have tracked Kowalski down to his wife, and the hospital. Dan also knew he could use the FBI's help now. This was his country, not some back post in the middle of Afghanistan. Him getting arrested for breaking the law helped no one. It wouldn't be hard. He needed to speak to McBride and get himself some creds.

Dan pressed the buzzer.

"Can I help?"

Trisha Dunne spoke into the intercom. "Is that Dan Roy?"

"Yes." He waited. After a pause Trisha said, "We need to ask you some questions, Mr Roy. Can we come in?"

"Not without a warrant, but you knew that already, right?"

CHAPTER

Trisha stepped back. Mark came forward. "I would urge you to open the door, Mr Roy. If you cannot, I would recommend you come with us to the station immediately."

Dan paused, then said, "I need five minutes to get dressed."

"We`ll be waiting," Mark said.

Dan got dressed into jeans, a button down shirt and black shoes. He gelled his hair and put some aftershave on. When he came out of the front door, he could feel Trisha`s eyes on him. She was smartly dressed in a black skirt business suit, with a similar white shirt, top two buttons undone.

Mark pointed to the parked Chyrsler saloon.

Dan looked at him. "Am I under arrest?"

"No," Mark said. "But we need to question you, in the…"

"Light of new evidence," Dan finished for him.

Mark`s face was impassive, but his voice hardened. "That's right. Now get into the car."

Trisha drove and Mark sat in the front. They drove to the WFO quickly. Dan got out slowly, making them wait at the door. Inside, it was a hub of activity. Analysts huddled over screens, pointing at them and talking, nodding into headphones. Trisha and Mark skirted the main floor and walked down the edge to a row of offices at the back. Mark unlocked a door and they went in. Same set up as last time. Grey blank walls, a small slit for a window at the ceiling, table and four chairs. They sat down. Dan waited for them to speak. He was good at waiting.

Trisha cleared her throat. "We have a witness that places you at the hospital where Victor Kowalski`s wife died. Were you there yesterday?"

"Yes."

"Why?"

"I told you," Dan said. "I wanted to find out who he was."

"I looked at your record."

"I knew that already."

"Like most special ops guys, you must have worked with intelligence agencies."

"Don't ask me for an opinion on them, please."

"I'm not." Trisha glanced at Bellamy who opened the laptop in front of him. He clicked on the keyboard and turned the laptop around. On the screen Dan could see the grainy image of a CCTV playing. He saw himself, walking down the street outside the hospital, then turn inside the park. Shortly after, the two men followed inside.

Bellamy turned the laptop back to himself. Trisha said, "Half an hour later, you emerge from the park alone."

Dan thought hard. If the two bodies had been discovered, Trisha would've mentioned them already. Or she might not, trying to lure him into a trap to confess. She might not even know what happened to the two men.

Dan said, "No harm in going for a stroll in the park, is there?"

"On a dark, rainy night? Most normal people wouldn't go for a stroll. What happened to the two men?"

Dan upturned his lips. "I don't know."

Trisha was holding his gaze, her hands on the desk. She held a pen in the right hand, and it didn't move. Dan remained similarly still.

Trisha spoke first. "I made a mistake. I thought you could help us. For some reason, you need to know more about Victor Kowalski. His death is now a federal investigation. By withholding information, you are committing a felony."

Still Dan didn't say anything. Trisha glanced at Bellamy, who nodded. Trisha said,"Dan Roy, I am arresting you on suspicion-

"Hold up," Dan said. He stared at both of them in turn. "I need to make a phone call."

"To call a lawyer?"

"No."

"That is the only call you are allowed to make."

"You want my help, right?"

In the silence that ensued, Dan watched Trisha scribble something on her notepad. When she looked up, he said, "The person I need to speak to will explain a few things to you."

She raised her eyebrows. "To me?"

Dan leaned forward. "This has gone too far. We need to work together. Trust me, you need to take this call."

Trisha rose. "OK. Come with me to get your phone." Dan walked out between them to the front desk reception, where his cell phone and keyrings were handed back to him.

Back in the room, he called McBride and explained the situation.

McBride said, "This had to happen. I did tell you in the beginning, Dan."

"I'm putting you on," Dan said. He handed the phone to Trisha who took it. Dan watched in silence as her face changed. She glanced at Dan, then averted her gaze.

"Yes," she said, and reached for the laptop. She tapped on keys, clearly writing down what McBride was giving her. Dan could guess what it was. His cover in the DOD was as an agent for Consular Operations, a small unit that on paper, acted as liaison between the DOD and the State Department. In reality, it didn't do anything but provide people like Dan with an ID card and a job title.

He watched as Trisha squinted at the screen. Then she nodded and hung up. Bellamy was hunched forward.
Trisha asked, "Who was that guy?"
"My VA man. What did he say?"
Trisha rolled her eyes at him. "VA, huh? Anyway, you got some creds. Should have a card sent over to us shortly." She stood and prdocued her cell from a pocket. "I need to get approval from my boss to let you in. Stay here." With Bellamy, she walked out. Dan waited.

They came back in ten minutes. Trisha slid over a card hanging from a lanyard. It said, "Temporary Non Official Agent." Dan shrugged and put it around his neck.
"Now," Trisha said softly, "tell us what happened in the park."
"Did you find any bodies?" Dan asked.
She shook her head slowly. "Should we?"
"Did you look?"
She didn't answer, but from the look on her face Dan knew they had. It figured. Dan said, "They had a backup team to removed the bodies. You didn't find them, did you?"
"No."
"Which meant they were on constant visual contact with the two men."
"Did you kill them?" Bellamy asked.
"It was self defense. Them or me."
"How?" Trisha asked. Dan explained.

"Any ID marks? Wallets?"

"Nothing."

"Tell me about the guns." Trisha said.

I Dan told her. "That serial number should be trackable. But I reckon I know already."

"What?"

"The two Colt M1911's I got from the dead guys are the type used by Navy SEALs. They have waterproof chambers. Picatinny rails for attachments, like sights. The hand grips were specialized too, and non-slip, for use in water."

Trisha was frowning. "What are you saying?"

"I am saying these guys were not your run of the mill thugs. The way they tracked me, their weapons, points to a certain type."

"What type?"

"Ex special forces. Seals, Rangers, Delta, Marine Recon, if these guys are American. They might not be. I don't know. I'm guessing."

"That's bad news."

Dan said, "Yes. I was lucky to escape before the back up team arrived."

Bellamy asked, "Why do you think this is happening? This team has you under surveillance as well, right?"

Dan clenched his jaws. There was a lot he didn't understand, but being under watch in his own country was not something he had expected. He shook his head. To be honest, why was he surprised?

Trisha was watching him closely. She said, "Now can you tell us more about Kowalski?"

Dan told them what he knew from McBride. When he finished, Trisha seemed lost in thought. "Funny that."

"What?"

"He did the same with us."

Dan's ears perked up. "He called the FBI?"

"Yes. Most calls to the switchboard we dismiss as prank calls, unless they want to meet face to face. Which is what he did."

"The day he was shot happened to be your appointment with him," Dan said.

"Exactly."

"What did he say on the phone?"

"It concerned national security. He did not have much time. It was urgent."

"Anything else?"

Trisha`s face blanched as she the memory hit her again. She became visibly pale. Her voice dropped a notch. "He said what was about to happen would make 9/11 seem like child's play."

Dan leaned forward, frowning. "Did he mention any dates?"

"No. But he said time was running out."

CHAPTER 4

Dan had to show his ID at the desk and enter his details. Bellamy stayed at the large and busy Washington Field Office, while Dan and Trisha walked to the parking lot. She got into a Ford Taurus and they drove to the Langhorne office block, the crime scene. Dan glanced at the spot where the old man had been shot down. Yellow and black police tape cordoned off the area. White chalk mark showed where the body had lain.

"What happened was not your fault."

"Not sure I follow you."

"The old man contacted you," Dan said. "And you had him under surveillance. But you weren't to know a sniper was tracking him."

Trisha had pulled up on the kerbside. She killed the engine and looked at Dan. Her green eyes were large, and they searched his face. Dan felt something tighten in his guts, then release. Was there something in her eyes, or was it his imagination.

Trisha said, "You think you have me all figured out, huh?"

"Not at all. We just met. But I can the passion you have for the job. Just don't be hard on yourself. There are others waiting to do that."

"I'll remember that."

Trisha opened the car door and got out. Dan followed. Leroy, the security guard, looked up as the approached the reception counter. He was standing behind a middle-aged receptionist lady.

"Hey Leroy" Dan said.

"You know him?" Trisha asked. Leroy was more confident than before. He rolled his shoulders inside the pale brown uniform and strode out from behind the reception. He hooked his thumbs in his belt.

"You the guy who came in here after the shooting?"

"Yes."

"Who is she?"

Trisha flashed her badge. "Special Agent Dunne, FBI."

Leroy swallowed and took a step back.

"Leroy, you want to take us to the fifth floor?" Dan asked.

"Sure," Leroy said. He moved towards the elevator.

"No," said Dan. "We take the stairs. They ran down after the shooting. We need to have a look around."

There was nothing in the stairwell. They went up to the fifth floor.

"How did you know it was the fifth floor?" Trisha asked.

"I didn't," Dan said. "Because of the tree cover on the avenue, I knew it could not be any lower than the fifth. It seemed about the right elevation. It could have been the sixth or seventh, but I found what I was looking for right here." He did not tell her about the soldier`s common and frustrating experience of being fired upon and not being able to find the source. It was second nature to him still, to look where the bullet was coming from. Without that, he could not fire back. No point wasting ammo that could save your life later.

Dan knelt before the open window. He pointed to the floor. "This is where the dust was disturbed by the knee pad. He was kneeling on one knee." He pointed to the wall. "See where the dust has shaken? He leant against the wall as well." Dan stepped back from the window at a diagonal angle. He crouched, and took out an imaginary rifle. He leaned slightly to the left.

"Like this," he said. "But with the barrel just out level with the window sill. Maybe he had a microphone embedded in his ear. Someone telling him to take the shot before the old man crossed the street. Sniping is always a two-man job. More sometimes, if a backup team is present."

Dan stood up and walked to the sill. He leaned closer without touching anything, then pointed to a black mark on the sill. It was about two inches long, and looked like shoe polish.

"Discharge from the weapon," he said. "He left in a hurry. He took the shell case, but he should have wiped down the window sill as well. Maybe your crime scene guys can uncover more from here."

Trisha looked impressed. "I am guessing the shooter used this building as it was the only one available?"

Dan nodded. "Your guess is as good as mine. The ones opposite where the old man was must all be occupied office blocks. This was the only free one, and distant enough for him to make an escape. But you can check on that. How long for the ME to do his report?"

"The case only started four hours ago. Tomorrow maybe."

They walked down the stairwell again. Trisha moved slower, checking the bannisters and landings to make sure she didn't miss anything.

When they got to the car, Trisha asked, "Do you remember the registration plate?"

Dan had it memorized. An out of state number. He gave it to her. Trisha wrote it down. She drove back to the WFO. Traffic was heavier now, and several times she had to honk to be let through. Dan could tell she wanted to flick her front bumper lights and siren on. When they finally reached the office, Trish parked and waited for a while before she spoke.

"What will you do now?"

"Ask around about the old man," Dan said truthfully. She seemed disappointed by the answer, but recovered quickly. "If anything happens, I will let you know."

"Right," Dan said, getting out of the car.

CHAPTER

Pechora
North East Russia

The Daryal is one of Russia`s flagship anti ballistic missile radar systems. Seven of these giant long phased array radar, or LPAR systems surround Moscow, designed to give early warning of any incoming ballistic missiles, whether nuclear, chemical or conventional weapons capable. And not just ICBM`s or inter continental ballistic missiles. The low mirrors of the LPAR`s look towards the low atmospheric levels, and can pick up US or NATO spy planes flying at 30-50,000 feet. The radars themselves are two huge collection of mirrors 80 by 80m across. They are separated by a distance of 1.5km. Each station occupies more than 5km radius in space. Only two are operational, one in Pechora and the other in Belarus. Inside an office of the HQ in Pechora, Field Corporal Asimov was hunched over his screen, looking at a display. He printed the display, rose and tore off the paper that came out of the printer and took it to his commanding officer. His boss, Field Lieutenant Timoshenko, acknowledged his salute, and took the paper from his hand.

Asimov said, "From the Zemlya satellite sir. Not seen anything like this before."

The Zemlya group of satellites, in geo stationary orbit high above continental USA, are Russia`s cold war brand of spy satellites. Released in the 1960`s by the older generation Soyuz rockets, and superseded now by the Bars M recon satellites that monitor American military installations, the Zemlya`s are still extremely useful to the SVR, Russia`s foreign intelligence service.

Timoshenko looked tired. He was three years from retirement, and he did not like the fact that the GRU, or the military intelligence wing, had not given him a plum placement in the Kremlin. He was having to see out his last years of service in this isolated post, listening to extra terrestrial squeaks. He brushed a hand over his white hair, and squinted at the paper. He said, "It`s a digital distress signal. What location have you got from the satellite?"

Asimov told him. Timoshenko`s face changed. He looked at the page again, at the numbers and letters in the signal that were undoubtedly a coded message.

"Dismissed," Timoshenko barked at his younger colleague. He turned and headed back to his own cabin. He took out the pressed black leather notebook embossed with the gold GRU sign that every GRU agent carries. He thumbed down to a phone number and then dialled it, staring at the paper in his hand.

****

General Grigori Evanovich was watching the frost on the trees from his window. His third floor office on the sumptuous, grand old KGB building, Number 2 Lubyanskaya Ploschad, afforded him a direct view of the imposing towers of the Moscow State University One. He was a similar age to Timoshenko, in his late sixties. He had served for many years in the GRU, and then left for the KGB, which had now become the SVR.

Evanovich had been the head of Unit 3, or space affairs with the GRU. Now, with the SVR, he looked after agents trained and working abroad in both clandestine and public capacities. He preferred working for the SVR. The GRU had, in his mind, an old school, sclerotic mentality where rank still mattered more than anything else. The SVR was not exactly a breath of fresh air, but it was still an environment where he was given more responsibility, and more pay. With his daughter in graduate school in Italy, he needed every rouble he could afford.

But Evanovich liked his old-world charms. Which is why he had insisted on having his new office in the large old KGB building. The SVR actually occupied the new sixty acre complex in Yazenevo, south Moscow. But many of the top brass of the SVR had secretly re located to the Number 2

Lubyanskaya Ploschad. The Ploschad, or Square, was discreetly tucked away in south eastern Moscow, and its rabbit warren of rooms afforded privacy. And Evanovich had the ear of the War Minister, and most other members of the Politburo. That helped in his relocation as well.

Evanovich startled as the phone rang. He was deep in thought about his daughter, and his wife`s illness. He stared at the phone for a second, then picked it up slowly. He did not want it to be a call from the hospital.

"Timoshenko here. Is that you, Grigori?"

Relief flooded through Evanovich as the voice of his old friend. "Sasha!," he exclaimed. Sasha was a nick name for most Russian men who were called Alexeyevich or Alexander. "You old bastard, how are you?"

Timoshenko said, "People in glass houses should not throw stones, Grigori. The last time we met you had less hair than me."

Evanovich smiled. They had been long time colleagues at the GRU. He had made the move, poor Timoshenko had not.

He said, "Are you in Moscow, Sasha?"

"No, still in Pechora."

Something in Timoshenko`s voice alerted Evanovich. "This line is secure. What is it?"

Evanovich listened. His hand gripped the received hard, and he flopped back on the desk chair.

"Jesus, Sasha," he said. "How many signals have you got?"

"Two so far. You have the key to decode them?"

Evanovich said, "Yes. But they only mean one thing."

Timoshenko said, "I know comrade. That is why I am calling you."

Evanovich let out a deep sigh. "We knew this day would come one day. Let me speak to the War Minister, and arrange a meeting with the politburo. I am sending a car down for you. Bring all the papers with you. And Sasha?"

"Yes?"

"This is top secret. You know that, right?"

"Yes comrade. I was there, remember?" Timoshenko hung up.

CHAPTER 5

Capitol Hill
Washington DC

General Peyton Mildred marched up the stairs of the
venerable building, his sharp heels clacking against the stone.
In his early fifties, General Mildred was the proud recipient of
the Legion of Merit with two gold stars, numerous service
medals and the Combat Action Ribbon, on top of being a two-
star general. As he looked down at his swiftly moving feet, he
reflected on how little all that meant to him now. In his
younger days he had believed in a higher cause. Yes, his
country. And his innate sense of leadership had led him from
being a legendary warfighter in the Marine Recon Force, to the
halls of the Department of Defense. That too, had been a
higher calling. He wanted to improve a soldier`s life, period.
Bureaucracy had not come easy to him. It did not to most
former soldiers. But some managed better than others. He
managed somehow, and that, with his service record, had
been enough.
But not any longer. He had chased stars and bars for long
enough. The DoD would survive without him. But the men he
had served with would not. Their lives, the miserable state of
affairs at the VA, these are what kept him going. Politicians
came and went, and it did not matter which side they came
from. Ultimately, they were all the same.
Corporate whores. Always had been, and always would be. If
there was anything about his country that Mildred could
change, it would be the nexus of big money and politics. An
unholy nexus, in his mind. He reached the top of the stairs
quickly, and breathed a deep sigh. He was supremely fit still,
and had not even broken a sweat. He pushed all thoughts out
of his mind, set his lips determinedly and walked into the
giant lobby of the Senate House.

The usher was waiting for him inside. The young man saluted crisply, and Mildred smiled at the excess of youth. He was in uniform, but this was a civilian site. The usher had no need to salute.

"This way please, General Mildred." He followed the usher down a bevy of corridors till they came to the large mahogany double doors of a meeting room. The usher knocked and the respectfully opened the door. He spoke before he stepped back.

"General Mildred, I would like to mention what an honour it is to see you in real life, sir. What you have done for the veterans is appreciated by the whole country."

Mildred raised his eyebrows. "Why, thank you, young man." Mildred walked into the long, rectangular room. Most Senate Intelligence Committee Meetings are held in designated rooms in Capitol Hill. Occasionally, they are held elsewhere, mainly in CIA HQ at Langley. They could go on for days, but this one, the Senate had promised, would be a quick affair. Opposite the bank of senators sat a lean, tall figure in Army uniform. Joint Chief of Staff Steven Harding stood up, and shook Mildred`s hand.

"Thanks for coming, Peyton."

"How you doing, Steve. Been here the whole week?"

General Harding smiled. He looked tired, despite the assured brevity of the hearing. "You know what it`s like, Peyton. We just got started," he added in a low voice.

"That I do," Mildred said, and took his seat next to another colleague from Pentagon. After handshakes with the Director and Assistant Deputy Director of the CIA, the meeting began in earnest. The meeting concerned a group of SEAL Team Six operatives who had a failed exfiltration from Syria. The mission had been a raid on a government building in Damascus, and it had been classified. Of the four member team, three had unfortunately died. The fourth had been captured, and was not heard from again. Everyone knew he was tortured for information in the infamous prison hospital of Damascus.

Eventually, the lead Senator of the Armed Forces Select Committee looked up from his report pages, and put his glasses to one side. His name was James Walsh.

"To my mind, there is only one course of action," he said.

General Harding said, "What is that?"

After a pause, Senator Walsh spoke. "Deny the whole mission." Around him, several heads began to nod in agreement.

Peyton Mildred felt his whole body stiffen up. He tried to catch Harding`s eyes, but he was staring straight at the politicians. Mildred put his hands on the table and cleared his throat. All heads turned to look at him.

"These men deserve recognition Sir. They are our most elite fighters. The mission was a success, you will recall. The target was neutralised. Yes, we lost the men, but they gave their lives for this country. We owe them a military burial."

"At what diplomatic cost, General?" The Republican said. "The Russians are hopping mad that we were there in the first place. Only last week the President signed a memorandum with the Russian Premier to cease hostilities involving special forces."

Another Senator, a House Democrat this time, said, "An escalation of hostilities with Russian will only go one way, General Mildred. You know that."

Mildred choked on his words. Horrible visions appeared in his mind. The forgotten special troops who had been forsaken in the South China Seas. The family and media were told they had died on a sunken ship in the Pacific. The list went on. The Marine Recon Force members left to starve in the deserts outside Iraq. Men under his command, that he had to lie to the media about.

All for what?

"General, are you ok?" one of the Senators asked.

Mildred gazed at him vacantly, as if seeing him for the first time. Maybe he was. For the first time he was seeing them for what they were.

"Yes," he said. "I am fine."

CHAPTER 9

The US Capitol Building stamps its authority on the eastern edge of Washington`s National Mall, rising more than three hundred feet in the air.

On a sunny day, the stunning white building evokes memories of Rome in its heyday, and that similarity is exactly what the nation`s forefathers hoped to achieve. The home of the House of Congress, and the seat of all federal legislature, one could argue it is the most important government building in America. Its perimeters are more than 750 feet in length, and 350 feet deep, and the building encloses a staggering sixteen acres of floor space.

The newly built underground visitor`s complex is similarly grand, comprising almost 500 thousand square feet of meeting halls, restaurants and visitor`s booths.

Nicholas Carlyle and his team walked in through the revolving door of the main lobby with their equipment. Nicholas, known as Nick to his friends and colleagues, stopped and looked up at the glass ceiling. He had not been to the visitor`s complex since its inauguration in 2008. Nick was not a man who was easily awed. But the sight facing his upturned face had only one adjective to describe it: awesome. The entire ceiling was made of glass, and discreetly placed lights did not obstruct the view of the illuminated Capitol Dome above it, rising like an ethereal white vision into the night sky.

Nick took a moment to appreciate the vista above, then transferred his gaze down. Despite this being the subterranean chamber, it felt as open and airy as out in the open. The ceiling did a lot for that, but the wide, stretching lobby helped too. Nick indicated to his three- man team, and they wheeled in the grey steel box in its portable trolley. A smattering of guards patrolled the area, and as expected, one of them approached them. The guard`s face was unsmiling, and his eyes cold and examining. As he approached them, he raised his hand. Nick thought it was meant for them, and he motioned for the team to stop. But the raised arm was a signal for something else. Two other guards who were standing motionless at the periphery suddenly galvanized into motion, approaching the group at a brisk trot. Out of the corner of his eye Nick saw a guard at the checkpoint desk speak to his buddy, and then head over rapidly. Nick nodded to himself. It was all expected.

"Good evening, guys," the guard said, hands on his belt, not far from his weapon. Nick looked at the name sewn above his left pocket.

"Hi Gomez. We are here for maintenance works."

"Can I see some ID please?" Gomez asked.

Nick took out his federal government sub-contractor ID and handed it over. Gomez looked at it carefully, while his three friends spread out and around them, keeping an eye on the team.

"We were not informed about any scheduled maintenance works this evening," Gomez said, handing back the ID card to Nick.

"I know, it was last minute. I got the call this morning. One of the frames of the "Capture of Narcissi" painting in the National Statuary Hall has come unhinged," Nick said. He was relaxed. He knew exactly what he was talking about. Someone had taken a pair of pliers to the 150 year old painting this morning, and broken the frame at its lower right edge. The whole operation had been planned to perfection.

Gomez shrugged and looked at one of his colleagues. "You know anything about this?"

"No," his colleague said. "But I can send someone to check. I`ll also call up the evening Maintenance Supervisor to check the detail." He looked at Nick. "What`s the name of your company?"

"A1 Restorations."

When the man walked off, Gomez turned his attention back to Nick.

"What`s in the case?"

"The frame, separated into sections."

"I need to see inside."

"Of course."

Two of the men put the trolley on the floor. The steel grey case was made of hardened carbon fibres to keep it light. It was ten feet long, and four feet wide. The men unlocked the metal clasps at either end and lifted up the lid. Gomez shuffled forward and peered in. Inside, Nick knew Gomez would be looking at an assortment of varnished timber frames, each in their own compartment of the sponged interior. He would inspect any closer, or lift them up to see what lay underneath. Gomez took out his portable metal detector and ran it over the wood frames. This was the only part that Nick had been wary of. He knew the technology worked, but he did not know if Gomez had a new type of metal detector. In a conventional metal detector, the electric coil in the detector created a magnetic field. When this magnetic field came into contact with a metallic surface, it beeped. But Nick`s hidden cargo had a magnetic field deflector built into it. He watched with bated breath as the guard took his time in passing the spherical, flat face around the entire case.

Suddenly there was a beeping, and a red flashing light from the detector. A knot of apprehension tightened in Nick`s guts. Instinctively, his right arm moved to his coat pocket, but he was not carrying tonight. None of them were. There was no point in getting stopped at the security checkpoint for packing a weapon. But he had to do something. Nick took a step forward, and bent over Gomez.

"Is there a problem?"

Gomez looked at him, then straightened slowly. He shrugged. "It beeped when I got to the metal locks on the side." He pointed at them.

Nick checked his sigh of relief. "Ah, I see."

"You need to bring that thing around the other gate," Gomez indicated a steel door that was the good entrance. "But the rest of you have to go through security first."

"No problem," Nick said. Gomez`s colleague came back and whispered in his ear. Gomez nodded.

"You got the green light," he said to Nick. "Do you know where the Statuary Hall is?"

In fifteen minutes, they were ascending in an elevator with their luggage and one of the guards as their escort. The guard opened the door to the Statuary Hall and they trooped in. The room was built like a Greek amphitheatre, with life size statues of great American standing in a semicircle. The hall was empty. The guard tipped his hat at them and left.

"Right guys," Nick said. "Let's get this show on the road."

CHAPTER 10

Dan had walked over from his apartment to the WFO. He didn't see a car parked opposite his house anymore, and no one followed him. His cell phone was dismantled, and he left it as his apartment. Trisha was waiting for him when he arrived.

She said, "Kowalski had a daughter, right? Antonia."

"That's what it said in the hospital records. Surprised you didn't look there."

Dan caught the sudden flush on her cheeks and grinned. "Sure it's in your files somewhere."

Trisha shook her head slightly, a look of irritation on her face. "There are hundreds of Antonia Kowalski's. When we narrow the search down to DC, there's only ten, and all of them are elderly. No one has signed in under that name in DC hotels in the last two months."

Dan frowned. "You sure? The nurse said she saw the daughter visit."

"Did you pick up any other details, like DOB or address?"

Dan said, "Nope. There was just her name and relation to mother."

"Kind of strange that she didn't leave her cell number at the hospital. Or address," Trisha mused, almost to herself.

Dan saw where she was going. "Almost like she didn't want to be found. She could have used a fake name?"

Trisha nodded. "To throw us off scent if she was trying to hide. But I'm sure we can find something if we go through her parents' medical records."

"They lived in that address all their lives, or moved around?"

"Moved around a fair bit actually. I have a record now of their addresses as they moved around. Mostly up and down the East Coast."

Dan pondered in silence. "He had to be kept safe, I guess. He must have been an important asset for the CIA."

Trisha asked, "Have you asked your contact about more information on him?"

Dan shook his head. "He doesn't know. But there are things that CIA don't tell anyone. Kowalski might well have grown tired of the CIA, and realized they couldn't protect him, or his family any more. Hence, he reached out to us, and the FBI."

And he must have known the General he spoke to for a while, Dan thought to himself.

Trisha's cell phone beeped. She checked it, then went to her laptop on the desk and clicked on the keyboard. She looked up at Dan. "This is interesting. There are several female Kowalski's with other first names in the DC area. We narrowed the search to young females and now have hits on fifty females."

Dan said, "And we have the photo from his bedroom. You could do a face match."

Trisha nodded. "It's ongoing right now. This is assuming of course, that the photo in Kowalski's house is his daughter's."

Dan shrugged. "Who else could it be? And even if it's not, she is a person of interest, right?"

"Uh-huh."

Trisha said, "I need to see the nurse at the hospital myself. Did she say if the daughter came to see her on her own, or with Victor?"
"I don't know. She didn't say." Dan thought to himself. "Hospitals have CCTV, right? Antonia, if that's her name, would have to sign on the visitor's book so we can get the date. Then its a matter of going through the images to see if we find her."
Trisha said, "Will be difficult if she came on her own. But the nurse might be able to identify her. Then it's a matter of matching her face on our databases."
"If we get the image right, then the NSA Signals Directorate at Fort Meade would be a better idea. Their supercomputers snoop for matches the world over. Your database will look for known felons only, right?"
"Yes."
Trisha said "Strange how apart from the photos no other documents were present. Like, anything with their names on it."
"Like he didn't want anyone to know."
They were both silent for a while. Dan said, "A lot depends on us finding the daughter. Let's hope we get a match from the searches. Do you want me to contact the NSA at Fort Meade. I can use back channels which might save time."
"You do that."
Dan had been in touch with Tim Dalton, the Director of the Signals Intelligence Division of the NSA in his last mission. He had Tim's personal number and called him. They spoke for a while, then Dan hung up. He told Trisha, "He'll start it on his MYSTIC and ID-300 databases. But he wants you to formally contact him as well, just so the request is logged."

"Roger that."

Dan asked, "What about Kowalski's employer, if he had one? Or was he retired?"
Trisha said, "He was retired, but prior to that he held down a number of different jobs as he moved around."
"What was his latest job?"
"There's no record of any recent employment."
Dan thought to himself. The only contact of Kowalski's he knew was the bar owner near the crime scene. He told Trisha. "Sure, you head down there. I have paperwork to catch up on. Call me if you find anything."

Dan walked out of the WFO and decided to walk the two klicks to the bar at the corner of K and 13th Street. There was a small lunch time crowd, mostly office workers from the nearby buildings. Dan took a seat at the bar, looking around him. Three waiters were going from table to table taking orders and behind the counter he saw two chefs busy at work. In a while, he saw the owner emerge from the kitchen, wiping his hands on an apron. He saw Dan and came over.

"Have you been served, sir?" He began, then stopped as he recognized Dan. "You're the guy who asked about the old man, right?"

Dan nodded. "That's right. His death is now a federal investigation."

The man narrowed his eyes. "See, I knew you were a cop."
Dan shook his head. "I am anything but, my friend. But I am helping the investigation. I was wondering if you could tell me anything more about him."
The man pursed his lips. His hands were still wringing the apron, and Dan could see the tell tale signs of anxiety.

"Listen, I'm not a cop, and I don't have any powers to arrest people. I can see you're a god guy, or you wouldn't have trusted me with Victor Kowalski's details. I appreciate that." The bar owner stopped wringing his hands and regarded Dan carefully. Dan said, "What's your name?"

He hesitated before replying. "Miguel. Look mister, I'm a simple man. I have a wife and kids. I run this bar as a business and that's all I do. I don't want any trouble."

"And there's none coming your way. Trust me."

"You sure?" Miguel asked nervously.

"Positive. Now, can you get me a drink while we talk?"

"Sure. What do you want?"

"Americano with a shot of espresso, white."

Miguel gave the order to a waitress at the counter, then sat back opposite Dan. "What do you want to know?"

Dan shrugged. "Anything. We aren't having much luck finding people Kowalski interacted with, so you're our best bet for now."

Miguel was lost in thought. "You know, in many ways, he was an odd guy. Loner, never said much. Hard to figure him out."

A waitress put Dan's coffee down in front of him. Dan thanked her and took a sip. "How did he come here? Walking?"

"I saw him get off the bus once, right opposite." Miguel pointed. Dan turned to look. Across the road a knot of people were waiting for the next arrival.

Miguel said, "Hang on. You just reminded me. He came once or twice in a car. I remember it cos it was an old, beaten up old jalopy the first time I saw it. Like an old Plymouth with those big fins."

"I know which ones you mean."

"Right. The second time, he had it all repaired and painted, and it looked nice. He told me he was into old machines."

"Did you get the registration number, by any chance?"

Miguel shook his head. "*Lo siento*. No, I didn't." Miguel tapped the counter. "But I remember talking to him about the car. He said he had a garage."

Dan thought about the garage where Kowalski lived. It had been searched and nothing was found. "You mean in his house?"

"No. He had a mechanic's garage, space he used to hire. I didn't get why he had to do that, but you know, none of my business." Miguel shrugged.

"Did he tell you were it was?"

"Nope. But he did mention it was close, within walking distance."

Dan felt an excitement clutch at his guts. This was new information they could use. He drained the coffee and stood. "Thanks Miguel. You did well."

Dan spoke to Trisha as he walked back.

She said, "We have an app for that. If these were professional garages for hire, even if it's just a lock down place, we can get to it."

"See you back at base," Dan said and hung up. By the time he had taken the metro back to the buzzing WFO, the March sky was darkening with clouds. A stiff breeze had picked up off the river.

Trisha was in her office when he knocked and walked in. Bellamy was standing with his back to Dan and he turned quickly. His features didn't relax when he saw Dan, who stared back at him before sitting in the chair opposite Trisha.

"Any news?" Dan asked.

"Yes," Trisha said. "There is an alley of garages one block away from where Kowalski lived. But none of them were rented out to him, or owned by him. Bellamy went through the list of owners."

"Great, at least we know where to start looking. Any news on his daughter?"

"Nope. You heard anything from your friend at the NSA?"

"Nada," Dan said. Bellamy was standing still to one side. Dan ignored him. He said to Trisha, "Let's check the garage out."

Bellamy said, "I gotta catch up on some paperwork. See you guys back here."

Trisha nodded at him, and Dan followed her down to the parking lot. Trisha said, "Do you think we need back up?"

Dan was thinking the same thing. It was possible they weren't the only ones to know about Kowalski's garage. But both of them were armed.

He said, "It should be fine. We can patrol the area before going in."

Trisha weaved her S line Audi A5 through the traffic till they arrived at the quieter residential location. The street in question was a cul de sac, with the garages at the end. Trisha had stopped the car at the mouth of the street.

"Drive around and stop at the next block" Dan said. When they parked and got out, Dan took some time to observe the buildings around the cul de sac. There weren't any high rises within easy visual reach. The glistening metal tower blocks of downtown were more than three klicks away and trees shielded the cul de sac from easy prying eyes.

Maybe Kowalski chose this spot for a reason.

He felt for the weapon in his belt line. "I go in first. Stay in my line of vision and I'll signal to you if OK to step in."

Trisha raised her eyebrows. "Who put you in charge?"

"Nobody. I'm used to doing things on my own. You know that. Hope you don't have a problem."

Trisha studied him for a while. "As long as you don't start breaking down doors or shooting people we should be fine."

"Sure," Dan said.

"I mean it. I really don't want a federal agent breaking the law."

Dan said, "I ain't no federal agent. But I'll remember what you said."

Trisha opened the dashboard and took out a rectangular box. Inside it rested four pairs of headphones. She gave Dan one and put one on herself. The radio device was small and fit into Dan's waistband. They did a comms check to make sure the line worked.

Dan nodded at Trisha, then walked off into the narrow street, keeping his eyes peeled.

CHAPTER

The street existed solely as a garage and storage area. Dan walked past a few lock up store rooms. He saw no one else. The whitewashed walls rose above the rows of garages and he looked at each one as he walked towards the end. Halfway down, Dan stopped. He didn't know which garage to look into, and he had found nothing that gave him a clue. He was looking for something well maintained, and large. Kowalski wouldn't have space to do up a vintage car without the space.

He also didn't like the thought of going to the end of this blind alley. The only exit was behind him and there was nowhere to take cover. But he hadn't seen anything to cause him concern. Dan touched his earpiece, creating a hiss of static.

"Can't see anyone here. That doesn't mean its risk free. Keep your weapon handy."

Trisha hung up and Dan pressed himself against the side of a garage, watching the ones opposite. His eyes travelled all the way down to the end, where the big trees rose from a line of back gardens. The screen of leaves hid the houses effectively. He saw movement to his right. It was Trisha, coming towards him cautiously. Her head moved suddenly and Dan detected a shadow opposite. He crouched immediately and drew his Sig. He was about to extend his weapon when his arm relaxed. A red garage door was opening further down. An old woman emerged, oblivious to the two of them.

Dan stood as Trisha came alongside. The old woman was locking the garage door up.

"Do you think she's seen us?" Trisha asked.

"I doubt it," Dan said.

The woman turned as Dan finished speaking. She saw them and stopped. Dan had put his gun away already and approached her slowly.

"Sorry to bother you ma'am. But we're here about a friend, Victor Kowalski. He had a garage here where he repaired old cars. Did you ever see him?"

The woman's white hair fell past her shoulders and was long but sparse at the top. Lines etched her cheeks and forehead and her face was sunbeaten. She stared at Dan for a long time. Age hadn't dulled the sharp glint in her eyes.

"Who wants to know?" she asked. She glanced at Trisha who was standing next to Dan.

"I'm a friend-

"If you're a friend you would know where the garage was, right?"

Trisha said, "So you knew Victor Kowalski?"

The woman stared at Trisha. "Is he in trouble? Are you cops?"

Trisha flashed her badge. "Special Agent Trisha Dunne." She explained what had happened to Kowalski.

The woman's shoulders sagged. Her head dropped downwards.

Dan said, "Ma'am are you OK?"

She lifted weary eyes to him. "When you've lived as long as I have not much surprises you. But Victor was a good man. I can't think of anyone out to kill him."

"You knew him?"

"Not very well. I use this place to store my old stuff and he had the garage down there. We used to chat when we met. He helped to fix my radio and computer once. I trusted him enough to invite him around."

Trisha said, "We would really appreciate if you would come down to the station. What's your name?"

"Brenda Sheldon."

"Well Brenda, do you know which garage belonged to Mr. Kowalski?"

"Sure. It's the one before the last one on the right. There's a line of them bigger garages near the end. I can't remember the number."

Trisha took Brenda's address and phone number. As they were leaving, Brenda called out. "I hope you find who did this to him."

Dan nodded. "We will don't worry." After a second he aksed, "Did Victor ever speak to you about his daughter?"

Brenda frowned. "I never knew he had a daughter. He never mentioned it."

"Thank you, Brenda. Won't keep you any longer."

Dan felt the old woman's eyes on his back as they walked away. Brenda was right about one thing, Dan reflected. The older he got, the less he was surprised by man's ability to cause himself grief.

Trisha had walked ahead of him, and stopped outside a black painted garage. There was only one more after this one, and then the high wall. It was wide enough to fit two cars in side by side.

Trisha said, "She said this one, right?"

"Size seems right," Dan said. He walked up to gate and peered at the crack between metal and wall. He could see nothing but darkness. The gate was a pull-down type and it was firmly locked. The handle in the middle of the door was bar shaped. It could be turned and lifted, Dan assumed, as there was a keyhole in the middle. Trisha had seen it too. "I have something in the car. Wait up."

Trisha was wearing flat shoes with rubber soles, and she jogged back to her car. Dan checked around the margins of the gate, and at the top, where the sheet of corrugated iron acted as the roof. He walked back and stared at the garage, noticing the entire row, separated by a two-layer brick wall. A sense of unease had come over him and he couldn't shake it.

One of the grimmest experiences of his Army life had been the random discoveries of Improvised Explosive Devices or IED's in Iraq and Afghanistan. Dead cows could be stuffed with C4. Landmines on the roadside would blow off soldier's legs. Nothing could erase from his mind the image of his buddy lying on the ground, leg hanging loose from the kneecap.

Dan came back to the present. He thought hard about Kowalski. A man he had seen for the briefest of seconds, before his head evaporated. K had been a Colonel in the Russian Army. Despite all the talk of Russian superiority, Dan knew well that the Russians copied western Army training and technology. K would've had training in explosives and ordnance.

Dan caught movement in the corner of his eyes. Trisha was hurrying back. She nodded at Dan and walked towards the garage, producing a large key ring.

"No," Dan shouted, running forward. Trisha stopped dead.

Dan said, "The door could be tamper proof. Trying different keys could blow the whole thing up." He explained his reasoning to her. Trisha raised her eyebrows.

"You think this place is booby trapped? Kind of extreme in a civilian neighborhood, don't you think?"

"You willing to take the risk it's not?," Dan countered.

Trisha moved forward and Dan grabbed her arm. "Come back here. I need to show you something." He let go of her.

They walked back and away from the garage, from where they could see the door at angle. Dan moved till they were a safe distance away. He pointed at the bar handle.

"Wires could be connected to the keyhole, that give way when a key is inserted several times. The wires break, triggering the charge that fires the explosive. It could be packed behind the handle."

Trisha shaded her eyes and looked. She opened her mouth to speak. But the words were swallowed in the sudden boom of the explosion that shattered the garage door.

CHAPTER

Dan had moved instinctively, draping his arms over Trisha, pushing her down to the floor. The orange fireball smashed the garage door, flinging its debris in the air. Dan lowered his head as the pieces of iron and wood rained down and hit him on the back. Trisha was spooned against him, her back pressed to his chest. Black smoke rushed out of the gaping hole where the door had once been.

As the smoke cleared Dan reached for his weapon. He pointed and jerked it around. The smoke was stinging his eyes and he could taste blood on his lips. He wiped the liquid off his lips and wiped his hands on his shirt. His attention was focused where the street opened to the main road, their only exit. He could hear Trisha speaking on her ear piece. She was connected to the base as well on a different channel, he realized.

"Let's go," Dan shouted. Sig pointing straight, Dan crouched and ran, ignoring the pain on his back and the blood that kept congealing above his left eye. They were sitting ducks here. As they ran, Dan looked behind him and up. The surrounding buildings were set well back, and the trees at the rear blocked a straight view. Panting, they leaned against the wall at the exit. A few people had stopped to look, and they shrank back with exclamations when they saw Dan and Trisha with their guns.

Sirens sounded in the distance. "Head for the car," Dan said. A few cars had slowed down as well. Passengers were pulling windows down to gape at the scene.
Trisha barked at the onlookers on the pavement. "Please clear this area. This is a crime scene." She held her badge up and said her name. Dan followed her, weapon trained, as she ran across the road. Trisha turned the engine on and took another call from the WFO.

A convoy of three SUV's arrived, sirens blazing. They were followed by two patrol cars, and they blocked the road in both directions. Dan saw a white van with the words Bomb Disposal Unit come to a stop opposite. A man in a white suit opened the rear door, getting equipment out.

Dan got out of the car, scanning the windows of surrounding buildings. Several were open now and he could make out faces peering down. Dan caught sight of Bellamy striding towards them.

Dan said, "We need to get a visual from above. And I don't trust this scene. A sniper could open fire on us."

Bellamy said, "We're putting snipers on the roofs around us already. A drone is getting scrambled. Should be above in ten minutes."

"Good," Dan said.

"What the hell happened?" Bellamy asked. Trisha joined them.

Before Dan could speak she pointed at his head. "You need to get that looked at?"

"Just a scratch," Dan said. "Don't feel anything, it should be fine." He looked at Bellamy. "To answer your question, we were expected. And lucky to be alive."

Trisha said, "Hold up. Are you saying the place wasn't booby trapped?"

Dan shook his head. "No. Whoever did this knew we were coming. The explosive was detonated from a distance, maybe with a cell phone call. I don't know. The bomb disposal guys can tell us."

Trisha frowned. "I didn't see any cars following us."

Bellamy looked around him. "Jeez, they had a line of sight. Maybe still around here somewhere. Good job we have the drone."

Dan said, "He's probably long gone. But yeah, still worth keeping a lookout."

Trisha and Dan went back to the garage. The place was now a hive of activity. The bomb disposal unit guys were joined by crime scene investigators. Four of them were kneeling over the destroyed door, and one stepped inside as Dan watched, taking photos.

Trisha handed him some gloves and pointed at the plastic matts that had been laid on the ground for them to step on. They gave the forensics guys some time then walked inside. Black soot coated the walls and the smell of cordite hung heavy in the air. In the middle rested a 1950's Plymouth. It was a convertible model, and the back had been demolished in the explosion. The front two seats and dashboard remained intact.

Dan said, "He put mod cons on this car. Look at the sat nav."
Trisha leaned over, next to him.
Dan asked one of the CSI guys, "Can I start the engine?"
"You can't sit down without a white suit. Let me do it for you," the man answered.
He opened the driver's door gingerly and sat down. Dan stopped him. "Have you seen under the chassis, and the hood?"
"What for?" the man was puzzled.
"For wires like the one that blew the door up," Dan said. His voice carried to the other members of the team. One of the bomb disposal guys stepped up. He had a name badge that said Saunders.
"We haven't got to the car yet," he said.
Dan knelt by the car. "Let me do it for you then." Before anyone could protest, Dan lay down on his back. Trisha handed him a flashlight. Dan slid under the chassis. He detected the fuselage first and the gas pipes. They looked fine and he couldn't see any tell-tale wiring that would make him think of an IED. He came out, opened the hood and repeated the process.

Dan nodded at the CSI guy who had the keys. "Try it now," he said.

The guy put the keys in the ignition slowly. He looked up at Dan. It had become very quiet suddenly. One of the CSI guys near the entrance shifted backwards. Dan looked up to see all eyes on him.

He said to Trisha quietly, "Go outside."

"No," she said.

"Trisha I-

"You think the car's safe, right?"

"Yes I do, but I'm only willing to bet my life on it." Dan gestured towards the man in the driving seat. He was sweating and visibly pale.

"Give me the keys," Dan said. "I'll start it. Rest of you can wait at a distance."

Dan was reasonably sure the car didn't have an IED. But never say never. He wasn't afraid to die. But he couldn't live with himself if his actions led to the death of others.

Saunders stepped up. "Can I have a look under the hood?"

Dan lifted the hood and moved to one side. Saunders shone a light inside the hood and checked the engine.

"Looks fine to me," he said.

Dan had the key in his hand and sat down on the driver's seat. Trisha was standing next to him, but the others had slowly filed out.

"Go," Dan said. "Now."

"No," Trisha said.

They held each other's eyes for a few seconds. Dan saw iron determination in hers.

"I don't want something to happen to you," Dan said.

"I'll be fine. Start the engine."

Dan closed his eyes and clenched his jaws. The key was in the ignition already. He turned it clockwise and flinched as the engine caught and whined. Then it died and he heaved a sigh of relief. He glanced at Trisha, who had her arms folded across her chest, face flushed red. Her eyes were closed too, and she opened them as Dan looked at her.

Dan gave her a smile, then turned the key again. It caught, then the engine came to life with a loud sound, echoed by the walls. Dan revved the engine, then kept it running. He sensed Trisha had come closer. He looked up at her, and caught the brightness in her eyes.

"Thank god for that," Trisha said.

There was a sound of clapping from behind and some whistles. The men filed back inside.

"Get in," Dan said to Trisha. He concentrated on the sat nav display. It looked out of place where the old radio should've been. It was a standard machine and he went to the stored addresses. He flicked through them. One address caught his eyes. It was the most recent and also local.

Dan asked, "22216 is a local zip code, right?"

"Yes it is. You got the rest of the address?"

"23634 Sandbrook Drive. If Kowalski was driving this car then it makes sense he had visited this address a few times last week." Dan scrolled down. "And a couple of months ago as well."

Trisha wrote the address down on her phone and sent it to Bellamy. She helped Dan to look around the rest of the car, but they found nothing. Dan reversed the car out into yard and got out.

Saunders called to him from inside the garage. "Come and have a look at this."

CHAPTER

Dan walked back inside the garage, leaving Trisha and Bellamy. Saunders was haunched on the floor and stood up as Dan arrived. Saunders had collected fragmented pieces of wire and metal in his hands. He held them to Dan who took the pieces in his gloved hands. Dan knelt and arranged the pieces on the floor. He wasn't an explosives expert but he could make an improvised device. What he saw on the floor was the remnants of a cell phone's antenna, with a wire wrapped around it.

Dan looked up at Saunders, who squatted down to his level. Dan said, "This cell phone was called, and the electric charge set off the device, right?"

Saunders nodded. "Someone saw you arrive and called this cell."

Dan said, "The place wasn't booby trapped. Kowalski didn't have time to do it maybe. Whatever."

Trisha had walked in and was standing behind him. Dan turned, holding up the piece in his hand. "Like I said, we were expected."

Trisha said, "We must've been followed?"
Dan frowned and transferred his gaze back to his hand. He hadn't seen a car. But that didn't mean they hadnt been followed.

He said, "We should check out that address in the sat nav, the local one?" He looked over Trisha to where Bellamy was speaking to the forensics guys. "And remember we could still be watched. The person who set this off could see us. He had a line of sight. Cover all the angles that lead to this street."

Bellamy looked up, "Like I said Dan, there's men on the roofs around us. Expecting drone images any minute now. We got this." He reached inside his coat pocket and took out his cell phone.

"OK," Dan said. He turned to Trisha. "Shall we make our way to 23634 Sandbrook Drive?"
Trisha raised an eyebrow. "This time we take protection."
"Sure."

Trisha rang the WFO and spent some time speaking to an analyst. She hung up and gesture towards Dan to wait. She spoke on the phone again, then hung up.
Dan was standing in front of the garage, arms folded across his chest as he watched the forensics guys do their job. Trisha walked over to him.

"The guy who lives at that address is called Robert Murphy. We got his social security details. Retired 76 year old. Lives on his own and owns the house. Stayed there for almost twenty years. Before that, he was in Canada."
"Any idea about his job or profession?"
"Nope, she's digging all that out right now?"
"How about Kowalski's daughter?" Dan asked.
"Same. I'm gonna get an email as soon as they locate her or get an ID."
Trisha went off to speak to the drivers of the SUV's who had arrived in the aftermath of the explosion. Men were leaning against the car, fingers on the triggers of their assault rifles. They straightened as Trisha approached.
Dan got into the car with Trisha. She drove. He watched in the rearview as the two SUV's indicated, then followed them.
"Did you get Murphy's telephone number?" Dan asked.
"Good idea. It's in my email." She lifted her phone for Dan to look at the number. Dan called from his cellphone as Trisha weaved her way through traffic.

The phone rang for a while before someone picked up. The person coughed, then cleared his throat noisily.

"Who is it?", an old, croaking voice asked.

"Is that Robert Murphy?" Dan said. There was silence. Dan waited for a few beats, then repeated the question again. Still silence. Dan said, "Mr Murphy, are you alone?"

With a click, the phone went dead. Dan griped the phone hard, then grimaced. "Drive faster. He's got company."

Trisha turned her siren on and floored the gas.

She slowed as the wheels crunched over fall leaves into a narrow road. Trees around them were turning red, yellow and brown. The houses on either side were white timber colonials with pretty porches and wicker chairs. They stopped outside the address and looked. The porch was in bad shape and the wooden steps leading up to it were rotting. Leaves needs sweeping out from the porch.

Dan saw the two SUV's pull up behind them. He nodded to Trisha and they both got out. Silently, they stared at the house. Trisha was the first one up the porch steps.

The porch creaked under their weight. Two magazines and a couple of white envelopes lay on the floor. Dan picked them up. Trisha knocked on the door as there was no calling bell. After the third loud knock there was a cough from inside. The door rattled on the chain, and a face peered out cautiously. An old man`s face. Wispy white hair on either side of an otherwise bald scalp. His eyes were sunken, and dulled. He tried to straighten himself, gave it up, and peered at them with a glare in his eyes.

"Who are you?," the old man rasped.

Trisha lifted up her badge. "Special Agent Dunne, FBI. This is my colleague, Dan Roy.".

"Are you Robert Murphy?" Trisha asked.

The old man stared at them without answering.

"Did you know Mr Victor Kowalski?" Dan asked. That got the old man`s attention. A glow came into his eyes

Dan took that as a yes. "I'm a friend of Victor`s. My name is Dan Roy."

"How do you know Victor?"

"I met him on the street," Dan said truthfully. "I need to tell you something about him."

The man gave Dan that futile, impassive, I-have-seen-it-all stare that some men have. Then he looked at Trisha for a few seconds. Then he took the chain off the hook.

"You better come in," he said.

The wooden door creaked open. They stepped into a paisley patterned carpet and peeling wallpaper covered hallway. The carpet was threadbare, and the house felt cold. A kitchen lay directly ahead, but the old man turned into the living room on the right. He stumbled into an armchair opposite the TV. Trisha walked around till she was facing him. Dan stayed behind the sofa, checking out the window. He noticed the curtains were open. A news channel was on, showing the war in Syria. Or rather, the flattened cities, and children playing soccer in the rubble of what was once their home.

Robert Murphy spoke without looking at Trisha. "Is Victor dead?"

Trisha glanced at Dan before answering him. "Why do you think he is dead?"

Robert Murphy lifted a gnarled hand, then put it down. "Well, we are getting old, you know."

"How did you know Victor Kowalski, Mr. Murphy?" Trisha asked.

Murphy ignored that. "Funny," the old man said. He pointed at the screen. They both looked. More images of destroyed city blocks. Murphy lifted dull eyes to Trisha. "What goes around comes around."

Dan felt a sudden chill, like the air in the house was getting to him. He shifted on his feet and looked around quickly. The window faced the street. Net curtains were drawn, minimizing visibility.

Dan looked at Trisha and pointed upwards. She nodded. Dan walked out slowly and made for the living room door. He got out into the hallway, and made sure the front door was locked. He went into the kitchen. An old formica counter, and a stand alone white hob and oven from the sixties. Breadcrumbs on the floor. A cat poked its head in through the cat flap of the door opening into the garden. It saw Dan, mewed, and moved into the kitchen. The cat sat on its haunches and looked at Dan expectantly. Dan looked at the rest of the kitchen. An old radio on the table. Four chairs around it. Dan opened one of the cupboards above the sink and found a steel bowl. He opened the white fridge door and took out the milk carton. He sniffed the milk, then poured some milk on the bowl and put it on the floor in front of the cat. Without a mew of thanks the cat started slurping the milk. Dan turned, and on his tip toes, went out into the hallway. He peered up the staircase. Apart from the muted sound of the TV and his own breathing, it was silent. The Sig appeared in his right hand. The stairs creaked when he tried them. He went up slowly, keeping close to the railings. When he got near the landing, he dropped to the floor, and went up the stairs on his belly. No sound. No movement. Three bedrooms and a bathroom opened up on the floor. Two of the bedrooms were full of junk. The third bedroom was used. The double oak framed bed had seen better days, but the covers indicated someone had slept in them the night before. Strangely for a single man, there was a dressing table in one corner. In neither of the bedrooms did Dan see any family photos.

Dan checked the bathroom. There was nothing of interest. He went down and into the living room. Trisha was seated closer to the seated Murphy.

Murphy stared at the TV screen. A bubble of spit formed in the corner of his mouth and drooled down the side of his chin. He lifted up a hand to wipe it, but an invisible force seemed to push it back down. His eyes never left the screen.

Dan walked around to face the old man and stand next to Trisha. Murphy glanced briefly at Dan before looking back at the screen.

"Three days," he said.

Dan frowned. "What?"

"Three days. That`s all you got."

"Victor is dead. They will come after you now. Look at me."

Dan sat on his haunches and faced Robert.

"Wrong," said the old man.

"What?"

"It`s not just Victor. In three days we are all dead."

Dan was about to say something but he felt Trisha`s hand on his shoulder. A split second later, he saw the red dot dancing on the forehead of Robert Murphy.

CHAPTER 11

Trisha pulled on Dan`s shoulder the same time as he pushed her back gently. He stood up and shuffled back from the window.

"Get down," he hissed to Trisha. Dan looked towards the window, but apart from sunlight he could not see nothing. Robert Murphy looked at them and opened his mouth to say something. It was his last movement. The window splintered into a hundred shards of glass as the round crashed in, and Murphy`s head erupted into fragments of red blood and brain. Dan flung himself over Trisha as the rounds pumped in. The sofa became pockmarked with bullets, white upholstery flying up in the air. Bullets thudded into the carpet and the woodwork around the window frame.

Trisha said something that Dan could not hear. He knew if they both stayed in the room they were dead meat. He had five feet roughly to cross to the open door, with the rounds flying in. He pointed to the open doorway and Trisha nodded. He waited for a lull in the fire, then sprang to his feet and dived for the door, along with Trisha. He hooked an arm around her midriff, and they both landed on his arms outside the door as the firing started again.

He dusted himself up, ignored the front and ran to the rear of the house. The frontal attack was now a diversion. They would either send someone in from the back to finish the job off, or fling grenades in through the window at the front. That`s what he would do. But the FBI guys were there to stop it from happening. The garden at the rear was a different issue.

Trisha had her Glock 20 out, pointed straight to the front door. "I`ll stay here," she shouted.

Dan ran towards the kitchen, staying low. The Sig was in his right hand, pointed up. He scooted towards the cabinets, then lifted his head up a fraction. The garden was overgrown. Apart from long grass and trees at the back he could not see anything. The firing had started again, and round were pinging inside the living room. He heard a round shatter the glass on the front door.

Dan shuffled closer to the garden entrance from the kitchen. He raised his head and looked. He caught a flicker of movement to his left and flinched backwards. It was one of the FBI guys who had come in from the side entrance. Dan opened the door and stepped out. The long trees at the rear moved in the wind. No one fired on him and the FBI man as they checked out the garden.
There was a sudden silence. The long-range firing had stopped. Dan asked the man if he was OK.
"Yeah, fine," the man wiped sweat from his brow. "When the firing started we couldn't respond to it. Came from behind and above us. So we took cover here."
Dan nodded. Bellamy joined them, and together, they went back inside the house.
Dan almost bumped into Trisha who lifted up her gun and screamed before lowering it.
"Whoa, don't shoot us" Dan said.
Trisha pointed her gun away.
"It`s not over yet," Dan said. "If there is a sniper somewhere, he might be waiting for us to make a move outside. He thought about the position. It was more suburban blocks around here. He was on a roof somewhere, with a clear sight into Murphy's living room. For that, he had to be in a street nearby. Maybe the next one along, or higher up on a slope.

"Can we get a bird up here?" Dan asked.
"Yes," Bellamy said. He was on his cell phone already.

Trisha took charge. She explained to the officers what had happened, and showed them around the house. Dan watched her as she barked instructions and spoke on the phone. Her left cheek had a bruise on it from where she had landed, and a small cut on her forehead which had stopped bleeding. He heard the rotor blades of the bird and looked outside without stepping out. It was a black civilian bird with a grey FBI mark on it. It hovered loudly over the neighborhood. A few people came out of their houses.

Trisha walked outside, and Dan followed. They stood on the sidewalk, watching the FBI guys hustle around them, anxious faces peeking out of windows opposite.
Dan shook his head. One hell of a thing to happen in this neighbourhood. He gazed up and around. He pointed to the southwest, above the trees, then looked back at the destroyed window of Murphy's house. The trajectory of the bullet was clear.

He said, "Shot came from there. Has to be on a hill, or an attic somewhere. Probably a deserted house."
"We can check it out," Trisha said. "It`s like they knew we were coming." She had a radio in her hand now, and she pulled the antenna up. Loud static hissed from it. Trisha relayed orders to the pilot and Dan watched the bird bank high above their heads and change direction.
"What the hell," Trisha said softly.
Dan said, "He was under surveillance. When they saw us go in, he was taken out."
Trisha shook her head, letting loose a weary sigh from deep in her lungs. "Let's get back to the WFO." She spoke to Bellamy who was going to stay back and coordinate the forensics and crime scene guys. A blue and white tape was being used to cordon off the street.

CHAPTER

While Trisha spoke to the FBI agents, Dan walked back to the house. The agent at the door stepped aside and Dan walked in. Debris scattered out from the living room. Bullet holes pockmarked the wall inside. Murphy still lay on his side, his face nothing but a congealed mess of blood and bone. Dan inspected his clothes carefully. He was wearing a bathrobe. Dan snaked a finger inside the pockets and found a reading glass but nothing else. He lifted up the sleeves of the bathrobe and inspected the forearms. He was looking for old wounds or any identifying features. There was nothing on the right arm, but on the left forearm Dan found an interesting tattoo. It was a blue star with five pointed ends.

Dan lifted the legs of his pyjamas and looked at the legs. He saw an old scar on the left ankle. It was deep and had been stitched in the past. It could have been a bullet wound. He heard footsteps then Trisha appeared at the door. Dan took some photos of the tattoo and the wound on his cell phone.

"I hope you're not destroying evidence," Trisha said.

"Nope," Dan replied. "Just having a look."

The room shook as the bird did a pass overhead. As the sound receded, Trisha said, "No one's been spotted acting suspiciously in the neighborhood."

"A lone operator," Dan said. "That's how he keeps escaping." His mind went back to the man he had seen coming out of the office block, after Kowalski's murder. A cold, dark hand passed over his eyes, and he shook his head.

Where had he seen that face?

Dan stood and looked around what was left of the room.

"Let's get out of here."

*****

Dan looked at Kowalski`s coroner report as soon as he got to the WFO. It was as expected. Death from brain trauma and haemorrhage. He looked at the photographs of the body parts. Nicotine stains in the fingers. He was a smoker. His attention was drawn to the fingers. He had a ring on his index finger. A white stone with a red star on it. Quite neat. He had a low right abdominal scar from an appendix removal. Dan turned the page and narrowed his eyes. The ME had noted the presence of a tattoo. A blue, five-pointed star on the left forearm.

The same tattoo Robert Murphy had.

Dan read the description carefully. There was a photo of the tattoo as well in the index pages at the back of the report. Dan took out his phone and compared the tattoos. There was no doubt. They were identical.

Dan closed the report and stared at the wall of Trisha`s office. It was 1500 hours. She came in with two coffees. Dan tasted them. He suspected coffee at a federal office might be bland, but the strong taste surprised him. He inhaled deeply and took a long swig. He told her about the tattoos.

He asked, "Any idea how long Murphy and Kowalski knew each other?"

Trisha shook her head. "Nope. But Murphy's Irish and K is Polish, right?"

"I was thinking that," Dan said. "Murphy sounds like he's got all his family back in south Boston." Trisha cracked a smile at that.

She said, "In fact, it seems Murphy had no family whatsoever." She opened a file resting on her desk and flicked through it.

"He came from Canada. Irish Immigrant. Worked odd jobs there. Factory, waiter, car salesman."
"When did he immigrate to USA?"
Trisha checked the folder online. "1988."
They were both silent for a while, thinking. Then Dan spoke. "Nothing unusual then, apart from what he had to tell you, and the way he died?"
"That was pretty unusual."
Dan nodded in agreement. He said, "Do me a favor, please. We have his Canadian passport, right?"
"Right."
"Can we make a list of every Canadian born on the same day. Then I want to see how many of them are still alive. How old was he?"
"76."
"Can we run that search?"
"One hell of a big search. You thinking he stole someone`s passport? Or got an illegal one?"
"All I know, there is more to Robert Murphy than what we have uncovered just now. You sure he doesn't have any family?"
"Yes."
"That's odd in itself. Irish pride themselves on big families. Murphy could well be a fake name."
Trisha said, "What do you think Murphy was trying to say?"
"About the three days?"
"Yes."
"Kind of matches what Kowalski was trying to tell you. He had no time. It was urgent," Dan said.
"What do you think the tattoo means? They belonged to some kind of club?" Trisha asked. Dan finished the last of his coffee and put the cup down on the table gently.

He said, "We know that Kowalski came to this country as an asylum seeker. Well, he walked into the US Embassy in Moscow and offered to help us. Then he moved with his wife and daughter. At no point is there any mention of his friends in Russia, or who he hung out with here."

"His daughter might know," Trisha said. "especially about her dad's contacts here."

"Good point." He looked at Trisha. "We need to find her. One by one, all of Kowalski's contacts are being killed."

Trisha didn't miss the look in his eyes. "And she's next."

CHAPTER

Valona Kowalski hurried down the road. She was still wearing the spare white coat that the doctor had in his room, and which had allowed her to walk out from the clinic unchallenged. The road ahead of her stretched in a straight line to the horizon. Behind her lay the white walls of the clinic and opposite, a forest.

Valona decided to continue down the road, despite the absence of houses or human beings. It would be dark soon, judging by the light. Going into the forest was tempting now. Someone would discover Dr Stainforth soon, and then they would be on to her. She needed to hide and the forest was ideal. But she didn't fancy too much being alone in the darkness of the forest. The men who would come after would have flashlights and weapons.

She felt the butt of the Glock in her pocket. Well, she had a weapon as well and she knew how to fire it, thanks to her dad. Pain twisted in her chest when she thought about him. Had her dad wanted to prepare her for a day like this? Valona remembered the lessons in the firing range. Dad would stand next to her and show her to get her "zero", the point at which her eyes lined up with the gun barrel and the target.

She walked faster, needing distance between herself and the clinic. She walked past the high walls eventually and looked back once. Barbed wire covered the top of the walls. She shivered. Why did the place look like a prison when it called itself a clinic?

The fall wind was biting and she wrapped the white coat tighter around herself. A car came down the road behind her. She turned, sticking her hand out to flag it down. It went past her and she caught a man's face stare at her from the driver's side.

Valona knew she looked silly. But apart from the white coat, she didn't have much to give her warmth. She saw another car coming in the opposite direction, facing her. An ear splitting alarm suddenly blasted in the silence. It came from behind her. Valona turned and her worse fears were confirmed. The alarm came from within the white walls of the clinic. She could hear voices shouting from inside the compound. She had barely put a hundred yards between herself and the place. Valona ran. She was wearing slacks, luckily and her flat shoes pounded the dirt track that gave way from the pavement. The alarm wailed on. The cold air stuck knives into her lungs as she breathed heavily. Sweat beaded on her neck. She kept running and the road curved to the right. Ahead of her, stopped on the side, she saw a car with its hazard indicators on. A man stepped out and he appeared to be checking the front tires.

He looked towards the sound of the alarm and went still as he saw Valona running towards him. She stopped, breathless, when she was ten yards away.

"Can you help me?" Valona panted. "A mental patient has run away from the insane asylum there," she pointed behind her.

"How can I-

"She went this way in a car," Valona said, wiping sweat. "If you can give me a lift, we could help find her."

The man frowned and came closer. "She was in a car? Don't you have other people inside who can help?"

Valona didn't have time for this. Any second now she expected someone from the clinic to arrive at the scene in a car. It was getting dark but she was easily recognizable in her white coat. Her fingers closed around the butt of the gun. She whipped the gun out and pointed it at the man. She flicked off the safety.

"Whoa whoa hold on!" the man said putting his hands up. "Don't do anything silly."

"Where are the keys?" Valona asked.

"In the ignition."

"Are the tires OK?"

"I think so."

"Get down on your belly, face down. Hands above your head!" Valona shouted. The man hesitated. Valona came closer with the gun pointed at his chest. "Do it now!"

"OK, just don't shoot." The man's face worked with fear. He laid down as instructed. She stepped over him, and ran to the nearside front tire. It seemed OK, but she didn't have time to make a detailed check and the other tires would have to wait. She jumped into the driver's seat and slammed the door shut. The engine was purring. She took the gear off neutral and with tires screeching, set off down the road.

CHAPTER

Valona didn't have the faintest idea where she was. She pushed the GMC Yukon's gas pedal down hard as she could and rocketed down the road. The central yellow line curved to the right. Pine forests crowded the road on either side. A few drops of rain arrived. Her headlights were on, darkness had fallen. Any minute now, she knew, the man would call for help. She rummaged around on the dashboard, then around the driver's seat. Her fingers touched the cell phone on her right. She glanced at it. It was on silent mode and no calls had come through. She lowered the window and threw the phone outside.

Headlights flashed on her rearview. Swallowing the wave of panic that surged inside her, Valona squinted at the mirror. She pushed harder on the gas. The car began to fall behind. She breathed a sigh of relief, as a police patrol vehicle or one from the clinic would be chasing her. In the distance, to her right, she saw a sign appear.

Four Springs.

Respect the Peace in our Town.

Valona slowed down. The town was still five miles away, and she needed to think about her next move. Was going into a small town, where everyone knew each other, dangerous? Her attackers had travelled two to three hours in the car, so chances were she was still in rural Virginia. How far was she from the nearest big town? Easily four five hours drive.

She looked at the gas tank. Her heart sank. Less than a couple of gallons left. She reached out and fiddled with the radio. She turned the knobs till she got the local radio stations, and turned the volume up. Eventually she got what she wanted.

...and now for the KNBC Live News Alert. News when you need it...

She listened with rapt attention as the reporter reeled off two accidents on the interstate, then about the closing of a gas station.

We also have this just coming in. A mental asylum patient has escaped from the Open Mind Psychiatric Hospital twenty miles outside Four Springs. The woman is Caucasian, dark hair, five feet nine and weighs sixty eight pounds. She might be wearing a white coat stolen from the clinic. She is considered armed and dangerous. The public is warned not to approach her if seen and to call 911...
The hard knot of fear inside Valona's throat tightened. Her breath came in harsh gasps. She was a wanted woman now? But she couldn't hand herself in. No way. The men who had grabbed her were law enforcement. At least, that's what they told Dr Stainforth. Her father's warning echoed in her mind. *Their reach goes all the way to the top...*
Valona shook her head, trying to dispel the wall of panic that was closing in. Never in her wildest dreams had she thought her dad's predictions would come true. Now they had and she had to deal with it. Panicking wouldn't help.
The lights of the town appeared to her right. She indicated and came off the ramp. From the opposite direction three cars whizzed past her in quick succession. The last car had a flashing blue light on its front fender. It was small, and the car was a black SUV, windows tinted. Valona took the exit quickly and sped towards Four Springs.
A drug store and strip mall appeared, with a gas station next to it. Valona drove past a street with shut down store fronts, and a couple of bars with men smoking outside. Motorcycles were scattered on the side walk. She kept going till she found a field without any lights. She turned her headlights off and bounced into the dirt track. The uneven ground made her head hit the roof several times but she kept going till she was in the brush. She checked to make sure she had the doctor's wallet and Glock on her, then took the car off neutral and opened the door. There was a flashlight on the glove box, she took that too. Branches and shrubbery blocked the door and she had to push hard to get out. There was no point in trying to push the car deeper, it was too big for her. She could see lights in the distance from the bars she had driven past.

Twigs scraped her hands and face as she fought her way out of the forest. She kept the flashlight off mostly. Occasionally she turned it on, facing down every time she heard a noise. Valona didn't like dense forests. She wanted to see where she was going, and not step on a reptile. The thought made her flesh crawl.

She made it out to the field, and promptly splashed on a puddle. Swearing, she climbed out. Her pants and shoes were now soaking wet to her mid shins. Valona grit her teeth and walked fast till she got to the road. Voices and music tinkled across to her from the right. She stood there for a while, shivering. Her wet pants were sticking to her legs like a frozen second skin.

She turned and walked towards the bar. The sign said Rooms Available, ask inside. Valona ignored the bearded bikers who looked at her and whistled as she opened the door and stepped inside. The music was louder and the bar busier than she expected. There was a group of bikers in one corner, and several tables with card players. A juke box played country and western and a dim dance floor to the far left had two couples slow dancing.

Valona walked up to the bar and caught the attention of one of the waitresses. She didn't miss the inquisitive look on the waitress's face.

"I need a room for the night." Valona took out the wallet and counted the cash. One hundred bucks. "How much?"

"Forty," the waitress said.

Valona gave her sixty. "Twenty says you never saw me. Got it?"

The waitress took the money without missing a beat. "Got it. Come this way."

"No. I'm going to step outside, like I'm leaving. Where's the back entrance?"

The waitress stared at Valona for a while, then nodded. She gave Valona directions. Valona walked out, feeling the cold more now. She had left the white coat in the forest. Folding her arms across her chest, she went past the bar, turned left and went down the side. She dodged a couple kissing and followed the lights till she came to the end of the building. A door opened and the waitress stood framed in it.

Valona stepped inside and the door shut behind her.

CHAPTER

Rashid Al-Falaj looked down at the green and blue shaded woods of Washington state as his Gulf Stream jet began its descent towards Dulles Airport. It took longer than usual due to the midday air traffic. Rashid checked his Rolex Daytona. Half past twelve. He wanted to be in his ranch outside DC but three pm. He had real estate business deals to close, two senators who wanted to see him before the mid-term elections later this year, and then attend to his Russian matter.

He sipped his yogurt smoothie as the jet landed smoothly and taxied up to it's private hanger. Rashid kept two jets in the East Coast, both capable of being airborne within an hour. As he came off the jet, nodding at the guard who opened the door for him, his satellite phone beeped.

Rashid put his briefcase down and looked at the screen. It was Nick Carlyle.

"It's me," Rashid said. "I heard the old man is dead."

"Both of them are dead," Nick said in a flat voice. "Murphy was the last man who knew."

"And Kowalski's daughter?" Rashid asked. There was a silence which he didn't like.

"I'm working on it."

"What does that mean? You can't track a woman down?"

"I got to her and admitted her to the clinic to see what she knew. But she escaped. She didn't get far, don't worry. We'll get her."

Rashid frowned and clutched the receiver tighter. "That woman is the only one who can mess up our plans. I haven't come this far to watch this fail because you can't do a simple job."

Carlyle paused before answering. "I've done everything else so far, right? Just give me another day, and I'll wrap this up."

Rashid grunted. "Have you been to the site?"

"Yes. It's all in order. We need to activate the signal and move the merchandise."

"We need to be in position by tomorrow. There's only three days left."

"I know that."

"You need to deliver on this, Nick. I trusted you."

Nick hung up. Rashid stared at his phone for a few seconds. Then he strode out of the hangar to the waiting limousine.

CHAPTER

General Peyton Mildred was in his civilian clothes. He wore black hiking boots, black cotton chinos and a warm pullover beneath his black jacket. His Ford Taurus hummed along the road, holding the curve as he kept within the speed limit. Tall vegetation grew on either side of the road, now getting sparse as fall arrived. The farm land undulated around him and the fall colors of the distant trees struck him with their beauty. Winter was coming, and summer was having its last hurrah. He clutched the steering wheel tighter. Karl used to love summer, like every child. Peyton remembered how excited Karl got when they visited the Lake of Ozarks. It was their family vacation spot and some of Peyton's fondest memories came from those warm sunshine days, walking with Clara and Karl up the trail, catching white bait in the Lake and barbecue's by the night fires. Days he would never forget.

His jaw clamped tight and a mist shook in his eyes. "I love you," he whispered. Almost automatically, his eyes caressed the photo on his dashboard. Karl standing between Peyton and Clara, on Graduation day from West Point. The proudest day of Peyton's life.

Peyton indicated for the right turn and stopped to let another car go past. This road was narrower, leading to a farm yard just outside the town of Waldorf, twenty three miles southeast of DC.

He parked in the front yard, noting the three other SUV's already there. He opened the door and stepped out. Men spilled out from the SUV and a tall, thin figure stepped up to Peyton. Nick Carlyle saluted. Peyton had been Nick's CO in Fort Benning when Nick was in the Army Rangers. Old habits died hard.

"General."

They shook hands. The men behind Nick stood to attention and saluted as well. Peyton looked at them for a while. Each of the fifteen men present were hand picked. Each had been trained by him personally at Fort Benning.

He nodded, then took the keys out of his pocket and headed for the front door of the ten bedroom log wood farm stead. It had been in the Mildred family for the last three generations. Peyton would be the last to own it.

He pushed open the heavy door and it creaked. It was cold inside. Peyton went to the large living room and got the fire working. He opened the door that linked to the conservatory and lead to the garden. The men were standing there. One by one, they filed into the living room.

A map of USA was stretched on the wall, with red and black pins struck at strategic locations. Peyton took his place next to the map. He stared at the men standing opposite, some seated, some standing. Carlyle was at its head.

Peyton said, "For too long we have tolerated the tyranny of the few against the many. Like you, I took an oath. To protect this great country against all foes, foreign and domestic. We cannot win against our foreign enemies unless we neutralize the domestic ones." He paused for effect, finding the eyes of each men in the room.

"In the process, we will make enemies. We will be hated and reviled. George Washington was hated by the English, when his blood cleansed the soul of this nation. One day, future generations will look upon as in the same light. We were the few who liberated this country from the corrupt shackles that hold it prisoner. But for now, we will have to live with the hate.

"So, I need to know that you are with me. That from this day on, there is no going back. A new America will rise from the ashes of the tyrants. Our blood will nourish the soil. If you have any doubts, now is the time to voice them."

His eyes bored into the eyes of every man in the room. All stared back at him unflinchingly.

Peyton closed his eyes and breathed deeply. He opened his eyes slowly. "To a new America," he said quietly.

The men spoke as one. "To a new America."

There was a knock on the door and Peyton turned his head sharply. A man poked his head inside.

"Sir, they've arrived."

"Good", Peyton said. "Show them in." He glanced at Carlyle. "Outside."

Carlyle ordered the men into the garden, out of sight. Peyton walked to the window and watched as wheel crunched gravel and a black Chevrolet came into view.

The angular, tall, slightly stooped figure of James Walsh emerged from the rear right passenger door. Peyton moved away from the window. Soon, Walsh and his aide, Sam Porter, were shown inside. Peyton shook their hands and they took their seats in armchairs by the fire. Carlyle and another man were placed discreetly in the corner, but Walsh had seen them.

"Would you like a drink, James?" Peyton asked.

Walsh rubbed his hands on his pants. He coughed once. "Well, General, I'm obviously interested in what you have to say."

Peyton could see the signs of nervousness in the Speaker of the House of Representatives. It pleased him. He had never made a secret of the disdain with which he treated politicians. Walsh was a prominent member of the cabinet, acting as the lead senator of the Armed Forces Intelligence Subcommittee. Watching him squirm was something Peyton savored.

"All in good time, James," Peyton said with a smile. He stood and looked at Porter, who as befitted his name, had a sprawling gut that bulged over his beltline. Portly Porter. "How about you Mr. Porter?"

"Call me Sam, please," Porter said. "What do you mean?"

"What would you like to drink? Wine or Scotch?"

"Scotch, please."

Walsh concurred and Peyton went to the bar at the side of the large room. He chinked ice into three glasses, poured a double measure of Glenmorangie in each one, and bought the two glasses over. He went back to get his own and nodded at Carlyle. Carlyle gestured at his man and they shuffled closer, unknown to the two guests, who had their backs to them.

CHAPTER

Peyton raised his glass in a toast. "To your health."

They sipped in unison. Peyton put his glass down and fixed the men with his dull, glazed eyes.

"Thanks for coming gentlemen. I wouldn't have asked you here if it wasn't something important." Peyton let it hang for a moment, watching Walsh's reaction.

The Senator leaned forward. "Peyton, you are a well-respected member of our armed forces. We seek your opinion often. But I don't get the need for secrecy."

"According to the US Constitution, you are third in line to become President, if both the President and the Vice President become, shall we say, incapacitated."

Walsh narrowed his eyes. Peyton thought he looked like a shark who had just smelt blood. "Incapacitated? What do you mean?"

Peyton spoke slowly. "You know what I mean."

Walsh held his eyes for a while, then sat back in the chair. His jaw was lax and the fire of curiosity was lit in his face. Peyton leaned in.

"The current President's policy of appeasing our enemies is getting us nowhere, James. We've reduced our missile protection systems in Eastern Europe. Now there's cuts to the satellite program. He wants to make friends with the Arabs while we fight them in Syria."

"We need to keep that friendship for oil security, Peyton. Fracking ain't enough."

Peyton fought to stem the bile rising inside him. "Then stop the war. What's the point of buying their oil while dropping bombs?"

Walsh spread his hands. "Destroy their defense capability and make them more reliant on us. For oil, defense, everything. What's not to like?"

"Why don't you ask the taxpayer who's stumping the bill for your wars? The VA medical bills are rising into the billions. You're fighting this war to win votes. I say the real enemy is China and Russia. They have enough nukes to blow us sky high. You want a real war? Fight them."

"And the point of that would be what? Mutual assured destruction. MAD. They nuke us, we nuke them. Humanity dies. No one wants that, Peyton. The whole point of having the largest nuclear arsenal is for it to act as a deterrent."

Peyton smiled. "So you want to use these phony, proxy wars to show our muscle while you claim the popularity vote. You see, James, the whole point of the war is to show Americans that we are united against a common enemy." Peyton lifted both hands and made commas in the air.

"So you can tell everyone how hard you're working against them. But we all know who the real enemy is."

Walsh frowned. "Who do you mean?"

"It's this administration's hopeless policy of fighting wars while appeasing the same foes. Our jobs are disappearing. Large swathes of America are unemployed. Instead of looking at these problems, we waste our money on this crap."

Walsh raised his eyebrows. "You want to make a run for office? Is that what this is about?" He lapsed into silence, staring at Peyton. The image of a shark came to Peyton's mind again.

He said, "No. I don't want to make a run for any sort of office. But we need a new government. One that will carry out the wishes of the people."

"The people voted for this government. Have you forgotten that?"

"The people?" Peyton snorted. "Take a look outside, James. This country is at a crossroads. We need change."

There was silence again. Sam Porter took a gulp of his whiskey, finishing it. He cleared his throat. "So, what are you saying, General?"

Peyton said, "We know the Vice President will never go against what the President wants. Isn't that right, James?"

Walsh nodded. "That's true."

"So we bring about the change ourselves." Peyton laid out his plan. He ignored the open mouths and stunned surprise of his guests.

"And when it's done, James, you will be the 54th President of USA. It makes sense, as you are third in line anyway. The people will accept that."

Peyton picked up his glass and drained it. He swirled the ice inside. The silence in the room was deafening.

Eventually, Walsh spoke. "Are you insane? This is...this..." The Senator was at a loss for words.

"It's a *coup d'etat*. Yes, I know. But the will of the people will be served."

Walsh stood. He buttoned up his jacket. "I don't know what's got into you, Peyton. I thought you were a patriot."

Peyton stood as well. "I am, James," he said softly. "I am."

Walsh screwed up his face. "Is this about Karl?" He closed his eyes and rubbed his forehead. "Look Peyton, I'm sorry we couldn't bring your boy back. You know better than me fucked up things happen in war. But he's a hero-

"Don't talk about my son!" Peyton's voice was like a whiplash. He stepped forward, teeth grinding, eyes flashing. Walsh and Porter moved back.

Peyton flexed his shoulders then relaxed. "I'm offering you a chance to make history, James. What do you say?"

Walsh shook his head, disbelief all over his face. "I can't even believe you're thinking this way." His lips set in a firm line. "I'll be seeing you, Peyton. Count me out."

The door opened and two heavy set men stepped inside. Walsh stared at them, and then back at Peyton. His mouth opened in shock.

"What the hell is this?"

Carlyle and the other guy stepped up and grabbed them from behind. Walsh and Porter struggled buy they were no match for the trained soldiers. Carlyle cuffed their hands with plastic ties.

Walsh's face was beetroot red and he panted. "I am the Speaker of the House, damn it. You won't get away with this, General."

"I don't intend to James," Peyton said in a whisper.

CHAPTER

Valona's head hit something hard. It seemed to press down on her skull and the pain grew, like someone was holding a gun against her head. Her eyes flew open and she scrambled upwards, breathing heavily. She was in a strange room. Faint light filtered in from behind the curtains. It took her a few seconds to adjust.

She was in a room above the bar. Memories of the night before washed over her like a tidal wave. She swallowed, shook her head and cleared strands of hair away from her face. There was a small bathroom attached to the bedroom. She washed, ignored the black rings under her eyes and tied her hair back in a ponytail. Appearances could wait. No point looking pretty if she was dead.

She tiptoed over to the curtain, stood to one side and parted it gently. The Four Springs Pikeway was a straight road that ran through the middle of this small town. She could see a post office in the opposite corner. The street was wet with rain that had now stopped. An elderly woman shuffled out of the post office, stuck her umbrella out and walked down the road. No one else stirred. Valona checked her wrist watch. It was seven am.

She craned her neck and caught sight of the gas station on the same side as the bar. The neon light of a drug store was visible just after. A movement caught her eyes. A black dot coming down the road, getting larger. A black SUV, moving fast. A weight caught at the back of her throat. Why in this sleepy small town, would a car be moving with that speed?

Her mouth ran dry as she caught sight of another vehicle behind the SUV. The blue and white stripes of the County Sheriff's car, and the still silent siren light on the roof, was unmistakable. The SUV pulled up at the gas station, and a tall man in black uniform got out of the driver's seat.

Valona didn't wait. She grabbed the Glock and wallet and ran out of the door. She skidded to a stop in the hallway as a door opposite her opened. A woman with frizzy blonde hair and no make up came out. Valona recognized the waitress from last night. They stared at each other for two seconds.

Valona was the first to speak. She had nothing to lose. "I need your help. The men who are after me killed my father. Now they want to kill me as well. They've arrived at the gas station."

The woman stared at her for a while and something like understanding flickered in her eyes. "You need to get out of here, right?"

Valona nodded. The woman went back inside her room and Valona followed. The room was identical to hers, a double bed and wardrobe with two windows opposite. A bathroom door was half open in one corner.

"My name's Maria," the woman said as she opened the drawer of the desk and grabbed something quickly. She stopped with her handle on the door. "Say, are you the person who beat up the doctor and escaped from the looney bin?"

"Do I look like a looney to you?"

"Sorry, that's just what we call the place. I know it's a psychiatric hospital. Some folk in town work there."

"Did you hear about me on the radio?" Valona asked.

"Yes," Maria replied.

Valona read the question in her eyes. "Look, it's gonna take a while to explain. I'm a scientist and I think these people are after my research."

"And they killed your dad?" Maria raised her eyebrows.

"I know it sounds crazy, but you got to believe me." Valona's voice trembled and she swallowed hard. "Please."

Maria dropped her gaze. She opened the door and they went down the stairs swiftly. The place was still empty, but Maria turned to Valona and put her finger on her lips. The bar was deserted, but Valona saw two figures through the window. They were striding up to the door. One of them had a uniform on, and she saw the Sheriff's badge on the right chest. Fear sparked inside her. She caught Maria's arm.

"They're here! I need to get to the car I left in the woods last night." Even as Valona said the words she realized how stupid it sounded. How on earth was she going to wade back into the prickly undergrowth and get the SUV out of there. For all she knew, the tires were stuck in mud now.

There was a knock on the door. Valona's heart rocked against her ribs, and her breath came in gasps. Maria and herself were behind the counter, shielded from view. They could see the bar floor and the door up ahead. A face lowered itself against the glass and tried to peer through.

Valona took the wallet out. She took out a wad of notes and thrust them at Maria without counting them.

"Do you have a car?"

Maria looked at the bundle of notes, then back to Valona. The knock came again from the harder, this time louder, harder. Then a male voice said, "Hello this is the Sheriff speaking. Can you open up?"

Valona gripped Maria's hand. "Please don't open the door. These people will kill me. The Sheriff's in with them. You *have* to believe me."

Maria sighed. She took the money from Valona's hand and stuffed it in her pocket. "Come this way."

Maria led her out to the rear entrance, and then to the staff parking lot. The air was chilly and Valona shivered. They ran to a grey Honda civic that had seen better days, with Virginia license plates. Maria gave her the keys. Valona slid inside and turned the engine. It caught on the first go, and she breathed a sigh of relief.

"Thank you," Valona said, putting the window down.

"Take the back road straight down for ten miles, then you come to cross road. Turn right for the interstate. Takes you towards Charlottesville. Tank's full."

Valona nodded. Maria ran forward and opened the back gate for her. Valona didn't rev the engine too hard as she slipped out of the gates. When she was almost a hundred yards away, she floored the gas.

CHAPTER

Valona gripped the steering wheel tightly, leaning forward as if willing the car to move. She watched the speedometer tick up to 100. She didn't care if a state trooper stopped her. She knew that if she ended up getting arrested without a licence she would end up in jail. And the men chasing her could influence law enforcement to give her up.

Because they were law enforcement too? Or above the law?

She didn't know what to think, but knew this was the situation her father had always warned her about.

Valona wondered if there was any safe place for her. Her mind ran loops till she suddenly thought of something. She kicked herself for not thinking of it earlier. When she was young, the family used to holiday. It was further west from Charlottesville, near the Applachian mountains. Valona racked her brains for the name of the town. It was ideal, she wasn't far from the I-64 and she knew it would take her there. What the heck, she thought, if she reveresed direction and headed for the mountains, she might recognize the signs.

She glanced at the rear view and her heart froze. A black SUV was gaining on her rapidly.

Valona squeezed whatever was left of the gas pedal. The old Honda's engine complained and rattled. The SUV in the mirror was gaining on her by the second, almost like she was standing still.

Valona slammed on the brakes. She lost speed rapidly and pulled on to the dirt kerb. Smoke and dust blew a cloud around her, engulfing the car. Valona grabbed the Glock, clicked off safety and made sure there was a round in the chamber. Then she opened the door and crawled out. Small rocks cut against her hands and hurt through the thin fabric of the coat Maria had stowed in passenger seat. She left the engine running.

She lay down on her back, head turned towards the approaching SUV. To anyone passing by, it looked like an accident, a car on the roadside, engine on, and a woman lying next to it. Valona hid the weapon behind her back and peered through half open eyes.

The SUV roared to a stop about twenty yards away. Valona flinched as the engine steam and dust hit her. She shut, then opened her eyes quickly. Visibility was limited now but that also meant her attacker couldn't see her well. One man got off the driver's side. She couldn't make out if there was someone else in the car. He came forward and the weapon in his hand was unmistakable. But it was pointed half way up. The man, dressed entirely in black, was jerking his head around.

She let him move closer. Her heart was beating so loud she thought her ribs would splinter. With a superhuman effort, she lay still, forcing herself to breath gently.

She heard the crunch of his boots. The warmth of his body as he leaned in. She could smell the leather of his coat.

"Hey you!," the man barked. Valona didn't reply. He reached forward and nudged her with his boot. He called her again. Valona moaned. She flickered her eyelids and groaned softly. It had the desired effect. The man knelt by her. The gun was pointed to the ground now, away from her.

Now.

Valona flashed her gun hand forward and pulled the trigger in the same instant.

The boom of the unsuppressed weapon was loud and the butt slammed back against her palm. She saw the man fly backwards as the round hit him almost point blank in the chest. He rolled over and came to a rest face down.

Valona didn't even look to see if someone came out of the SUV. She jumped back in her car, shut the door and sped off.

CHAPTER

Nick Carlyle was getting a headache. His knuckles were bone white as they gripped his cell phone tight against his ear. "Gone? What do you mean, gone?"

The voice on the other end was apologetic. "Your man followed her, but she shot him."

Carlyle heard the story in silence, fury rising within him like lava inside a volcano. "You're the goddamn Sheriff of the County. What the hell did I pay you for?" He hissed.

"I was looking around the rest of town for her-

"Shut up!" Carlyle gripped his forehead, then kicked the chair in front of him. It hit the wall and one leg broke. Izmir had been one of his best men. One who had fought alongside him in Afghanistan and Iraq. And now a woman…he swallowed his anger.

"Did you even see which way she went?"

After a pause the Sheriff said, "I'm sorry, he was the only one in the car."

Carlyle gnashed his teeth together. "She's a scientist for heaven's sake. How hard can it be for you guys to get her?"

"She's clever. We found the car she took from the farmer. She drove it into the woods where we couldn't see it. Then paid off the waitress at the bar to take her car."

"I guess that makes you dumb, huh? No wait, don't even answer that."

Carlyle took the phone off his ears and seethed for a while. He closed his eyes. He needed to think. This situation was getting out of control. If Valona Kowalski went public with her research, the whole operation had to be called off. All she had to do was call a media outlet and let them know. He shuddered at the thought of Facebook and Twitter feeds spiking with the news. True, if they moved at speed, it wouldn't matter. But the operation that General Mildred had in mind wasn't a quick job, regardless of the efficiency of his operators.

In three days the bulk of it would be done, but the real mess came after. And Nick had Rashid Al-Falaj breathing down his neck as well. Somehow, he had to keep all the plates spinning in the air.

His mind went back to the killing of Victor Kowalski. The shot that sent this operation into motion. When he drove out after the decoy car, he saw the face of that man staring at him from the side walk.

A face he had never forgotten.

Dan Roy.

The way Dan had stared at him, Carlyle knew something had sparked. He was wearing his glasses luckily, and baseball cap. But there was every chance Dan recognized him.

He ignored it as coincidence at first. He had heard rumors that Dan had quit the field, even Intercept. Laughable as it sounded, he was trying to live as a civilian.

Men like Dan Roy could never live "normal" lives as civilians. Without speaking further on the phone, Carlyle hung up. He rubbed the scar on his left cheek. *That night in Ramallah, ten years ago.* When they were waiting to ambush the chief bomb maker of Hamas.

The operation went badly wrong. They were expected. Carlyle knew what happened next, but he kept it a closely guarded secret. The IDF and Dan Roy saved him. He had a chance to kill Dan then, and she should've done it. Now he was paying the price.

"Shit!" Carlyle whispered. He sat down on the sofa, hands in his hair. He knew Dan would be involved somehow and he wasn't wrong. Seeing him again at Kowalksi's garage, then at Murphy's house, with the FBI, wasn't exactly a shock. And he should have killed Dan this time. It was only by luck Dan had escaped so far, and so had the FBI woman with him.

But Dan presented a real problem. In the shadow world of black ops, his name was still revered. He had to be stopped, at any cost.

Carlyle's phone rang again. He looked at it and grimaced. It was Rashid Al-Falaj. He had to answer.

"Is it done?" Rashid asked.

Carlyle's slight hesitation was enough for Rashid to get it. "I want the truth."

"She escaped. But not for long. This time, I'll go after her myself," Carlyle said.

Unexpectedly, Rashid chuckled. "Honestly, you guys. Can't catch a simple woman?"

"She ain't as simple as she looks," Carlyle growled. "She's got brains, and knows how to shoot."

Rashid snorted. "Really? Sounds like you're making excuses, Carlyle."

"No, I'm not. Trust me, she's as good as dead."

He hung up and called the Sheriff back. "Which road was she last seen on?"

When Carlyle heard the name, a light dawned at the back of his mind. He put the phone down slowly.

Valona was on the I-64. With any luck, she was heading for the secret location. Did Victor tell his daughter before he died? Or had she always known?

It didn't matter. Carlyle knew what he had to do.

CHAPTER

Dan watched as Trisha leaned over her screen. Her phone rang for the third time, and she switched it off. The desks of Bellamy and two agents who shared the space with her was empty. Beyond the glass door, Dan could hear the perpetual rash of feet, voices, phone rings – the usual hub of sounds in the Washington Field Office that he had got used to.

Rather you than me, he thought, looking at Trisha.

He felt bad immediately. Trisha was tough, smart and deserved respect for handling her job in this mammoth bureaucracy with such chutzpah. Rising up in a world where 80% of agents were men.

Form filling and box ticking would never be Dan's thing. But everyone was different. He could see Trisha's passion for her job. He knew the country needed more individuals like her.

And maybe less of damaged, torn individuals like me.

The confession surprised him. It was not something he dwelt on. Dan knew he was incapable of holding down a regular job. Wearing a suit, shaking hands, saying hello and thank you like he meant it. He didn't even know what he was good for any more. Sure, he could fire a variety of weapons. He was deadly with a kukri knife. Skills he could only use in special situations. But he had no contacts with the real world. He had broken off from his old Army life. Intercept was a disaster zone, he would never have any friends there.

What did that leave?

Dan got up and walked to the window that looked out on the balcony that wrapped around the fourth floor of the building. He played with the blinds and looked out at the sunlight glinting from the traffic inching on the black asphalt snake down below. Beyond that, in the distance rose the tall finger of the Washington Memorial, a nascent, gleaming finger of purity, glowing in the sun.

And the white dome of the Lincoln Memorial. The lake and fountains whose waters rustled in the wind. It was a sight that once filled him with life. With energy. Even now. Because it was beautiful. He couldn't deny that, and he never would.

"Come and have a look at this." Trisha's excited voice penetrated his thoughts. Dan walked over to her side. Trisha pointed at the screen which showed a mug shot of a man in his forties. He looked vaguely familiar. He read the name on the side – Robert Murhy.

Trisha said, "We tracked him down from his social security numbers and IRS files. The address, DOB and description all match. It's him."

"Looks similar to the old guy," Dan said.

"It is. We traced him back to when he came over from Canada. That's where it gets interesting."

"He's not from Canada?"

Trisha leaned back and steepled her fingers. "Well, we spoke to the Canadian Passport authorities. A Robert Murphy was indeed born in Ottawa on that DOB. But he died at the age of two."

Dan was listening hard. "Carry on."

"Twenty years ago, a passport application was filed for him. For the dead boy, I mean. The Canadians managed to dig out the original application. Its filled in properly, with two witnesses, a local businessman in Ottawa and lawyer."

Trisha clicked and the old form came up as a scanned image. Dan glanced through it, then paced the room.

He said, "So someone impersonated the dead boy, Robert Murphy, and got a passport. That became his new identity. And we saw this man die yesterday."

Trisha stared at him. "So he could be anyone."

"We know a couple of things. We was close to Victor Kowalski, a Russian informer. He has a tattoo that is exactly the same as Kowalski has, on the same arm."

"And he was killed shortly after Kowalski," Trisha finished.

"From the satnav data, it's clear that the two met up the week before they both died. There must've been a reason."

Trisha said, "The same reason why Kowalski rang up the FBI? Something bad happening?"

"Bad, like a terrorist attack? Or an assassination? Just thinking aloud here." Dan wandered back to the window, and looked out without seeing. "What about the daughter?"

Trisha picked up her phone and spoke to someone for a while. Then she beckoned Dan over. "I'm through to Simpson, the NSA Signal Directorate Chief. You said you knew him right? I sent his analysts the data on Kowalski's daughter."

"Sure, I'll speak to him," Dan said. He took the phone and said his name.

Simpson said, "Dan Roy. Still trying to save the Vatican?"

Dan grinned. "That was last year. Might have something brewing closer to home this time."

Simpson said, "Here's what we got. The FBI analysts got hold of fifty females with the last name of Kowalski in the DC area, right? Of which thirty were outside the upper age limit of 50."

"Right. That leaves twenty."

"What else do you know about this woman?"

"She changed her name at some point. I'm now thinking she didn't just change her name, but her whole identity. She was the daughter of a spy, and might well have known a guy called Robert Murphy, who also has a fake ID." Dan told Simpson about the dead Canadian boy.

Simpson said, "Well you might be in luck. There's only three female Kowalski's in DC under the age of thirty. Two are married with children. Does that rule yours out?"

"I think so. Kind of hard to have a fake ID if you're in hospital giving birth."

"That leaves only one." Simpson clicked on a keyboard and paused. "A woman called Valona Kowalski."

CHAPTER

Trisha drove in her Audi A5 while Dan kept up a 360 degree sit rep, Sig on his lap, finger on trigger.

They arrived at a suburb of Arlington, where Valona Kowalski lived. The residential street was lined with two and three story tall, white, wooden colonial buildings. Birch and oak trees rose from the sidewalk, scattering fall leaves on the ground. Trisha drove past the address. The porch out front was empty, but looked well cared for. Lights were on in the first floor. Windows above were dark. Trisha turned left and did a circle, then came back to the street.

Dan got out first. He kept the Sig in his coat pocket, with his hand on the butt. His black jacket was cotton with a felt lining inside and the pockets were large. Just the way he liked them. He observed the house from across the street for a while, then crossed. The porch stairs creaked under his weight. The building was split into three apartments, one for each floor. Valona lived on the top. Dan pressed the buzzer, but nothing happened. After three tries, he pressed the first floor and saw a light come in the hallway. Dan stepped back and beckoned at Trisha. She locked the car and strode up quickly.

An old woman with silver hair opened the door. She wore jacket and slacks, and her hair was done up. Her eyes behind the glasses were sharp and she looked from Dan to Trisha, who just arrived as the door opened.

"May I help you?" the old woman said.

Trisha held up her badge. "FBI, ma'am. Looking for a lady called Valona Kowalski."

Dan said, "She lived on the top floor."

"Is she in trouble?" the woman asked, her eyes narrowing.

Trisha said, "She could be. Do you know if she's in?"

"I barely see her, to be frank. She comes and goes. Haven't seen her in the last week."

"Did she have anyone come to visit her, that you can recall?"

The woman knotted eyebrows together, thinking. "No. Wait, hang up, that's now what I meant. Yes she did have visitors, but its been a while."

"Do you know who they were?"

"An old man and woman. Looked like her parents. She held their hands."

Trisha took out the photo of Valona with her parents and showed it to the neighbor. The woman nodded.

"Yes, that's them alright." She looked at Trisha carefully. "Something's happened to them, right?"

"The investigation is still ongoing, Miss…"

"Barker. Trudy Barker."

"Miss Barker we can't comment right now, but you should know what's been in the media already. Valona's father, Victor was shot a day ago."

Miss Barker's eyebrows shot up, taking the glasses with it. "Mother of Mary. Who would do such a thing?"

"That's what we're trying to find out, ma'am. Do you have keys to the top floor apartment by any chance?"

"No, sorry." Miss Barker stood to one side as Trisha and Dan stepped inside. Another door led to a broad staircase that went up to the top floor.

They said goodbye to Miss Barker and she closed the door behind them. Trisha took her weapon out, nodded to Dan and started climbing. Dan waited, weapon still inside his coat, watching her. Trisha kept her back to the walls and disappeared round the bend, Glock pointed up the stairs. Dan waited till he couldn't hear her steps anymore.

He climbed in the silence. Sunlight filtered in from the stained glass window, dust motes dancing in the air around him. He could smell old carpets and wood. He strained his ears, but could hear nothing from Trisha. Which wasn't a bad thing. He went around the second floor landing, and caught sight of her at the top, opposite the door. She was crouching, and had a set of keys in her hand. She saw Dan and put a finger to her lips.

Dan came next to her and shuffled forward to the door, putting his ear against it. He couldn't hear a thing. He shook his head at Trisha. She put the first key in the keyhole and tried to slide the lock. After her third attempt there was a click. She pushed the door and it opened. Dan signaled to her and she stayed put.

He knelt, gun pointed ahead. Bending low, he entered, scanning with his weapon. The open plan living area and kitchen was modern, different to the rest of the house. The granite top kitchen counter gleamed in the light. Dan went down the small hallway and checked the two bedrooms and kitchen. The bedrooms were furnished with wardrobes, beds, and the place looked lived in. But it was empty.

Trisha opened the balcony door and stepped outside. The balcony ran the length of the apartment, and she could see the street below. She moved backwards and checked for any new cars. Then she looked at the building's opposite. She was looking for half open windows, curtains drawn, blackened. The snout of the sniper's rifle would be behind, out of sight. She turned when she heard a sound.

Dan joined her. "Place is empty. Time for a search?"

Trisha took out gloves and gave them to Dan. He put them on, and they went around the apartment. Trish went into the bathroom and opened the cabinet doors. She checked in the wardrobes.

"All her toiletries and most of her clothes are here. I don't think she was planning on a long trip," she said.

Dan was looking under the bed and he stood up. "There's two suitcases down there, too. You're right. She left in a hurry."

Trisha had walked to the table. She picked up a plaque resting on a pedestal. It said:

Best Scientist of the Year Award.
Environment Protection Agency.

Dan came over and joined her. Gently, he nudged her elbow. "Let's get away from the window. Remember what happened in Murphy's house?"

Trisha took the plaque and they walked back into the kitchen. Dan had looked into Valona's file while they drove down. He looked at the plaque and said, "Isn't that where she worked?"

"Yes." Trisha looked thoughtful. "This is a nice apartment. Valona was doing well for herself, I think. Maybe a rising star in the EPA."

"We should go check the place out," Dan said. "You know anything about it?"

"Only that it's a big agency."

"Yet another giant tax payer funded agency no one knows about." Dan said drily. "At least it can't be as big as where you work. The FBI is a money drain, right?"

"You want to compromise on the nation's safety?" Trisha said, her voice hardening. "Besides, what do you know about the FBI? It does a lot of good for a lot of people."

"Sure," Dan said, moving away. "We should get going. See if we can catch her boss before he goes off to lunch."

The EPA turned out to have a sprawling campus of over ten acres, thirty miles outside DC. As they approached, Dan couldn't help notice the barbed wire on the fences that encapsulated the scattered buildings. Armed patrol cops with sniffer dogs stopped them as they reached the outer checkpoint.

"I wonder what they do in there," Trisha muttered. "More security than we have."

She put her window down and showed her badge, then told them what she was here for.

The man took her ID, and Dan's too. He spent longer with Dan's ID, checking it matched his face. Dan stared back at the man with stone cold eyes. The guard took their ID's into the hut while they waited.

He came out and without a word, returned their ID cards. The bar lifted and they were waved through. They parked in the spacious and mostly full parking lot, then made their way inside. Inside a vaulted lobby, the long white reception desk seemed to glow against the black coated figures hovering on the other side.

A woman in her forties, with a perm, looked up as Dan approached. She opened her mouth and shut it, then swallowed.

"How can I help?"

Dan said, "We need information on an employee. Valona Kowalski. She's been missing for a week."

For a beat, the woman didn't speak. Then she cleared her throat. "Just give me a moment to make some enquiries."

As she walked off to a screen on the table, Trisha nudged closer. "Do you have always have that effect on women?"

"Didn't see it working on you."

The woman came back, patted down her black dress suit and smiled at Dan. She held his eyes for a bit longer than necessary, and completely ignored Trisha. Dan read her name badge. Dana.

Dana said, "Chris Walker is the Chief of Radnet, the department Miss Kowalski used to work for. He will see you in his office. 3rd floor, Room 320."

Dan leaned over the counter. "Thank you, Dana. You've been a big help."

She grinned. "Oh. Anytime."

Trisha had walked off already. Dan nodded at Dana and followed her. Trisha was waiting at the elevators. She looked at Dan and shook her head.

"What?" Dan asked.

CHAPTER

Trisha knocked on the brown mahogany door that said Room 320. A short, bespectacled man with wisps of hair on his balding head opened the door. He stood his ground, staring at them for a while.

"What's this about?" he asked.

Trisha said, "Are you Chris Walker?"

"Who are you?"

Trisha showed him her badge. He glanced at it, then towards Dan. He pointed. "Who's he?"

"A colleague," Trisha said. Dan stood still, saying nothing. Something about Walker's stance bothered him. The man was being defensive. He could see the wheels turning in Walker's head. Did he have something to hide?

Dan took out his ID, and in silence, passed it to Walker. Walker looked at it, then sighed.

"Come in," he said.

They sat opposite Walker, who took his time, opening and closing drawers before sitting down. He extricated a handkerchief from one of the drawers and wiped his forehead. Dan could feel the normal temperature in the room. Mr. Walker had no reason to feel warm.

Trisha said, "You were Valona Kowalski's boss?"

"I am the chief of Radnet. She was our senior scientist. So yes, I was her boss."

"What is Radnet?"

"Short for Radiation Net. We capture all forms of radiation in the atmosphere, making sure there's no harmful stuff for human beings."

Trisha asked, "Did you know that Valona was missing?"

"No." Walker wiped his forehead again. He loosened his tie.

"She didn't come to work for the last few days. You weren't concerned?"

"I tried to call her. She didn't answer. I figured she'd call back when she was ready."

"What exactly did Valona do here, Mr Walker?"

"We're all scientists here, right? Valona was a gifted researcher. She had this ability to know what data would be useful. Most of the data analysis is done by the machines these days, but you have to know what to feed them."

Trisha and Dan remained silent. Walker continued. "We measure air pollution levels, OK? The number of heavy metal molecules in the air, ionizing radiation, that sort of stuff. We look at water pollution, and soil as well.

Valona's specialty was ionizing radiation, and she devised a monitor for it. Well, we devised it, the department, with our engineers. But she came up with the design, and then got the data as well."

"What's ionizing radiation?"

"Radiation that is strong enough to break molecules. Like, of any matter. Radiation that can knock electrons off an atom`s orbit, and make them charged."

Dan asked, "Where does this radiation come from?"

"A number of sources. X-rays are a source, and medical devices like CAT scanners. In fact, developed nations like ours have a higher ionizing radiation levels purely because of the medical devices around us."

Trisha said, "Yeah, but it's kept to a safe level, right?"

Walker said, "Yes. That is what our monitors are for. We make sure the radiation levels are not going higher in our cities, and in the atmosphere in general."

"Hold up a minute," Dan said. "The stuff used in CAT scanners are radioactive, aren't they?"

"Of course. That`s what ionizing radiation is. It's very powerful, and if the level is high enough it can cause us to…"

"Die?"

Walker loosened his tie. "Yes." He sank back in his high arm chair, which made him appear smaller.

Dan's brain was whirring away, like a camera shuttering in rapid speed. There was something here. He could feel it, almost touch it. But it just eluded his grasp.

He asked, "What else causes ionizing radiation?"

Walker seemed to be more at ease now. This was obviously a topic he was comfortable with. He shrugged. "There's plenty of it in the atmosphere. Stars colliding, big explosions, supernova, that kind of stuff."

"What about on ground?"

"Well, there is the biggie." He paused and glanced at both of them. "Nuclear explosions."

CHAPTER

Dan felt the temperature in the room drop a few degrees. Something slapped against the base of his spine, making him sit straighter.

He asked, "A nuke will cause ionizing radiation?"

Walked said, "Not just that. There's also gamma, neutron and other types of radiation. All of it is high energy, and Valona's device measure all of it."

He continued, "It also measured gamma radiation from radioactive decay."

Trisha asked, "What does that mean?"

"So, all radioactive minerals give off radiation as they get older. That's how they are found in fact, by a machine called the Geiger counter. Valona's monitor could pick up those as well."

Dan said, "So say there was a lot of leakage from a CAT scanner, would that increase the levels of gamma whatever, or radiation? And would Valona's machine be able to pick it up?"

Walker raised his eyebrows. "It would have to be a serious amount of radiation, or radioactive decay, but yes the device would pick it up. That was the beauty of the device, you see. It was very sensitive. It could give us advance warning in the case of an accident."

They were silent for a while. Trisha looked at Dan, and he saw understanding in her eye. She turned back to Walker.

"Who else knows about this device? Valona's monitor, I mean."

"No one apart from us."

"Has the device actually been made? Is it working?"

Walker nodded. "Oh yeah. It's working alright. But it's used only by myself and Valona. We drive to different parts of the state and take readings." He stopped suddenly, a faraway light in his eyes.

Dan asked, "What is it?"

Walker recovered quickly. He cleared his throat again. "Nothing at all."

Trisha hadn't missed it either. She leaned forward. "If you're all scientists, you publish your findings, right? That's how you get funding."

Walker seemed uncomfortable again. "Yes. But we get normal Federal grants too."

"Whatever. Did you publish your findings about the device? Or the data you collected?"

Walker opened and closed a drawer again like he was looking for something. Trisha said, "Mr Walker, can you please answer the question?"

He rubbed his eyes. "No, I didn't. Because it wasn't mine to publish. It was Valona's. She had the rights." He stood and stared at them with red rimmed, tired eyes. "Look, are we done here? I have other business to attend."

Trisha and Dan remained seated. Walker stared at both of them with a hostile look in his eyes.

"Didn't you hear what I said?"

Trisha asked calmly, "Do you know where Valona Kowalski is?"

Walked shook his head, face working. "Did you just ask me that? Oh God, I can't believe it."

Dan said, "You're nervous, Mr Walker. You weren't happy to see us but realized you can't hide from the FBI. What are you not telling us?"

Walker clenched his jaws. "I told you everything I know. Now just leave."

Dan looked at Trisha and nodded slightly. Trisha fixed Walker with a stare. "Mr Walker, I am arresting you on suspicion of the kidnapping of Valona Kowalski. You have the right to remain silent. You-

"What?" Walker gasped. His face was purple, a vein standing up in the middle of his forehead. Sweat poured down his face. "Are you kidding me? I didn't do anything." He collapsed on his chair and put his head in his hands. "Oh Jeez. Come on."

Trisha said, "Why don't you tell us what's going on, Mr Walker? That way I don't have to arrest you. But I want the truth."

Walker's head remained downcast. Trisha said, "If you haven't done anything wrong, then you'll be alright. I promise."

Walker looked up, his face pained, drawn. He stared at both of them. "I got a young family. Two kids in middle grade."

Dan said, "Someone threaten you?"

Walker sighed, wiping his face and head. "Jeez. What the hell am I gonna do?" He jabbed a finger at Dan. "They told me...." He left his sentence unfinished.

"Not to speak to the cops."

"The FBI. Like they knew you were gonna come."

Dan said, "We can protect you." He glanced at Trisha.

She said, "That's right. No one's going to harm you, or your family. You have my word on that. I can put a security detail outside your house this evening."

Walker seemed to relax. "OK." He wiped his moist forehead. For a while he remained motionless, staring at the carpet.

Trisha said, "Mr Walker?"

He looked up at her with vacant eyes. "I'm worried."

Dan intervened. He knew it took a man a lot to admit he was scared. He was concerned about his family. Dan got that. He leaned forward.

"Give me your address. I will personally head down there tonight and check the place out. No one's going to touch your wife or kids, I promise you."

Walker sighed. "Fine. Guess I need your help in this now. Two days after Valona didn't turn up to work, a man rang. Valona and I were in the process of submitting the research to Nature magazine and other scientific journals. Valona had picked up high traces of radioactive decay in rural Virginia. Where exactly, I don't know. But she had the data and was excited about publishing it."

He continued. "This man said if that data was ever published then my wife and two sons would disappear. No one would ever see them again. Then they'd come after me."

CHAPTER

Dan asked, "What did he sound like?"

"American, East Coast. Said I would never trace him. I didn't try." Walker's face was pale now, drained of color.

Trisha asked, "So could you publish the data even if Valona wasn't here?"

"She named me as co author in the paper. So yes, I could." He gripped his forehead. "What am I gonna do now?"

Trisha said, "Like I said, we're gonna help you. Do you know what happened to Valona's dad?"

He nodded. "Yes. The man told me. Said I would die much slowly than her Dad did." Walker shivered.

Dan said, "Walker, I need you to think about this. Where in Virginia did Valona get the readings of radioactive decay?"

Walker said, "High decay. You will find traces of radioactive decay everywhere. Mostly it's not important. And mostly, it comes from the health institutions, or near a nuclear research lab."

Dan said, "Or, close to a big pile of natural uranium."

"Yes."

All three were silent for a while. Dan repeated his question.

Walker shook his head. "She didn't tell me." He frowned. "To be honest, that's what I didn't get about her. Once she got those readings, she was different."

"Different how?"

"She was quieter. Started avoiding me. Then she stopped turning up to work. That's when this man started calling me."

Trisha said, "We need your phone. Our guys might still be able to triangulate the call, using the cell network. And you need to come down to the station to give a statement."

Walker looked nervous. "You're not gonna arrest me, are you? Look I have a reputation to keep. I'm the boss here. This looks bad."

Trisha allowed herself a smile. "You don't have to walk out with us. Come an hour later to the WFO." Her voice hardened. "But if you don't come, then we have to arrest you."

"Of course, I'll come," Walker said hurriedly. He got a cell phone out from his pocket. He held it in his hands, rubbing the screen. "You won't look at my personal data, will you?"

Trisha didn't mince her words. "Mr Walker, I have no choice. This is a serious matter, and its getting worse by the second. We need to cover all angles. If you have nothing to hide, then don't worry. All your data will remain confidential to the FBI, I promise you."

Trisha and Dan walked out, leaving Chris Walker slumped on his chair, staring at the table. They didn't speak till they were out in the parking lot. Wind whipped around their ears.

Trisha said, "Valona took off, right? Her father was killed 2 days ago, so she went before that." Trisha counted. "Five days before the shooting."

They sat down in the car and Trisha turned the engine, but didn't move. Dan said, "Someone told her to get out. Maybe they were after her already. Maybe her dad told her to haul ass. I don't know. But she had a good reason to do it. You heard what Walker said. She was skilled at her job. From what we saw in her apartment, she ran out scared. Left most of her belongings."

"The guys who killed Kowalski and Murphy are chasing her too, right?"

The sun was out and Dan had his shades on. He watched the trees bend in a stiff breeze. He took his time before answering. "That means the same guys threatened Walker to keep the research quiet."

"But why?"

Dan came from Montrose, a sleepy small town near the base of the Applachian Mountains. He knew the country around it, to his mind, it had some of the best wilderness he had ever hiked and hunted in. He knew how remote some parts of rural Virginia could get.

He said, "We need to find out where Valona used to go to get her readings. Where in Virginia, I mean. The place she never took Walker to. Sounds to me she wanted to keep it a secret. Like she knew what she would find there."

Trisha stared at him in silence for a while. "Where you going with this?"

Dan shook his head. "Not sure. But my gut's telling me we find Valona, we find the solution."

Trisha started to back the car out. "Lets get back to base. Maybe the missing person alert found something about her. She took a train from somewhere and the cameras caught her."

Trisha's phone beeped and she had to stop. She glanced at the screen, then frowned, put the car on neutral, and scrolled. "What is it?" Dan asked.

"You better believe this. Remember that license plate number you memorized? Of the car that came out of Langhorne Office Building after the shooting. The tan sedan."

Dan's spine tingled. A sudden blinding white light hit the back of his eyelids with massive force. The world turned black for a second and tilted. His head dropped forward on his chest, and his mouth opened in shock. His forehead felt it had been blown apart by a grenade.

"Dan?" Trisha's voice was sharp with concern.

The world was swimming in Dan's eyes. Visions came and went abruptly, like a chainsaw cutting through a movie screen. Screams and shouts. A bloody hand reaching for his face. Clawing.

"No," Dan whispered.

"Dan what is-

Dan opened the car door and stepped outside. He took his shades off and breathed deeply. He walked a few steps, feeling his gait wobbly, uncertain. The light was harsh on his eyes, so he put the shades back on. He stood at the edge of the parking lot, looking out over the green fields to where the trees moved serenely, like they were tugged by an ocean current. Strangely peaceful to watch.

I know that face.

He didn't know how the memory suddenly came back, without even trying. Just Trisha's mention of the tan sedan blew some cobwebs away, and the truth flashed upon his mind.

He felt Trisha standing a few steps behind him. He appreciated that she gave him some space. He turned around eventually.

"Sorry about that," Dan said. It was weird that he was sweating. When he wiped his sleeve on the forehead, he noticed his hands were shaking. He made fists and shoved them in his pockets.

Trisha came forward. Her hazel green eyes were soft. "You look pale, Dan. Think you should see a doctor. Something you need to tell me?"

Dan nodded. He was regaining his balance. "I don't need a doctor. But I do need to tell you who that man in the tan sedan was. I remember him now."

"You *know* him? The man you think is the shooter?"

"His name is Nick Carlyle. He used to work for Intercept. Former Army Ranger."

Trisha's face showed her confusion. Dan sighed. "There's things I need to tell you. They're top secret. You can't get security clearance for this. Because according to the Pentagon, or the CIA, these events never happened."

Trisha folded her hands across her chest. "Black Ops huh? I knew there was more to you than meets the eye. Consular Operations my ass."

"Let's head back. I'll fill you in over a coffee."

Trisha raised her eyebrows. "Guess what the message was? About the tan sedan you saw."

"Sorry, I forgot."

"We heard from DMV. They tracked the tan sedan down. It's overdue on tax. But they found the car registered to an address in a small town called Mackton. It's sixty miles west of Culpeper."

Dan narrowed his eyes. "That's north Virginia. Quiet place, holiday spot in the summer."

Trisha's eyes flared and Dan was hit by the same thought, at the same time.

"Valona," Dan whispered.

CHAPTER

Lubynaka Square
Meschansky District
Moscow

Boris Timoshenko stared at the fumes that rose from his black coffee. The sharp smell was invigorating on this cold day, the first frost of a desolate winter suddenly closer. He lifted the cup, took a gentle sip and grimaced. He put the cup down and turned his head to look at the grey cobbled stone expanse of the famous Lubyanka Square, with the grand baroque Lubyanka building occupying the center ground. Still a captivating sight. Late afternoon sunlight gave the huge, rectangular building a yellow orange glow.

Colonel Grigori Evanovich spoke from opposite him. "When was the last time you came here?"

Timoshenko turned hard eyes towards his old friend. "The day they told me to leave. To Pechora, of all places."

"Pechora is very important, *tavarish*." Comrade. An old, nostalgic word from the days of the Soviet Union, a word that remained popular. "Our best early warning radar system. It needs someone like you to run it."

"Spare me the bullshit, Grigori. If its that good then why the hell don't you take the job?" Timoshenko cursed under his breath.

"We are past patronizing each other, Boris. But you know we all have to do our bit."

Tim curled his upper lip. "What you mean is kiss ass and keep my mouth shut even when I know something's not right."

"Now, now."

Tim jabbed a finger towards the old KGB building. "They were bastards. Still are. You know that."

"Then what does that make us?"

Tim grinned. "Well, you're an old bastard, aren't you?"

Grigori smirked. "Piss off comrade." The mirth didn't touch his eyes. "Are you sure about this signal?"

Tim took a sip of his coffee, then shook out a packet of Marlboro Reds. They were American and hence not easily available in Russia, but the SVR agents generally got what they wanted. Tim lit up and took a deep drag.

"The LPAR doesn't lie, my friend. The signal is correct. I verified it with my codebook. As you know, the code for the signal is not in a computer database for security."

"It used to be, back in the day. But those databases have long been destroyed." Grigori's eyes clouded over. "Who the hell could know about this?"

Tim shook his head. Smoke from the cigarette mingled with the coffee fumes. "I don't know, Grigori. But I'm worried. Viktor and Vassily left for America, I know that. The others are dead. That leaves me and you. I sure as hell didn't tell anyone."

"You're forgetting our War Minister. He was around back then. He knows, I bet you. And he's old school."

"Ilyich Gennady?"

"Yes. But forget about him. He's not going to be the leak. It has to be the two who defected to the bloody Imperialists. Viktor and Vassily. I looked up their names as soon as you told me. It wasn't easy. I don't want to trigger an alert, looking for old spies. Luckily one of my underlings still works for the Department 6, and they had a record."

"Viktor became Victor Kowalski, and Vassily changed into Robert Murphy, right?"

Grigori was thoughtful. "You looked them up too, huh?"

Tim shrugged. "Actually, I just remembered. There was only twelve of us originally. Strange to think only four survived."

Both were silent for a while. Pedestrians crossed the large square, strolling leisurely, a few sightseers stopped to take photos. That was allowed now, given that Lubyanka wasn't the HQ of the SVR anymore. But some die hards like Grigori still preferred the charms of the 400 year old building, and had kept their offices in Lubyanka.

Grigori said, "This is bad. I don't even know what it could mean."

"It means a mainframe computer somewhere is making contact with the Zemlya satellite. The frequency at which the contact is being made is the same frequency we know of. The one in my code books."

Grigori took out a packet of Belomorkanal cigarettes, a Russian make. He accepted the light from his friend. He blew smoke away.

"So, where the hell is this computer?"

Timoshenko didn't reply for a while. He brushed back the white hair that fell over his face. He suddenly felt exhausted. Maybe he was getting old for this. He never thought of it that way. But decades of looking over his shoulder was getting tiresome.

Grigori pushed. "The satellite feedback would have given the GPS location, right? Where in Russia is it?"

Tim fixed his old friend with a stare. "It's not in Russia, comrade."

The two men locked eyes, and Tim didn't have to say any more. Realization dawned in Grigori's eyes, and with it, blatant, surging fear.

"No," he whispered, leaning forward, mouth open in shock.

Tim closed his eyes and exhaled. "I'm afraid so. The computer is located in a town in Virginia, USA."

CHAPTER

Dan was back in the WFO, staring out the window at the same scenery. He felt like a caged animal. He needed to be out there. The old scent was back in his blood, the hunger to be on the road, watching the black miles slip beneath the wheels of his ride, weapons strapped to his chest.

Something very big is going down. And I ain't gonna solve this sitting in a freaking FBI room.

Trisha threw open the door behind him and walked in, clutching sheafs of paper in her hand. She dumped them on her desk and without a word to Dan, reached for the desk phone that just started to ring. She spoke fast and went into a maelstrom of calls and emails.

Dan walked over and tapped her on the shoulder. She put a hand over the phone receiver.

Dan said, "I need a secure cell. And we need to get in touch with Simpson from the SID."

Trisha opened the drawer on her desk and pulled out a black metal case. She pressed her thumb on the keypad, it buzzed and the spring lock opened. Inside, lay two new cell phones, batteries and SIM cards lying next to them. Dan picked one, powered it up and inserted the SIM card.

"Give me 5," Trisha mouthed. Dan nodded and left the room. He avoided the elevator and went rapidly down the steps. He took a left outside the WFO and went inside the park alongside. He walked till he came to a shady spot under a tree, away from the couples and tourists. He rang the number he knew by heart. A metallic machine voice answered.

"Please. Say. Your. Code."

"Oh-seven-one-oh-eight-three."

There was a click, and a whirr, then the pause of static. Apart from the code, Dan knew his voice was getting analyzed by the machine. After ten seconds, a dial tone came, then a ringing sound. Eventually someone picked up.

"Who is it?"

"It's me, Dan."

McBride coughed, then cleared his throat. "Where have you been?"

Dan gave McBride a quick Sitrep. Then he paused, letting the silence between them sink in.

Dan said, "We need to find out more about this Murphy guy. His ID's fake."

McBride rasped, "You know that's like a needle in a haystack right? We need to get the Canadians to cooperate, that alone will take a while. Besides, what if you're wrong?"

"The dead boy wouldn't come alive now, would he? And someone took the boy's name and got himself a passport and social security number."

"That's not what I mean. What if he really is Irish, and we need to start asking questions in that direction?"

Dan frowned. "What do you mean?"

McBride didn't say anything for a while. Dan understood where this was headed. He said, "You're talking about the IRA, right?"

"Right."

"Kowalski was Russian, why would he be in cahoots with the IRA?"

"This goes back a while. Before your time, young Dan."

"I ain't young anymore."

"You are compared to me. So shut up and listen." McBride cleared his throat. "When the IRA started their bombing campaign in London, the western world had never seen anything like it. And the IRA were strong supporters of the PLO."

"Palestine Liberation Organization?"

"The same. Both groups shared Soviet weapons, and bomb making skills. Urban terrorism as we know it in fact, started with the IRA."

Dan said, "I know some of the SAS men had a tough time in Belfast. They had Irish guys in the Regiment."

"I know. There aren't that many links between the IRA and the Russians today, but back in the day the Soviets did send them weapons. It's not crazy to think that an Irish dissident and Russian defector could be friends."

Dan thought of the tattoos that Kowalski and Murphy had. He told McBride.

Dan said, "But I think you're wrong there, for two reasons. One – why would Murphy have to go through all that effort to hide himself, if he was Irish? He could just change his name, get a new Irish passport and fly into Boston. Some IRA men did flee North Ireland like that, didn't they?"

McBride grunted.

Dan said, "And second, that tattoo, and Kowalski going to see him days before he was shot, points to a closeness that's greater than casual friendship. I think these men fought in the same operations, looked out for each other." Dan paused. He still had blood brothers in the army. He didn't see them often, but he knew how it worked. He wouldn't hesitate to help one if the need arose.

He continued. "Given that Kowalski was a known KGB commander, I would say Murphy was KGB as well. Maybe they emigrated at the same time. Ask the CIA. They should know. Whether they tell you is another matter."

McBride was silent for a while. Then he coughed. "Yeah, it makes sense. That bit you said about them meeting just before Kowalski was shot is interesting. It's like they *had* to meet."

Dan sat down on park bench. He needed to. "I saw Nick Carlyle," he said quietly.

"Who?"

Dan didn't answer but McBride caught on. "Oh, Jesus. Carlyle from Intercept. You saved his ass in Ramallah, right?"

"He didn't see it that way. You know, I still think he was selling out. Hamas had him surrounded because he wanted them to. I turned up and destroyed the scene."

McBride was quiet for several seconds. "He came back but Intercept didn't want him. I know some of our guys stayed in touch with him. Then he went dark.

McBride continued. "Dan, this doesn't look good. Why is Carlyle involved in this?"

"I don't know. But I'm working on it."

"Good."

"Find out who Murphy was. Then let's touch base." Dan hung up and walked back to the WFO.

Trisha was in her room, staring at the screen. Her eyes lit up when she saw Dan. Bellamy was next to her, watching the laptop screen as well. He nodded at Dan who returned the gesture.

Trisha said, "I got in touch with Simpson. They used their supercomputers on all the chatter coming out of Virginia. One odd thing stood out – an armed woman escaping from a psychiatric hospital." She turned the laptop so Dan could see. Dan watched the image on the screen. A white coated woman was walking out the sliding gates, and her profile was caught as she paused. Trisha froze the frame. She minimized the screen and brought up the photo of Valona from her father's house. It was identical to the woman on the cameras.

"Where did she go?" Dan asked.

"She's a tough cookie. She ambushed a farmer's car, rode it to the next town, then bribed a waitress for her car."

Trisha looked up at Dan. "It gets more serious after that. She shot and killed a man, found on the roadside. The Sherriff's Department reported it. No one knows where she went."

Dan rubbed his cheek, staring at the photo. A thought occurred to him. "Wait. Mackton, where the getaway car from Kowalski's murder scene, is registered. How far is it from where Valona was last seen?"

Trisha brought up Google Maps and typed in the name. Then she clicked on the report sent from the PD.

"About fifty miles. Not far." Dan held her eyes, and she nodded in understanding.

"It's time to go."

CHAPTER

Valona eased off the throttle as she travelled westward past Charlottesville. Trees shrouded the hills as far as eyes could see, and the yellow, gold and orange fall colors were mesmerizing. It reminded her of her happy childhood. The searing pain of never being able to see her parents again suddenly hit her hard. And despite the situation she was in, or maybe because of it, tears stung the back of her eyes. She wiped them away angrily. Emotions swirled inside her like the sunset clouds, but the predominant feeling was anger. Rage boiled in her veins.

Glancing at the rearview, she started to check the countryside again.

She was closer to the hills, she knew that. The temperature had dropped and sunlight was fading. She had to find a place to rest, or she'd freeze. A truck lumbered past the opposite lane, its lights temporarily blinding. She flinched, feeling the muzzle of the gun on her lap.

Lights appeared up ahead, and a road sign came into view. Waynesboro. The name sounded familiar, but she didn't know why. The lights up ahead moved to her right.

Waynesboro must be a small town, she thought, as darkness swallowed the land further up. Another sign came and with it, a stronger lurch of memory.

Blue Ridge Parkway North Entrance.

Valona frowned, then her eyebrows cleared. She had been to the Blue Ridge Park. But not with her parents, it was for summer camp. She had played in the lakes as a twelve-year-old. Images started to play in her mind, a silent cinema of near forgotten childhood days.

The Parkway Entrance was less than a mile away. She drove past it. No point in heading inside now, and driving down a desolate road for ages till she got somewhere. She checked the rearview again. A car caught her eye. A family carrier, travelling slowly. She had seen it before, and it had stayed at the same distance. Still no threat in sight but she knew it was a matter of time.

The sign for Waynesboro came up again and she indicated and took the exit ramp. She drove past a gas station and entered the Pike way that ran through the center of town. A Holiday Inn and Best Western appeared next to each other. Valona checked the gas. Half a tank left, which meant she had to fill up soon. Virtually no food in her stomach – that tank definitely had to be filled, she was famished. A parade of shops came into view, with the lights of a bar and disco open. People milled outside. Friday night, she thought to herself. She parked carefully, not too close to the bar, or to where she intended to stay, the Holiday Inn. She walked into the hotel chain, and washed herself in the restroom. The money was all gone, but she still had the credit card. There was no other option.

She didn't go to the reception, but sneaked back outside. She walked past the bar, on the opposite side of the road, and found a small department store. Using the credit card she bought scissors, a black hair dye, make up and two new T shirts, yellow and red. She saw the cameras pointing down, but there was nothing she could do about it.

Back in the Holiday Inn Restroom, she locked herself inside a cubicle. She took off the pullover and T shirt. Bending over the commode, she cut her blonde hair till it was shoulder length. She scooped up what was left over and flushed it down the loo.

When she came out, the place was still empty. She applied the die quickly in front of the mirror, and put heavy black mascara around her eyes. When it was done, she looked back at herself with satisfaction. Far from a proper job, but she had become a darker version of her former self.

She turned the jumper inside out, and put the red T shirt on. The old white shirt was now tied around her waist.

The male receptionist looked at her with a bored expression. "Can I help you?"

"Yes. Do you know where the restaurant is?"

CHAPTER

Valona sat near the entrance of the restaurant, partially hidden from the doorway by a counter. She kept an eye on the door, ready to duck underneath the table. She ordered steak and fries with an omlette on the side, and surprised herself by devouring the whole meal. She washed it down with apple juice, although she craved a nice glass of red wine with the steak.

She paid and left the Holiday Inn, and walked to the Best Western Motel. She got a room on the ground floor, next to a fire escape door. The room faced the street and she could see the cars through the net curtain. The double bed looked inviting and when she lay on it, she realized how exhausted she was. But sleep wouldn't come easy. She ejected the magazine of the Glock, to find it had seven rounds left. She racked the slide, checked the barrel, and put the gun underneath the pillow. She dragged a chair and jammed it underneath the door handle. She made sure the window was shut, turned the lights off, and watched the road in front. Her eyes gradually grew heavy, and her head sunk downwards.

*****

Valona almost fell off the bed when she awoke. Morning light was bright through the window and she blinked. For a few seconds, she had no idea where she was. It was one of the strangest moments in her life. Her mind tried to grasp where she had seen the lavender colored walls, soft bed, desk and window before, and came back with a blank. Then it all came back, a rush of memory that left her disorientated, fragile. She gulped and reached for the gun underneath the pillow. It was strangely comforting to feel the hard metallic surface.

Heart pounding, she jerked her eyes around the room. It was empty. She checked the bathroom, then washed and got ready. The short black hair looked alien in the mirror, and she guessed that was a good thing. She changed into the new red T shirt she had brought the other day, and pulled the jumper on before leaving the room.

The woman at reception greeted her with a smile. Valona took directions to the breakfast room, and ate quickly, eyes on the door again. When she came back to the lobby the same woman was still at the reception. Coffee had woken Valona up. She had a better idea now of where she was.

She asked the woman, "What national parks are around here?"

The woman took out a map from under the counter and spread it. "Behind us you have the Wintergreen Resort, which is in the George Washington and Jefferson National Park area. The Park's a big place." The woman pointed on the map.

The names meant nothing to Valona. But her eyes were drawn to a highway going northward. Number 340.

An electric flash sparkled inside her brain. She saw a sight from many years ago. As a teenager she had seen a road sign with that number, sitting in the back of their family car. The road was surrounded by deep green forested hills.

The vision faded but her memory marched down the road. Arriving at the banks of a lake. Log cabins, dense woods. Putting meat on the barbecue. Starry, starry night. Holding hands with her mother, walking down the lake.

Her father saying to her, remember this place, Valona, lapochka.
Why Papa?
You might need to come here one day.
Remember…

"Ma'am are you OK?" a voice inquired opposite her.

Valona transferred her gaze back to the receptionist. She swallowed, shook her head gently and smiled.

"Yes I am. Sorry." Valona pointed to Route 340, which ran almost parallel to I-81. "I have a sat nav but forgotten the name of the place now. Does this road go towards any holiday spots?"

"Yes. The Shenandoah National Park, right here."

Valona had seen it already, and somehow, the name was familiar, not because it was well known, but because she knew something else about it. The memory remained frustratingly out of reach. She should have paid more attention to what her father had said, all those years ago.

But you did. That's why you came down here to take the readings with the new monitor.

Valona thanked the woman, took the map, and left. She paused at the doors, watching the pedestrians and vehicles. No cars parked outside. No man staring at the hotel. That man with the scar on his left cheek. She would never forget him. She walked to the car quickly, and walked past it. She went inside the department store and stood at an angle near the glass display where she could observe the car. It was empty, of course, and she didn't spot anyone watching it. Her eyes travelled to the shops on either side, most of which were shut. But the two hotels were open. If someone was watching from the windows, at least she had time to get out of here.

Valona got into the car quickly and drove off. At the traffic lights, she followed signs for I-340.

She thought as she drove. She had come to a forest near Culpeper to check out the new radiation screening monitor. The device she had spent so many years preparing, since her days at MIT. It was her baby.

The Applachian Range had always held a special place in her mind. Mainly because of the family holidays. But why had she come here, on her own, to test the new monitor? Was it because of what her father had said?

She didn't remember, until this moment, what he had said. The words were lost in the mists of time.

You might need to come here one day.

Cryptic as hell. No wonder she didn't remember them. But they must have been in her subconscious, driving her to test the new monitor here.

And what she had found would change Virginia, maybe even America.

Her throat was suddenly bone dry and her heart thumped painfully against her ribs.

Like the Devil's own jigsaw, pieces of this nightmare were falling into place.

CHAPTER

Lubyanka Ploshchad
Moscow

Boris Timoshenko drained the remainder of his coffee and put his cup down. Grigori Evanovich was still staring at him.

"Do you have the precise location?" Grigori asked.

"Yes. Alexandria, a city on the Potomac River. South of Washington DC."

"So not far from DC, is it?"

Timoshenko shook his head. "Not at all. Access by river and road is very easy. I don't know precisely, but maybe 2-3 hours by road."

Evanovich was deep in thought. He asked, "Who else have you told?"

"Only you. I figured as a senior Colonel in the GRU, one who has the ear of the War Minister, you might know what's going on."

They both grinned. Evanovich swore at his old friend affectionately. Then he became serious. "We have to be very careful, Boris. Obviously, the War Minister needs to know immediately. But more importantly, is it Americans who are using this computer?"

"That stands to reason, given this is inside their country. But I have not made enquiries."

"Our hackers can break into the computer with an IP address, right?"

"Yes comrade, but that will also warn our enemies that the game is up. And no matter how many third party servers in Timbuctoo and Kazakhstan we use, the Americans seem to find the location of our hacking groups eventually."

"So, what do you suggest we do?"

Timoshenko was quiet for a while. He watched his friend carefully, then said, "Maybe it's time we came clean. Tell the Americans what happened all those years ago."

Evanovich rubbed his face and reached for his cigarette packet. He was getting a headache.

"Can you imagine the reaction? Never mind expel our diplomats, they might even move to DEFCON1."

"Can you imagine not telling them and getting blamed for it later?" Timoshenko countered.

"*Balyet!*"

"My sentiments exactly. I suggest you speak to the War Minister to arrange an interview with the American Ambassador in Moscow. Both of us can be present in the meeting if necessary." Timoshenko leaned forward. "Grigori, this is serious. Someone has the code book, and is sending the signal to the satellite. The satellite is relaying it back to receivers in the US mainland, and to us. Sooner or later, someone in the US Geospatial Intelligence, or in NORAD, will pick this up. You know they will."

He settled back in his chair. "Unless the unthinkable has happened by then."

Evanovich lifted his eyes and nodded. "You are right, comrade. Time to put this to rest. Because if the unthinkable does happen, Russia will cease to exist."

"*Eta pravda, Tovarish.*" That is true, comrade. Timoshenko leaned back in his chair.

Evanovich asked, "What have you done with your copy of the code book?"

Timoshenko tapped his left breast. "In here. I have it in a locked safe when I don't need it. I thought it might come in handy this time. Where's yours?"

"At home. Locked in a safe, as you said." Evanovich seemed to relax, as if a weight was removed from his shoulders. He took a deep drag on his cigarette.

"Right. So we speak to Gennady, the War Minister, and disclose everything. Then we beg him to tell the Americans."

Timoshenko said slowly, "Right. I hadn't thought of that. He might refuse."

"Exactly. Then what? I suppose he will speak to the Premier. Who might also refuse. You know how it works in politics. They might love the fact that we know something the Americans don't."

"Something that could destroy America." Timoshenko stared at the empty cup of coffee. With an effort he lifted his eyes, and stared sightlessly at the open Lubyanka Square. Pedestrians had picked up in volume.

He said in a quiet voice, "Grigori, then we have a duty to tell the Americans."

His friend was startled. "Us? Tell the Americans?"

Timoshenko shrugged. "What's so hard? We do what Viktor did. Walk in at the American Embassy and tell them who we are. Job done."

Evanovich frowned heavily. "Be careful of what you're saying, comrade. Good job there's no one here to listen to us."

"What is your plan if the War Minister refuses to speak to the Americans immediately? We can't wait on this. For all we know, this is already happening. Tomorrow might be too late."

Evanovich slumped. He held his head in his hands, looking, Timshenko thought, weirdly helpless for such a powerful man. When Evanovich looked up, his face was red, nostrils flaring, contorted.

"Boris, I will never betray this country, you know that."

"And neither will I. But if the politicians do not resolve this, are they not betraying the Russian people?"

The two men stared at each other for a long time. Evanovich was the first to look away. He sighed. "Yes. You are right. Ultimately, it is the people we serve."

"*Sovietski Soyuz.*" United Soviet Russia.

"*Sovietski Soyuz.*"

Timoshenko scraped his chair back and stood up. They shook hands.

Evanovich said, "I will speak to Gennady immediately. Then let you know this evening. It's best if we meet, without speaking on phone."

Timoshenko nodded. Evanovich asked, "Where are you staying."

"In Sporchivnaya." Timoshenko gave him the address.

"Good, that's on my way back to Yazenevo." He glanced at his watch. "In fact, I could head there now. Would you like a lift?"

Timoshenko shrugged. "Sure, why not?"

They stepped out into the cobbled stones of the charming old Square. Evanovich took out his cell phone and called his driver. Roughly two hundred meters away, they saw the colossal gates of the Lubyanka open and a Zil limousine join the road that went around the Square.

They waited till the car came abreast. The driver got out, saluted and opened the back door for them. Timoshenko got in first, followed by Evanovich. The driver set off.

The armor-plated car made its way onto the South Ring Road, powerful 5 liter engine purring smoothly.

Timoshenko was looking outside his black tinted windows at the traffic on the Ring Road. The car took an exit and turned down a ramp into a quieter street. He turned to look at his friend.

"Long way to get to Sp-

His words were cut off when he glanced down and saw the barrel of the snub nosed Makarov pistol that had appeared in Evanovich's fist. The gun was pointing straight at him. His mouth fell open, eyes bulged. He stared at the gun like he had never seen one before, then turned his saucer eyes to Evanovich.

Grigori Evanovich spoke softly. "I am sorry *tovarish*. I really am. I wish there was another way."

There was a sudden sharp noise, like air bursting out of a cycle tire. A bullet tore out from the suppressed weapon and slammed into the chest of Boris Timoshenko. Another followed, and the last thing Timoshenko remembered was the stony face of Evanovich, holding his eyes.

Then the world turned dark.

CHAPTER

Evanovich stared at the body of his old friend without emotion. After the third bullet had thrust the body against the upholstery of the seat, then eyelids lowered and the head dropped down to the chest. Evanovich tapped on the glass sheet separating him from the driver. A panel on it opened. "Drive to the dumpyard. We have an object to dispose."

"Yes sir."

The panel closed and Evanovich settled back in his seat. He turned his cell phone off and detached the battery from the phone. From his inside coat pocket he took out another phone, powered it up and unwound the antenna. He dialed the number and waited.

Rashid Al-Falaj answered from the other end. "Is that you, Angel?"

"What is the code phrase?"

Rashid said, "Angels are dying everywhere."

Evanovich relaxed. Voices sounded different on the satellite phone. "This is Angel. You need to know something." He explained what had happened.

There was silence on the other end. Finally Rashid said, "How?"

"You didn't take steps to use a GPS jammer when the satellite sent its signal."

"You didn't ask me to do that." There was anger in Rashid's voice.

"These are basic skills. It is easy to jam GPS signals, you can buy them commercially. I am surprised you don't know this." Evanovich continued. "For example, I am speaking to you from an encrypted phone."

"The satellite link is also encrypted," Rashid said. "You told me that, remember? Was that a lie?"

"I have nothing to gain from lying to you."

"Then they broke through the layer of encryption?"

"No. When the satellite sends the signal, it's encrypted. But you have a receiver, the satellite dish, right?"

"I see. When the dish receives the signal, and transfers it to the mainframe computer, the IP of the computer is not encrypted and visible to anyone."

"That's correct. Given how important the computer is to send and receive information from the satellite, I suggest you hide it immediately."

The car had turned into a large disposal yard, enormous cans full of rubbish all around them. Evanovich said, "I have to go. Remember what I said."

Rashid's voice was biting. "I will. But I need the codes. You said you would send them to me."

"I was waiting for a mistake like this to happen. Aren't you glad I did?"

Rashid didn't say anything. Evanovish said, "Send my proof that you are disguising the mainframe online effectively and using a GPS jammer, then I send you the codes."

"Remember you don't get the rest of the money without the codes," Rashid said softly.

"I know that. Do as I told you first." Evanovich said tersely. He hung up.

*****

Rashid stared at the phone in disbelief. Did that old Russian *kuffar* just give him an order? He swore and shoved the phone inside his pant pocket.

Fuming, Rashid opened the concertina doors and stepped outside into the garden. He needed to calm down. The operation was progressing as planned. Three years had gone into the planning. Now he just had to execute.

He didn't know Angel's real name, despite having met the man in Riyadh. He thought he had managed to intimidate him in that instance. But he didn't give up his name. What he was offering was so important, that Rashid was forced to accept his terms. And it was working out. The data from the satellite was getting to him. That was all that mattered.

One of the data scientists in his team came running. His name was Aftab. "*Sheikh,* there is a call for you."

Rashid nodded. He liked the guy. Aftab had a masters from Renessaler Polytechnic in New York and had returned to Saudi Arabia to serve his country. Most of his staff were trained at western colleges.

"Thank you *habibi*." Rashid reached for the cell Aftab was holding out. He answered. Carlyle's voice came on the other end.

"Hello."

Rashid asked, "Have you got the woman?"

"Not yet but I will soon. Don't worry about her."

Rashid exploded in anger. "Don't tell me not to worry you moron! Do you know what just happened?"

Carlyle hesitated. "What?"

"We got exposed, that's what! Luckily, Angel was watching out. Now, it's the woman's turn. If anyone gets to know about her research, we are finished."

Carlyle said, "Even if she did speak, it will take sometime to get to the top. Our operation will be over by then."

"Don't make assumptions. Your stupid media loves to make a mountain out of a molehill."

"Don't worry about her. But there is something you can help with, as you are close to DC."

Rashid narrowed his eyes. "What's that?"

"A man called Dan Roy. We need him out of the picture."

CHAPTER

Dan stood with a tray in his hand in the WFO canteen. Trisha was one step ahead of him in the queue, which at lunch time, was getting longer by the minute. Finally, he got to the hot food section and got himself a piece of roast chicken and fries. Trisha waved at him from a table by the window. Dan dodged the people filing into the canteen and got himself over to the table. He didn't miss the askance look many gave him as they passed by.

With his T shirt, jeans and ball cap, Dan didn't exactly fit the image of the hard-working Federal Government employee. He sat down opposite Trisha in the table for two, and took a sip of his apple juice. Trisha was picking at a green salad.

"That gonna last you all day?" Dan asked, and regretted it when Trisha looked at him.

"Unlike most men, I can't eat what the hell I want. Try walking in my shoes sometime, Dan. You might learn something."

"I'm sorry. Just looking out for you. Came out the wrong way."

"Forget it," Trisha said and took a mouthful. Dan followed suit.

"I guess you have a lot to tell me, right?"

"Yes and no. I can tell you about Nick Carlyle, but not much else."

Trisha stared back at him. "Who are you?"

"Question I ask the man in the mirror every day." Dan wasn't joking. The older he got, the more he wondered about who he was. A trained assassin. Built to kill without compunction, inflicting maximum damage.

But there was more to him. What exactly, he was still trying to find out. Was it the same for everyone else? Did fifty-year-old men and women wonder who they were? He didn't know the answer.

On the beaches of Thailand, and in the mountains of his home in Montrose, he had started asking himself. *Who am I?*

"Cut the crap. You know what I mean." Trisha gave him a hard glare.

"OK. I'm a former member of the SFOD-D. Delta Force, as it's known. Then started to work in Black Ops. For now, that's all you need to know."

Trisha gave a slight shake of her head. "OK. Then tell me about this guy, Nick Carlyle. How do you know him?"

A raincloud of memories settled over Dan's mind. He had time to think about this, and the answer was practiced. But he couldn't keep the bad thoughts at bay. Like most soldiers, Dan didn't like speaking about past operations.

"Carlyle was a sniper. A very good one. A CIA group were on Hamas' money trail. They were getting a lot of money from Saudi Arabia, and they finally traced it to a banker from Dubai. He was financing some big jobs for them. He came to Ramallah, and Carlyle was given the order to shoot him."

"What happened?"

"Somehow, Hamas found out. I don't know how. To this day, I think there was a leak. And I think the leak was Carlyle himself."

"Why do you say that?"

"I was lookout for him. We got dropped off by IDF at the border of the West Bank in Ramallah. Then they navigated us as we went in. I speak some Arabic, enough to ask for a drink, and I'm tanned enough to pass for an Arab. So I went up ahead and sat a café, having a drink. The café was in the square where the financier was meant to be."

"And?"

"What I saw was heavy Hamas security. Luckily, they didn't stop me, or my weird accent would've given me away. But I knew something was wrong. Like they were expecting us."

"Carlyle was behind you? Taking up position to shoot?"

"Yes. Up on the fourth floor balcony of a building. The financier never showed, and I got a distress call from Carlyle. I ran to the building, and almost got killed in an ambush."

"Ambush?"

"Like I said, I think they knew I was coming. If it wasn't for the IDF, I might have died. Anyway, we killed four Hamas men, got Carlyle, and jumped into the armored car the IDF had. We changed cars at the border, and I drove off to the airport with Carlyle."

"Didn't you speak to Carlyle?"

Dan leaned back in his chair and looked out the window. The iconic sights of DC weren't visible from here, just traffic and buildings stretching out to a blue haze in the distance. He turned his attention back to Trisha.

"Talking isn't something you do in these situations. But yeah, I asked." Dan clamped his jaws and his nostrils flared, briefly. "When I burst into that room, he had the gun pointed at me and almost…." Dan trailed off.

"Almost shot you?"

"He did shoot," Dan said flatly. "I dived, took cover. The round hit the wall."

"Maybe he didn't recognize you."

Dan shook his head. "I was the only one up there. The IDF guys were still coming up the stairs. I shouted my name, three times. I knew it was only him in there." Dan swallowed, then rubbed his eyes. He stared at the floor.

"I just had the feeling…..the feeling he tried to kill me. He would've killed me, if the IDF soldiers hadn't been there." Trisha was silent. Dan said, "All through the operation, he never said a word. It was weird. I've had friends in the Rangers before. They're great guys. They're Army, like us Delta guys, right? But Carlyle, he was weird from the start."

"He had an agenda."

"A hidden agenda," Dan said softly.

"We need to get Nick Carlyle's records," Trisha said. "I'll put in the request."

"Save it. It'll take a while to get to you, and most of it will be redacted. I can get you the unofficial version from my handler. I mean my old handler. Officially, I'm retired." Dan grinned despite himself.

He remembered what McBride had told him once. *Rocks like us only go downhill.*

Trisha said, "Valona Kowalski. We think she's the woman who escaped from the psychiatry hospital. She's in trouble, Dan."

"Yes. I need to get some stuff from my apartment. Then see you back here in 1 hour?"

"OK. I'll have to get permission for this, and a crew."

CHAPTER

Dan was heading out when he thought of something. He went back up the stairs to Trisha's office.

She glanced at her watch. "That was a very quick one hour."

Dan folded his arms across his spacious chest. "Everywhere we been so far, the sniper's been ahead of us."

"I guess so."

"I bet you any money they had eyes outside the EPA as well. On Walker. I should have thought of this already, I'm sorry. Remembering Carlyle made me lose focus."

Trisha was reaching for the phone already. Dan stopped her. "No. I go alone. You stay here. Does this building have a back entrance?"

"WFO is actually a nineteenth century building. It also has a basement and a tunnel that links us to the next building."

Dan raised his eyebrows. "You're kidding."

"Nope. You know that Capitol Building and its surrounding offices have underground tunnels linking them?"

"Isn't that an urban myth?"

"No, it's real. The Library of Congress, Adams Building, Russell, they all link up with each other, and to Capitol Hill."

"Guess the, what does this building connect to?"

"Number 2412 next door. We have most of our back office operations there."

Dan said, "Can you take me down there? If I can get to the next building, I can leave from there."

Dan turned his jacket inside out, changing the color from blue to brown. Trisha gave him a ball cap, and a pair of clear glasses.

They went down to the basement. Trisha used her ID card to buzz them through the heavy steel doors. A loud electric hum filled Dan's ears before he stepped into the basement. Then he saw the banks of servers. Lights came on as they walked through the air conditioned space, and kept going till Trisha stopped at another steel door in a wall. She used her card on the keypad again, and the handle clicked when she turned it.

Dan stared into a brick walled tunnel, paved with concrete, lit with bright white lights. It stretched straight on for a hundred yards at least.

"Let's go," Trisha said. Dan looked around him as he followed her.

His face echoed in the space. "You've done this before."

"Yep."

They went through a similar door on the other side, then climbed a set of stairs, ignoring the elevators. Trisha opened the back door which led into a garden. She crossed the roughly fifty feet of the garden, then opened the gate that led into the street.

"Be careful," she said.

Dan adjusted his glasses. "I'll call you when I'm back here. You need to let us in. It's better than walking with him to the front."

Trisha nodded. Dan walked to the metro, following a surveillance detection route or SDR, to ensure he wasn't being followed. He called Walker on the way.

When he got to the EPA, he waited outside till Walker drove past him in the car. He screeched to a stop and Dan jogged over.

"Did anyone see you leave?" Dan asked.

Walker looked pale. He licked his lips. "No."

"Did you get the disk drive with the data?"

"Yes."

*****

Back at the WFO, Trisha plugged the disk drive into a secure computer. The drive was password protected. Walker entered the digits and the file opened.

They looked at the screen. There were masses of numbers arranged in rows and columns.

"What the hell is this?" Dan said out loud.

Walker said. "This is data from a Fidler sensor."

Trisha said, "What is that?"

"It's a scintillation detector for radioactive contamination. Basically, the machine we used."

"And?"

"And hooked up to a Ludlum 2220 electronics package, it gives us readings on a graph that shows how high the resulting radiation is."

Dan jabbed a finger at the rows of numbers on the screen. "So, what does this mean?"

Walker said, "It'll look a lot better if I can make it into a graph." He glanced at Trisha. "I can access the net?"

"Sure, go ahead," Trisha said. "What site do you need?"

"I can download the open source software for spectral analysis from the internet. Feed this data into that programme and we have the readings."

"Let's do it."

Walker's fingers flew over the key board. His brows were knotted together.

"This is weird," Walker said eventually.

Trish asked, "Why? Haven't you checked this data already?"

Walked glanced from Trisha to Dan. "This is the data that Valona got from Virginia. The place she never told me about."

"She sent it to you?"

"Well, it was in the machine, so I could download it."

Dan asked, "Why did you say it's weird?"

Walker stared at the screen for a few seconds without replying. Then he checked another website on the laptop and shook his head, as if agreeing with something.

He said, "The graph shows very high levels of Americum 241."

"What's that?" Dan asked.

"Am-241 is a breakdown product of Plutonium 239."

A space cleared inside Dan`s head. That feeling returned: he had something almost in his grasp, yet just out of reach. Tantalizingly close. When they had patrolled near Saddam's palace in 2003, they were told to wear NBC suits. Nuclear, Biological, Chemical. It was a precaution, as the place was a wreck already and most men either half wore them, or played silly games with the masks. But Dan had heard that word being mentioned at the time.

Plutonium 239.

Dan frowned, trying to get his brain clicking. "Plutonium, that's radioactive, right?"

"It's enriched uranium Dan. Weapon grade. It's the hardest part of making a nuclear bomb. When you enrich uranium, it becomes Plutonium-239, a highly volatile form. If you can bang two molecules of Plu-239 together at high speed in a reactor…" Walker lifted both hands and brought them together in a clap, "Ka-boom."

Dan's mouth was dry and he was getting a headache. Not much phased him these days. But this had the potential to be a disaster of epic proportions.

He looked at Trisha, who was staring at him, color draining from her face.

Walker said, "To summarise, Plu-239 decays by emitting Americum-241. That's what the Fidler sensor can pick up."

Trisha had both hands pressed to her forehead. "Shit. Hold up here. Are you saying, there is nuclear weapon grade Plutonium being emitted from somewhere in Virginia?"

Walker looked at them with level eyes. "That's exactly what I'm saying."

Dan shook his head, "No, wait. In 2003, we got to Saddam's missile silos. In the desert, on the road between Tikrit and Baghdad. The intel we had at the time meant we had to treat every missile as a nuclear warhead." He glanced at his Trisha and Walker. They both nodded.

Dan said, "I heard at the time that nuclear warheads are designed to hold the radioactive stuff in. So that they don't emit radiation. When they explode that's a different story, you got radiation all over the place, for fifty years or something crazy."

Walker said, "Yes and no. If the warhead is made of heavy metals – and all of them are – like lead or mercury, then the fissile material will not leak out. But, not all warheads are created equal. Especially the early ones, or if they were made in haste, on a low budget."

"What would happen in that case?"

"Well, you would get higher radiation. Like what Valona found." Walker stabbed a finger at the screen. "Like this screen shows."

Dan said, "We need an expert opinion on this." He looked at Walker hopefully.

Walker smiled sheepishly. "I'm no expert on this but my college buddy now works at the nuclear reactor in the Pantex Plant in Texas. His name's Mike Crais. We can call him."

Dan nodded. "Let's do it."

Walker got his friend on the line and put him on a loudspeaker. Mike Crais listened to the story in silence.

"Are you kidding me?" Crais said in a strained voice. "If you have Americum-231 it can only come from one source. Weaponised or enriched uranium. This is serious shit."

Walker said, "Yeah, but without an explosion, can it leak out of the warhead?"

Crais thought for a while. Static crackled from the long distance line. He said, "In practice, no nuclear warhead I have ever designed emits radiation more than a few meters, and that too, low grade, alpha radiation. Not gamma or ionizing radiation."

Trisha said, "I can sense a but coming."

"You got that right. When the nuclear arms race was at full speed in the 1970's many warheads were made without the right materials. Oh, only heavy metals were used, but no one thought what would happened after 20 or 30 years. Would there be gaps in the joins of the surface? That's just one example. Wrong material was used as well, not strong enough to stop a radioactive leak for miles."

He paused, and a deathly silence ensued. No one looked at each other, but each knew what they were thinking.

Crais continued. "Most of these defective warheads were decommissioned early. But some might still remain. Especially in other countries."

Dan said, "Like in western Europe or Russia?"

"Don't forget India and Pakistan."

"Yeah but there's not much chance of a nuke from Asia ending up here, is there?"

Crais was silent for a while again. Then he said, "No. But that doesn't get rid of your problem. There's not been a test explosion or an accident in US soil recently."

Walker finished for him. "That means the radiation Valona recorded is coming from a defective warhead."

Dan said, "If it's defective, can it still be functional?"

Crais spoke. "You bet your ass it's functional. By defective I don't mean there's anything wrong with the weapon – just the design of the outer case. All warheads, even the ones I'm designing now emit radiation prior to explosion. But its well contained, only leaks out for a few meters, and low energy. But in your case, that high a reading of Am-231 only means one thing."

"Oh shit," Walker said, gripping his forehead. He thanked Crais and hung up.

Dan excused himself and walked out of the room. He called McBride on his phone.

"Sitrep, Dan?" McBride's gravelly voice demanded. Dan told him.

Then he asked, "Do you know of any missile silos in Virginia? Like secret ones."

McBride was silent for several seconds. Then he spoke slowly. "No. The minute man silos are in Montana, North Dakota and Wyoming. They are still operational, but most of our nukes are in submarines."

"Well, seems like we got a nuke in Virginia somewhere. And Valona Kowalski, the Russian spy's daughter found out where. Now she's on the run. What does that tell you?"

McBride said, "You need to find her Dan, fast."

Dan gripped his phone harder. He had iron in his voice. "I'm doing my best. But you need to tell me exactly what Kowalski told you."

"Believe me!" McBride hissed. "Why the hell would I lie to you about this? All he said was that we had to meet. And that this thing was very big. I'm starting to understand how big. Damn."

Dan wasn't a man who scared easy. But his mouth was dry, and he could feel his heart dashing against his ribs in a staccato beat.

"I got a bad feeling about this, McBride."

"We got to do something, Dan. Now."

CHAPTER

Dan came out of the metro, but didn't walk down the pavement. He pressed himself against the side of the station and watched commuters' stream in and out. Dupont Circle was a short walk away, and his apartment was close to it. He couldn't see anyone loitering outside the station, or pretending to read a newspaper. Eyes in the sky he could do nothing about, and these days drones were easily bought in RadioShack.

His mind was preoccupied with what Walker said. Trisha was calling up the Nuclear Regulatory Commission to verify the data. The FBI Director was already informed. On verification, the matter would be forwarded to the ODNI, White House and Pentagon on a critically urgent basis. McBride would use his own contacts to get the news into the right ears, Dan knew that.

Nukes hidden in Virginia? It sounded bizarre to Dan's mind. Virginia was a vast state. They still had no idea where to look for the source of radiation. That made it all the more important to make sure they found Valona.

Dan joined the throng headed towards DuPont. He took the side path that led to the street of his apartment. It was quieter here, the roar of traffic fainter behind a bank of tall office buildings. His ears took some time to adjust, and he almost missed the footsteps behind him.

He glanced over his shoulder quickly. A large, heavy shape was twenty yards behind, closing the distance fast. A man, moving with intent. Dan sped up. The road forked into a small T junction ahead. There was an alley before that, on the same side as him. An alley he hadn't noticed till another man suddenly appeared out of it.

One in front. One behind.

A car sounded behind him, and he looked quickly. That would be his play. Box him in, then bundle him inside a car. But this SUV went swiftly past him, braked at the T junction, then went right.

The guy in front wore a New York Knickers sweat shirt, black jeans and sneakers. He was thick around the shoulders, but not as tall as the guy behind Dan.

Dan crossed the road and felt the two men follow. There was a blind alley opposite and he walked into it, imaging the delight of the two thugs. No witnesses. No way out. Groovy. Dan walked fast and stopped abruptly in front of a trash can. He heard the men closing in, and he could sense their confusion when he suddenly halted. Dan reached for the lid of the trash can, and lifted it. He stood still, back to the men behind him.

"Hey you," one of the men growled. Dan remained immobile. One of them whispered to the other and Dan's ears picked up. Different language. Not English.

He felt a body move and step up right behind him. Dan turned his head slightly. From the corner of his eyes he saw a big, meaty hand reach for his right shoulder. Was the other hand holding a gun? It didn't matter.

Grabbing someone's shoulder to spin them around is one of the worst moves. The attacker opens himself up, and surrenders his hand. A man cannot fight without fingers. Dan moved like lightning. He spun the other way, and threw the trash can lid like a metallic frisbee, aimed at the Knickers sweatshirt guy, standing behind. Knickers didn't expect it, and his startled eyes met Dan's for a second before the lid hit him in the jaw, knocking him back against the wall. His right hand still held the gun as he fell.

Dan rotated full circle, grabbing the big guy's wrist with his right hand. With his left he twisted the fingers back till he heard them snap. The thug gave out a howl of pain, then slammed his knee into Dan's stomach. Pain exploded in Dan's midriff and breath left his lungs. He fell to his knees, dazed. He saw a leg stretching back for another kick.

Dan leaned forward and hugged the man's knees. His head was still groggy, but his hands were strong, and he pulled the knees towards him. The big guy lost balance and fell backwards. He smashed on the road and Dan jumped over him. He saw the left hand lift up, and a gun point at him. Dan kicked with his right foot, bending the arm back as the gun fired. A suppressed round flew out of the muzzle, way above his head.

The mist had cleared from Dan's head. He grabbed the gun wrist and hit it on the tarmac. Twice was enough to shatter the wrist bone, making the man scream again. He tried to punch Dan, but the blow went off Dan's shoulder. Dan grabbed the man's hair, lifted his head up, then hurtled it downwards on the road. There was a sharp crack and the man lay still.

From the corner of his eye Dan saw movement. Knickers was rising up, gun in hand. Dan rolled over to the gun from the man's hand. The butt felt heavy. He cocked it, pointed and fired in the same movement, aiming for mid mass. Knickers slammed against the wall for the second time. He slid down to the road, not to rise again.

Dan got up, feeling a wave of nausea inside him. He heaved, and a thin trickle of bile came out. He wiped his mouth, fought the dizziness and stumbled over to the dead man. The yellow Knickers sweatshirt had a patch of red blossoming in the center chest. He had a fuzz on his chin, and his features were Middle Eastern. Dan went through his pockets, found a switch blade knife and cell phone. He took those, and the gun, which was a Glock.

He crossed back quickly to the big guy. He was still breathing, and had a pulse on the neck.

Dan slapped him across the face. No response. He slapped him again, then rubbed his knuckles on the breast bone, hard. It was one of the worst pains to inflict, and the man's face twisted as his nerves screamed against Dan's knuckles and his sternum.

Dan slapped him again, then held his face up. "Who are you?"

This guy was Middle Eastern as well. Dan knew the features well and he tried to work out if he was Persian or Arab. Persians were Iranian, who generally hated Arabs. To Dan's eye, this guy looked like an Arab. He was well built and tough. Also well trained, it seemed. Dan frisked the guy, and came up with a cell phone and another hand gun in a shoulder holster.

Dan glanced at the mouth of the alley. No one there yet. He heaved the man against the wall. He held the switchblade knife under his eye, and slapped the man twice again. This time, his eyes flickered to life.

"Don't," Dan said. "I'll push this into your eye all the way." He held the knife against the man's cheek, pressing on the left eye.

Both eyes bulged with fear. "No," the man whispered.

"Min ayi balad 'ant, habibi?" Dan asked in his broken Arabic. Where are you from, friend?

The man narrowed his eyes, staring at Dan closely. Dan pushed the tip of the knife till it a trickle of blood appeared at the bottom of the eyeball.

In an anguished voice the man said, *"Min ajl allah…"* For God's sake.

"I'll do it. No one to stop me. Tell me who sent you." Dan increased the pressure and the man howled.

"Tell me!" Dan whispered fiercely.

CHAPTER

Dan took the Knicker's sweatshirt off the dead man. He sliced one arm off and used it to tie the man's hands. He put him face down and pondered his next move.

He had a name, but it didn't mean anything. The Sheikh. Anyone could be a Sheikh, from an Imam of high standing, to Bin Laden. It was just a moniker of authority, like Sir in the west. It figured that the thugs wouldn't know the master's real name. It acted as a circuit breaker if they got caught.

But Dan did have an address, and from the big guy, car keys of a GMC Yukon parked around the corner. He rang Trisha who didn't answer. He left a voice mail message, then walked to the car.

Dan reversed the big machine, did a K turn, and joined the traffic, heading for his apartment first. He picked up his kukri, Sig Sauer and three new mags, a flashlight and precision gloves. From the fridge, he extracted two bottles of water, a packet of ham and bread and put it all into a backpack. He went back to the car and put the address into the sat nav.

Thoughts ran through his head as he drove. These guys weren't routine run of the mill thugs. From the man's accent, he knew the guy wasn't American. He had come from Saudi Arabia.

Why? Not to kill Dan, that was for sure. He was acting under orders. He didn't know what the mission entailed, but he told Dan what he knew. A lot of them were here. Living in a big house. Something big was planned.

Traffic flowed well, and he crossed the Potomac at Arlington River Bridge, and went further up north into Fairfax county. Civilization became sparse, till he was winding his way down narrow two lane country roads, with no other cars in sight. Wheat and barley fields stood barren in the fall wind. Dan felt like he was driving down a village road in South England, of all the places in the world.

Old, majestic houses, colossal timber, bricks and mortar structures appeared in large isolated compounds. Some had lights in them, others stood empty.

Downton freaking Abbey, Dan muttered under his breath.

He drove down a winding road that got close to the river. Then he saw the house. A mansion, like the rest of the houses around. An old one, similar to its neighbors. The windows had blue shutters, and the house was made of white timber frame. A woodland stretched behind the house, leading to the water`s edge. Dan could see two outhouses, a barn with its doors open, and a large well for drinking water.

Dan drove right at a fork in the road and travelled up, leaving the house behind. After two kilometers, he stopped. He was in the shadow of a hill. The house was hidden from his vision. He drove off the road, into the yellow brush that rolled downwards. He took his feet off the brakes a tad, and let the car roll into the thicket. Twigs and small branches covered the car. Dan killed the engine, put the handbrake on and took his kukri out. He lowered the window, and with the long knife, hacked at the branches around him. When he had cleared some space, he could open the car door and step out. The vegetation crowded him, but he was able to use the kukri to clear his way out. He put the kukri back in it scabbard, checked he had everything he needed, and then pushed the car`s rear bumper further into the brush. It was heavy going, the ground was soft.

He gave up after a while and walked around, and chopped more twigs and branches. He picked up an armful of them and scattered them around the car. He did this several times, till the car was hidden from casual observation. He sprinkled branches to hide the tire marks as the car came off the road. After half an hour, he was satisfied the no one would notice the track marks, or the hidden car. He walked off into the forest around him, taking care to hide his trail.

He moved from tree to tree, till the house came into his line of sight again. When he was a hundred meters away, he stopped, and crouched down. The house stood isolated near the river. He bet his bottom dollar there was a boat moored at the back, for easy escape.

The nearest neighbor was a good seven to eight hundred meters away. Steam emerged from a downstairs window. It looked like the kitchen. The roof was made of slate tiles. The big front door was solid, and it appeared locked.

Several windows downstairs face the front courtyard. That was an obvious point of entry, but also easily visible to anyone keeping a watch. Dan looked around him, doing a 360 degrees sitrep. He could not see anyone. He went back to his vigil. There was space around the sides, and the barn with its open doors looked as though it had a car in it. A black SUV. He could see bullet marks on the side of the vehicle.

He found the cameras facing the front wall easily enough. The house was three story, and the cameras were about half way up. There would be more at the sides and back. Feeding into a bank of screens, and someone keeping an eye on it inside. He saw the motion sensor lights on the wall as well.

He heard a sound in the distance. A Lincoln town car was approaching from the left, down the main road. As it turned the bend, he saw another. Stately and elegant, with black tinted windows, the two cars moved smoothly on the road, and braked to enter the courtyard. The front door opened and a man stepped out. He did not move from the porch, but stood square and gazed out at the forest opposite. Directly where Dan was hiding.

Dan took the binos out again as he saw the drivers step out of the front car and open the passenger door at the back. A man stepped out. He appeared short next to his bulky bodyguards. Dan looked long and hard. The man appeared to be Middle Eastern. He wore sunglasses that weren't necessary at this time of the year. A trio of bodyguards stepped out from the other Lincoln. The man did not wait long. Two of his bodyguards covered him, and they stepped inside the mansion.

CHAPTER

Before the men went in, Dan refocused on the cameras. He watched them move. Motion sensors built in. The powerful LED security lights were similar, and they would turn night into day if even a fox strolled across the courtyard.
Dan looked up into the sky. He found what he was looking for quickly enough. Electric cables, looping across the brown fields, populated by small birds. Strung together on old fashioned wooden posts. No doubt leading to a central steel pylon somewhere nearby. This place was remote enough to have a big pylon, but the wealthy denizens here would not tolerate it within sight. That was OK.
 Dan stood up slowly, keeping himself behind the shadow of the tree.
He flitted from tree to tree, silent as a ghost. He crossed the road when he was a long distance away from the house. He went across the grass verge, and set off towards the field where he could see the wooden post with the cables. He got to the post and looked up. Electricity cable wires are relayed in straight lines. Three wires crossed at the top, and a thicker, galvanized wire came straight down at an angle and went underground.

Dan could see the house in the distance, roughly two hundred meters away. He looked at the wire going underground and got closer. Cutting into it was a serious health hazard. He needed non-conductive clothing. He could hack at it with the kukri, which would work, but could also get him electrocuted. He did not have a choice. The sound would spread in the quiet air, but hopefully the cold fall weather was enough to keep everyone indoors.

He took three steps back, and took the Sig out. He rested his right hand on his left forearm, and took careful aim. He crouched on his right knee. He missed with the first shot and the second.

He got up, stretched, then crouched again. This time he hit the target.

There was a bright shower of sparks, and a sharp twang as the round hit the wire. The tension in the wire made it snap, and it recoiled powerfully, emitting white light into the air. Dan moved backwards quickly. This was live electricity, enough to zap him alive.

He walked back fast, heading back to his lying up point in the woods opposite the house. There was activity now in the courtyard. The tall square man he had first seen in the doorway was out, looking around. He had an AR15 rifle slung on his shoulder. His movements were quick and precise.

He did a perimeter circle, then moved away to the back. Another man was with him, but they separated. The second man stayed in the courtyard. Something about his shape was familiar to Dan. In the fading light, he could not make the face out.

Dan got up slowly. It was time to make his move.

CHAPTER TWENTY-SIX

Dan darted to the left, heading for the barn. He stayed under the cover of trees as long as he could, but eventually he had to cross the road. Light was being squeezed out by approaching night, and the sky was deepening into black from a rusty shade of iron.

When he was fifty meters from the house, he went to ground. The dark shape of the barn was in front of him now, the house beyond it. He shuffled on his elbows till he got to the back of the timber structure. He saw a security light above the barn, but he did not have to worry about that now. He prised the sharp tip of his kukri into between two slats of old timber. They were both damp, and the nails holding them together snapped easily. He repeated the procedure till the hole was big enough for his head and shoulders to get through.

He could see the front grill of the SUV in front of him as he crawled in. Gasoline stank out the air inside the barn. A smell he liked, for the reason he had planned. He crawled straight underneath the SUV. With his flashlight, he found the fuel pipe after some rummaging. He came out, and looked around the barn. He only shone his flashlight when he needed to, cupping the mouth, and pointing it to ground. The barn door was locked, but it could be opened any moment.

He opened the car`s trunk, and found what he was looking for. A sheet of cotton had been spread on the trunk floor, and it had flecks of dark amber on it. Dan took the cotton sheet out, then quickly cut it into a long strip with his kukri.

He crawled back underneath the car. He found the fuel pipe again, and used the kukri to make a hole in it. Drops of petrol leaked out, making a puddle on the ground. Dan used the cotton strip to soak it up. He left petrol to leak out, and stretched the cotton strip out. He came out of the car, holding the cloth in his hand. It was wet with petrol. It would have to do as a rough made detention cord.

He opened the barn door a fraction and peeked outside. The front door was shut. The windows were all dark. The cameras on the wall were not moving, and no lights came on. No electricity.

Dan took out his zippo lighter and lit the end of the cotton strip he was holding. It caught fire easily. He dropped the cloth and ran across the courtyard, heading for the far corner of the house. He crouched behind a bush, protected by the corner wall. Ten seconds was his rough estimation.

How many men were inside. He had counted six going in, including the bodyguards. Judging by the three cars, maybe fifteen altogether?

His count was out by two seconds. A heartbeat after ten seconds, the SUV exploded.

The explosion shattered the ground floor windows nearby, and lifted the barn roof high in the air. A sharp sudden cataclysm ripped through the air, the boom deafening Dan`s ears. Glass and other debris smashed against the wall and fell around him.

Dan looked behind him. No movement yet. Could they have NVG's? Of course, and he had none.

The front door moved. The three big, beefy bodyguards tumbled out, as he had expected. Dan was to their extreme right, and his Sig was pointed on the first man's chest as he reached the last step. Dan fired twice and saw the body jerk sideways and fall. The beefcake behind him tumbled on his partner and fell, too. He did not get a chance to get to his feet. Dan double tapped him again, and his head exploded into a miasma of blood and bone. The last bodyguard was firing wildly around him, aiming at the front.

What he should have done was take cover. Dan took him down quickly, then turned around. This was the easy part. He had known the three stooges would be sent out first. The real danger lay inside. He ran to the back of the house swiftly. Another small explosion from the front, and then the sound of fire crackling.

The back of the house was wide. He could not see the far end. But he could make out long patio doors that opened to the outside. The two upper floors loomed high above him. Dan pressed himself against the wall.

It was quiet, no shouts, no running feet. He didn't like it. Above him he could see an open window. More than one in fact. Two windows, side by side. He watched for a while, but no one came to them.

He looked around him, then saw the tree. An old oak tree, with thick sturdy branches that he could walk on. One of those fat branches got close to a window on the first floor. Dan got to the tree, jammed the Sig back into his belt, and started to climb. He got to the branch. It was indeed wide enough for him to balance on two feet. The ground was more than five meters down. A fall would not be pleasant. He looked ahead, and saw that he could reach the ledge easily. He could stand on the ledge, and lever himself into the window.

Dan stretched his arms out, and stepped into the branch gingerly. One step first. He was heavy, and even a thick branch would snap under him. He pressed down. It did not give way. Dan got to the end quickly. He looked at the open window, less than two meters away now. Dan crouched on the branch. It tipped forward. He stepped back quickly, and revised his plan.

He walked back to the wider portion of the branch. This took his weight better. He walked all the way to the end. He steadied himself, then broke into a sprint. He accelerated, pumping his thigh muscles. As he got to the thinner edge of the branch he bent down, then hurled himself full tilt at the window sill. He flew in the air, and smacked against the wall, his fingers clawing desperately at the window sill.

CHAPTER

His palms found purchase. He gripped the old wooden timber sill tightly.

His boots felt for the ledge beneath him. One foot, then the other. Then he stopped and listened for a while.

Voices. At the front of the house. A flashlight beam searched around the bush where he had been hiding.

With both hands, he grabbed the window sill above him. He gritted his teeth and raised himself. He hooked an elbow over the sill as soon as he could, and raised himself up. He stopped for a fraction, looking inside. Granite darkness. The voices below him were getting louder. The flashlight came again, lighting up the ground below him.

He had no choice.

Dan went through the window. He crouched against the wall inside, and took his Sig out, pointing it ahead. If there was someone in here, they were keeping very quiet. His eyes got used to the dark. The room was spacious. Dark shapes stood in one corner. He felt a creaky floorboard underneath him. The voices below him got louder. The flashlight beam got brighter. Dan tiptoed away from the wall. The voices stopped underneath the window. The beam pointed upwards, spilling light inside the room.

A voice he did not recognize said, "Why the hell is that window open?" There was an accent to the voice.

Dan did not wait to hear the rest. If the question had been asked, action would be taken. He needed to get out of the room. He now saw the long table with chairs around it. A door next to it. His flashlight moved away, and the room was sunk in darkness again.

Dan moved towards the door. He tried the handle, it moved down. He opened a crack and peered outside. Darkness, as he had expected. He came out and stayed low. He was in a hallway. It appeared to circle around. There was emptiness in the middle, he could sense it. A grand staircase, going down. Dan crept forward. He could see doors leading off the hallway. He had taken a few steps when he sensed it before he heard it. A faint creak of a floorboard. He scurried forwards, reaching for one of the door handles. It was locked. He heard a rattle behind him, and glanced down.

An oblong object had landed less than a metre from his feet. One glance told him what it was. A flashbang. Stun grenade. He ran, but the air around him morphed into a million shards of light, totally blinding him. His senses were overpowered by the smell of the exploding mercury and magnesium gas, and it felt like he was pulling knives into his chest. The explosion threw him against the wall. He felt his head crack, his eyes go black, and he slumped to the floor.

CHAPTER TWENTY-SIX

A ringing sound. In the distance. Persistent, demanding. Layers and layers of darkness that allowed no visibility. More sounds. Mumbles, like voices in distorted microphones. Dan felt his head move, then fall, and move again. Then suddenly, like a slap from the devil, a cold and wet sensation on his face. His eyes opened. It was blurry. Redness rimmed his visual field. He had a headache, and felt sick. The ringing sound in his ear was louder. He blinked, and found himself looking at something. A bucket. Half full of water. As he stared, the bucket drew back, then splashed water onto his face again. He did not have the strength to avert his face.

Fingers gripped his cheek, and pointed his face up to a white light. Dan blinked, and was forced to open his eyes. Two men stood around him. He recognized one as the tall man he had seen in the doorway. The other man was shorter. Dan recognized him as well. The Middle Eastern guy he had seen step off the car.

The tall guy was holding Dan`s chin up. His lips moved, then he stepped back. His voice was muffled, and Dan could not hear well. The blackness returned, and his head slipped forward on his chest. He wanted to be sick again. Water splashed on his face, forcing him to take a deep breath and look upwards at the light. He squeezed his eyes shut, then opened them.

The tall guy leaned forward and seemed to ask him something again.

"…hear me?"

Dan shook his head. Some of the mist was clearing from his head. The tall guy bent forward again. This time Dan heard him, but his voice still came from a long way off.

"Can you hear me?"

Dan did not reply. He tried to move. He felt a pain in his shoulders. His arms were pinned back. He moved his wrists but they were tied together behind the chair. Dan sat up. The ringing was fading from his ears, but he still felt dizzy as hell. It was almost ironic, he thought. Every time he had been exposed to a flashbang, he had a protective mask with a respirator on. Except this time. When he was alone, with no backup.

The tall guy leaned forward again and repeated the question. This time Dan looked up, and met his dark eyes. Then he spat on the floor.

"Fuck you," Dan whispered.

The blow took him by surprise. There was someone behind him. A heavy fist slammed into the right side of his neck, making him wince. Stars appeared bright in a sudden darkness, then faded.

Dan swallowed, then breathed in and out. He looked up. He still could not hear properly, and his own voice sounded dull, distant.

Dan said, "That the best you got?"

Both men in front of him smiled and moved back. They looked behind him. Dan steeled himself. It came from the left this time, an iron fist plunging into his left cheek like a sledgehammer. The pain mushroomed like an exploding red ball in his head, and he slumped forward. He felt his jaw crack. His mouth hung open, and blood, mucus and fragments of a broken tooth dripped out of it. The blackness came back, inky and absolute.

Dan shook his head again, and straightened himself. He opened his eyes, The two men in front of him swam around for a while, hazy. Then his sight steadied. Dan cleared his throat.

Dan said, "You really need to invest in some man power. Getting a fag to throw punches is so old school."

The tall guy snarled something, and moved forward. Dan saw him removed something from his pocket. The flash of a blade was unmistakable.

"That's enough," a voice rang out behind them. The two men stopped, and the heavy hands that gripped Dan`s throat from behind stayed there, but relaxed its grip.

Dan looked as the two men stepped aside. To the right of him, in an old brown leather armchair, the shorter, Middle Eastern man was seated in an immaculate blue suit. The expressionless brown eyes stared back at Dan without blinking.

He looked above Dan`s head. "Dimitri, get him some water."
Dan felt the ground move, and a shadow seemed to lift off
him.

A huge, ham like fist gripped a glass that looked ridiculously
small. The fist appeared in front of Dan`s eyes. Dan opened
his stiff mouth. His jaw hurt like mad. The glass was thrust
into his mouth. He retched, but swallowed his bile down with
the blood stained water. He swallowed, then breathed.
The man opposite him, who was clearly the boss, spoke. "So,
you are Dan Roy."
Dan stared back at him without expression.
Dan could still hear him. "I took a photo of you and sent it to
my friend. He knows who you are. Don't make this hard on
yourself Dan. You must know what we can do. We have a
basement where we can get very, very creative."

Dan swallowed. He had to clear his throat before any sound
came from it. "You know my name, but I don't know yours.
Not good manners."
The man smiled. "You're going to die soon, so I might as well
tell. My name is Shehzad Al-Falaj."
Dan stared at him, trying to work out the name. He came up
with a blank. "That your real name?"
Shehzad nodded. Dan said, "You're the *Sheikh,* right?"
The smile faltered. Shehzad's eyes narrowed. "You killed
Altaf. One of my best men."
Dan didn't say anything. Shehzad said, "What about
Abubaker? Is he alive?" A snarl spread across his face.
"The other gimp you sent after me? He needs replacing. He
told me about this place. Your hideout."
Shehzad closed his eyes and muttered. *"Haramzadeh."*
"That's what I told him, *Sheikh.*"
Shehzad opened his eyes, gripped the sides of the chair and
stood. "Shut up, you idiot!"
Dan said, "Who sent you after me? Carlyle?"

Shehzad circled around Dan and then faced him. "How much do you know about us, Dan?"

From his polished accent, Dan knew he was English educated. In his blue suit blazer, and folded handkerchief, he was every inch the former public-school boy.

Dan remained silent. Shehzad cocked his head to one side. "Don't feel like speaking?" He reached inside his pocket and pulled out a cell phone. He held the screen towards Dan. It was a photo of Trisha. But it wasn't on the street, or at her office. This was a long distance zoom photo of her in her apartment. She was wearing loose vest and slacks and standing by the window, a glass of wine in hand. Shehzad flicked the screen to another photo. Trisha coming out of the bathroom, towel tied around her hair, and another tucked in at the breasts.

Dan flexed his jaws, a burning rage spreading slowly in his limbs. Shehzad took the phone away and watched the screen himself. "Rather nice, don't you think?"

Dan looked away. Shehzad. "Tonight, when she comes back home, Dimitri will be waiting for her. Isn't that right Dimitri?" Shehzad looked at the giant standing behind Dan and smiled. Dan heard Dimitri laugh.

CHAPTER

Dan flexed his fingers, trying to get some blood flow in them. His wrists were strapped very tight to the back of the chair. He fought to control himself.

He looked at Shehzad with dark venom in his eyes. "Leave the girl alone. She knows nothing."

Waleed gave Dan a shit eating grin. "That's why she's FBI, right?" His expression became serious. "You think this is a joke? You're going to die slowly, horribly. Your girlfriend here, will die even slower, after my men have their fun. Is that what you want?"

Dan held Waleed's eyes. "When this is over, I will kill you."

Waleed raised his eyebrows in mock horror. "Ooh, aren't you the hero."

"I know what you're planning."

That wiped the mirth from Waleed's face. Dan pressed on. "You're looking for the scientist, right? Victor Kowalski's daughter. Well, I know exactly where she is. And I also know what her research shows."

Waleed went very still. "You're lying."

"You touch Trisha, and I don't tell you a word of what I know."

Waleed flicked his eyes above Dan's head. Huge fingers tightened on Dan's neck, gradually increasing pressure. He felt blood rising to his face, throat constricting till he couldn't breathe. His eyes bulged and mouth opened. A croaking sound came from his mouth and his tongue hung out.

Waleed came closer and leaned towards Dan. "I can just kill you know. Then go after your girlfriend."

Dan couldn't breathe. He was gagging and jerked in the chair, trying to move. Waleed stood up and the pressure reduced on his throat. Dan gasped as he drew air into his lungs.

Panting, he looked at Waleed. "Are you going to talk of killing me, or actually do it?"

Waleed's expression didn't change. Dan said, "You're a dead man, Waleed. Your friend Carlyle is too. Everyone knows about you, and your stupid plan."

"Oh, it's not stupid, believe me. The whole world will know soon. America's time is up, Dan. We are here to conquer."

"Conquer?" Dan spat on the floor. "You can't even kill me. How the hell you going to manage an entire country?"

Waleed's eyes glinted. "By paralyzing it. I know you're bluffing. You don't know shit. This has been years in the making. We are making history."

His eyes bore into Dan's with fanatical intensity. Dan said, "Your last name, Al Falaj, suggests you're Saudi. You come from a rich family, right?"

Waleed remained silent. Dan continued. He had to speak, even though it was an effort. His throat felt raw and dry. But he needed to buy time.

"Funny thing is, you work for us. If it wasn't for American petro-dollars, you wouldn't have any money."

"I work for you?" Waleed asked, shaking his head.

"Yes. Think about that sometime, *Sheikh*."

"Enough talk," Waleed spat. He gestured to the men in the room. "Take him downstairs."

Dan said, "What`s going to happen in three days?"

No one answered for a while. Waleed said, "You will know when it happens."

Dan asked him, "Why did Kowalski say it would be worse then 9/11?"

He smiled. "This time we finish the job." The man lifted his right fist and smacked it into the other palm.

Dan watched his face, feeling his blood run cold.

CHAPTER

To walk, Dan had to be untied. He considered his chances as he felt fingers brush against the ropes on his wrist. A man held an AK-47 pointed at his chest. The man stood next to Waleed. To his left he could see another man, holding a similar weapon. Behind him stood the giant. As he watched, Waleed's hand went inside his coat and pulled out a hand gun. It looked like a Colt M1911, but the butt was gold, and it shone in the light. Waleed pulled the hammer back and pointed it at Dan.

His hands were freed and Dimitri, the giant, pulled Dan to his feet. Then he felt plastic ties going round his hands again.

Dan said, "I need to pee."

Everyone stopped and looked at Waleed. Waleed said, "Take him downstairs. Finish it off there."

The metal of another gun muzzle poked Dan in the neck.
Dan exchanged one last look with the three men in the room.
He considered his options. The distances. The force of impact.
He glanced at the window.
Waleed said, "I know what you are thinking. But there are others in this house Dan. They`ll come after you."
The plastic ties went around Dan's wrists.
Damn, he thought to himself.
He had a few seconds, and he had wasted it. It would be a suicidal move, but any move was better now considering Trisha's life was in danger.
Dimitri held the back of Dan`s shirt collar with one hand, and rammed the gun muzzle deeper into his neck.
"Move," he said.
Shirt collar chafing his neck, Dan stumbled forward. One man opened the door for them, and went down the stairs rapidly.
He stopped at the landing, pointed AK-47 at Dan and nodded.
Dimitri pushed Dan again. The duo moved slowly down the stairs.
They reached the ground floor. A spacious hallway, with the main door in front of him. Heavy, tall oak door with black iron bracings. Dan noticed the two cameras on the ceiling. He heard a humming sound.
They walked through the doorway into another landing. The humming was louder, and Dan looked to his left. An electric generator thrummed away in the corner. So that was how they had electricity, despite the cable being shot down.
They walked down a dark, yellow walled corridor, plaster flaking off the walls, lit by naked yellow bulbs.
Dan said again, "I need to pee."
The two men in front stopped in front of a door. One of them opened it and turned the light on. It was a small latrine, with only a commode and wash basin. Dan felt a knife cut the plastic ties and his hands were free. Two AK-47's were pointed at him, and the muzzle of the gun pressed against his neck.

Dimitri's fetid breath came on his face, and the giant whispered, "Try anything funny and I'll put a bullet in your neck."

Dan nodded. Dimitri prodded him forward till he was inside the bathroom. It was a small space, but enough for Dan to get in. He moved inside, Dimitri following with the gun.

"That's enough," Dimitri ordered. "Now do it."

Dan had sneaked a look at Dimitri. The guy was huge, more than six feet five and as wide as Dan.

Dan bent his head to lower his belt. For a second or two, the gun wasn't pressed against his neck. He whirled with lightning speed, slapping the gun away as he turned and cannoned into the giant's body. His finger gripped the gun wrist. Dimitri fired but the round smacked into the wall. Dan knew the two men outside wouldn't fire. The bullets would kill Dimitri first.

Dan pushed the big man back with all the strength in his body. Dimitri resisted, but the speed of Dan's move took him by surprise. Dan squeezed the gun wrist and propelled Dimitri backwards, pushing him into one of the men. The guy slammed into the wall, and all three of them went down in a heap.

The AK-47 had fallen from the man's hand. Dan let go of Dimitri, grabbed the butt of the rifle and pulled it towards him. The other man was getting ready to shoot, but the jumbled of bodies meant he had as much chance of killing his friends as Dan.

Dan flicked the safety back and squeezed the trigger. The rifle was set to semiautomatic mode, and a stream of metal flew out from the muzzle into the standing man. He was pointing his rifle at Dan but had no time to aim. The rounds flung him backwards and he collapsed, rifle falling from his hands. Dan aimed the muzzle downwards and pumped rounds into the two bodies at his feet. Spent cartridges flew in the air, and the two men jerked, then went still.

It was very quiet all of a sudden. Dan got to his feet quickly. He looked up and down the corridor. It ended in a blind wall, and a series of doors were present to his left.

Dan frisked the men quickly, removing weapons. One of the men had an ID card from King Salman Air Base in Riyadh. Dan pocketed that, and the handguns he found. He went to the first door and listened. Silence. He tried the handle but it was locked. There was no point in looking any further. Getting out of here was more important now than hunting for evidence.

He picked up the Glock that Dimitri had dropped, and strapped one of the AK-47's on his back.

Weapon raised, Dan went slowly up the stairs to the ground floor landing.

CHAPTER

He could not hear a sound.

The concrete steps were silent under his feet. He passed the generator. The ground floor hallway was empty. Dan looked out at the dark courtyard. Both the Lincoln town cars had gone.

The house was sunk in darkness and silence. There was a coat hook next to the door, about two metres tall. Dan grabbed it and put it in front of the door. He picked up a rug from the wooden floor and draped it over the coat hook. Then he opened the door, and keeping himself protected, put the coat hook outside. He shrunk back against the wall.

No shots were fired. Dan locked the door. He stole out towards the back of the house. The kitchen had a pantry, with a door next to it. Dan turned the key and the door opened. Finally, he outside.

He got his bearings quickly. The woods were opposite. Beyond the woods, to the far left, lay the bend in the road, where he had hidden his car.

Dan ran through the woods as fast as he could. He went to ground before they got to the bend, watching carefully. After five minutes, there was no movement. Dan crept down, pulled the twigs and brush away from his car. He was inside the car soon, backing it up on the road. He put the lights on, and Antonia knew that was the signal. She flew down the slope and jumped into the open passenger door. With a screech of tires, the GMC Yukon took off, heading south towards DC.

*****

Lights were still on at the WFO. Dan did not have any creds, neither did he have a cell. But security rang upstairs for him and called Trisha. She came down the stairs.

Dan was relieved to see her.

"Where the hell have you been?" Her voice had reproach, and disappointment. "Two cars are ready and I got permission to move out. Waiting on you." She came closer and her eyes widened.

"Jeez, what happened?"

"Did you get my message?" Dan was referring to the voice message he had left before driving off to the hideout.

"Yeah, we picked those two up. Who are they?"

"I think the big guy is called Abubaker. The dead one is Altaf." Dan told her about what happened as they went into the spacious lobby, and then took the elevator up to Trisha's fourth floor office.

There was an aching in Dan's head, and a throbbing in his neck. The adrenaline was subsiding, and he realized suddenly he was hungry. They went up to Trisha's office, and she ordered a burger takeout.

Trisha fixed him a coffee, which Dan accepted gratefully.

She said, "Dan you need to have your face looked at. I can't fix this in our medical room." She reached forward and touched Dan's swollen left jaw. Dan winced and moved away.

"Don't worry. There's no bleeding. I need some painkillers and fluids, then I'll be OK." He glanced at his watch. It was 19.00 hours. He felt exhausted, but also wired, aware that they needed to get moving.

Bellamy came in with an ice pack, Trisha had asked for it. He saw Dan's face and grimaced.

"Ouch."

Dan took the ice pack from him and pressed it against his face. His forehead creased in pain. He told Bellamy, "You should've seen the other guy."

Bellamy grinned. Dan popped two Vicodin's with some water. His mouth hurt like when he opened it. But he knew his jaw wasn't fractured. He could still swallow and chew. It just hurt like hell.

Dan said, "They're going to kill that girl unless we get to her fast. She might be dead already."

Trisha said, "We have the licence plate of the car she stole. I ran it through our supercomputers. They're not as good as Echelon over at the NSA, but it helped that we focused on Virginia only. We got a hit."

Dan looked up, excitement clutching at his guts. "You did? Where?"

"Town called Waynesboro. Not far from Mackton, where Carlyle's car is registered, according to the DMV."

"Then let's move. Do we have a team?"

Trisha nodded. "The FBI Hostage Rescue Team will send three of their guys."

"Good." Dan had never worked with the HRT but he knew of their reputation. They were all of Special Forces, and conducted the same operation that Dan had done in Afghanistan and Iraq, the only difference being they were domestic. The HRT only operated inside USA.

Dan's burger arrived, and he packed it for the drive. They went down to the armory and Dan finally got the kit he wanted. Kevlar vest, chest rig for handgun and extra ammo, NVG's and his choice of rifle, a Heckler and Koch 416. They loaded into a Chrysler SUV and moved into the perennial traffic of DC.

Dan watched as the car headed south. He turned to Trisha. "We need to head out west, right?"

She shook her head. "No air bases there. We can take a flight from Joint Base Anacosta-Bolllings."

"That's under the Navy now. You did well to get permission."

"I am the senior agent in my unit. Don't sound so surprised."

Dan watched her face warily, but she grinned.

"The base has a helipad. It's where the HRT will ride from, and we go with them."

"Cool."

The SUV swept in through the security barriers and within minutes, was at the runway of the former air force base. Two black Apache helicopters were waiting, engines on but rotors still.

Dan hauled his duffel bag out of the trunk, then followed Trisha and Bellamy to the three men waiting by the birds. He felt the tightness in his guts, that low rumbling of anticipation before a mission.

CHAPTER

Valona kept within the speed limit. Other cars overtook her, and she stayed on the right lane, watching the scenery as it unfolded. The 340 was a lane wide only in some places, and several times she braked rapidly to let a car through from the opposite lane. The Blue Ridge range undulated for miles around her.

A sign ahead said:

Shenandoah National Park
Thirty-five miles.

Valona began to see familiar sights from her last scouting. It was only three months ago, but so much had changed. Once she got the readings on the Dragon device, she couldn't believe it. The numbers were off the scale. That sort of radioactive emissions only happened near a huge deposit of uranium. And not just uranium…

When she told her dad, he had literally fainted. His eyes glassed over and she had to help him sit down. Once he had a swig of his brandy some color returned to his cheeks. He had leant forward and grabbed her hands.

"Not a word of this to anyone, Valona. Anyone. Do you understand?"

No, she had not understood. What would her father have to do with this? How did it affect him. Three weeks later he was dead, and she was being hunted like a wanted criminal.

She was so immersed in her thoughts she almost missed the old wooden sign, leaning so far to one side it was almost parallel to the ground. Valona slammed on the brakes, pulling over. No cars behind her. She got out and ran to the sign.

She had to wipe the surface with the sleeve of her jumper, kneeling next to it. Then the words appeared.

Shadow Valley Camping Ground.

Shadow Valley…where had she heard that name?

She frowned, gripping her forehead. She knew this.

Suddenly, an electric shock reverberated down her spine. Her scalp tingled and her brain shook. A memory flashed on the dark side of her mind, lighting up what had remained hidden for decades.

A little girl, asking her dad a question.

"Why is it called Shadow Valley, Daddy?"

The man pointed to the mountains all around them. "Because it lies in the shadow of these hills."

Valona straightened. She smoothed her hair back slowly. This had to be the place. But where was the entrance? The land just sloped off to the right, falling into the lap of a hill. There was no road. Had she missed it?

She got back on the car and drove slower, but forward. She was pretty sure she hadnt missed something as obvious as a disused road.

She saw it a mile away. The entrance was overgrown with weeds, and a tree had fallen across it diagonally, blocking half the entrance. But it was enough to let her small Honda through.

She drove into it, tires crunching dirt and plants that hadn't been touched in years. Some of them rose up to the window. But she managed to roll on as the road sloped gently down. The woods around her became heavier, and the hills suddenly seemed a lot closer, bigger.

The slope became steeper, till she was looking out over a large valley. She stopped the car. A river ran through the valley, a silvery cord that twisted around the yellow green mass of land. Around a section of the river, there was a large clearing. Easily two hundred meters across, she guessed. Trees clustered on the clearing, standing in clumps. Valona got back in the car and drove down further.

She stopped when something strange caught her eyes. Between the trees on the clearing, she could make out a shape. Like a mound of earth, but big enough to be spotted from this far away. She peered closely, and saw the mounds between the clusters of trees.

What the hell?

She drove farther on. The weeds and plants had been flattened by heavy tires on the road, she could tell. The slope levelled out soon and she drove more cautiously. She braked when she saw a tree house. She got out of the car. The breeze was stiff, flowing down the hills. She wrapped the jumper around her, and took the Glock in her hand. Glancing around, she crossed the road. The place was deserted. What she thought was an isolated tree house was in fact a derelict playing ground. There was more than one tree house, and she could make out swings, and climbing frames. Ivy grew over them, moss and lichen had followed.

Memories were assaulting Valona's mind. Occasional bursts of light, like strobes, glinting on forgotten parts of her soul. She had been here as a child. Perhaps she would recognize more if the weeds and overgrowth were cleared away. She shook her head and went back to the car. As she drove down, the road curved to the right and she saw an arrow sign. Cabins.

Her heart quickened. The log cabins were what she remembered most. She drove faster, noting the road was clearer now, but had pot holes like the rest of it. The path had brought her closer to the water's edge. Valona got out of the car slowly. There was no mistaking the line of log cabins by the water, separated from each other by several yards to afford privacy.

Yes. A shiver ran up her spine. This was the place she had tried to find. For some reason, she wanted to take readings with her device here. Why? Her father had never said anything specific.

Some day you might need to come back here.

What did he mean by that?

Valona sighed and looked across to the clearing. Her eyes narrowed. The mounds of earth were clearly visible, and it looked like someone had been digging. Her finger tightened on the gun's butt. She did a 360, but couldn't see a soul.

The time was mid-day. She had a few hours still, but after that she had to get out of here. She didn't fancy being here without the right equipment, on her own, when darkness came.

She parked the car in the lot near the cabins, then set off on foot towards the clearing. When she was close to the mounds of earth, she stopped. She counted five of them, and they all faced the river.

Why had someone been digging here? She held the Glock out, moving it around as she scanned. She got closer to the mound of earth, and stopped when she felt something hard beneath her foot. It was a long, round wire, thick in the middle. It was cased in steel, and the wire ran towards the mound of earth. She gasped when she got close enough to see.

There was a hole in the ground, like a grave. Only this was much bigger, large enough to five graves. In the hole, she could see a rectangular, flat object. It was green with moss, but she could make out the steel exterior. She walked closer till she was a couple of feet away from the hole.

There was a sound behind her.

Valona turned, but she wasn't quick enough. A dark shadow rushed above her, then she was on the ground, breath knocked out of her chest, a pressure on her back pushing her into the wet earth. The gun was removed from her hand.

"Thought I'd find you here," a voice said.

CHAPTER

Dawn was yet to break. A shy pink glow lay dormant at the edges of horizon, smothered by the last vestiges of velvety night.

Lights were on in the farm house outside Waldorf, Virginia.

General Peyton Mildred turned up the stiff collar of his uniform, then folded it neatly. The uniform fit him perfectly. His eyes were drawn to the stars and ceremonial medal hung on the left chest wall. His right hand came up and touched their metallic surface. For some reason, it gave him a sense of calm. He picked up his hat and pulled the beak of the cap lower, watching himself in the mirror. On the mantelpiece there was a photo of himself with Karl and Clara. Karl was in the middle, and had his arms spread, resting on his parents' shoulders.

Peyton picked up the photo and brought it close to his face. Emotion flared inside him as it always did. But today he also felt an unnatural peace. After months of planning, it was finally happening. There would be no going back. After he had achieved his mission, he might not be present to see the new America that emerged from the dust and rubble. But he knew that his name would live forever in the history books. He wasn't afraid of dying. Truth be told, after Karl's death, a part of him had died. The fact that Karl's body was never returned from Syria still enraged him. But then, the entire operation had been denied. To ensure no political feathers were ruffled. These cowards in the Senate had sold out his son, himself and their country. Peyton would make sure Karl's death was avenged.

And Clara? His dear, beloved companion. Many military men lose their wives when they're abroad on missions. Hell, marriages break up, period. But his had grown stronger with the years.

His tours of duty only made his marriage stronger. As he rose through the ranks of Pentagon, trying to change the system, Clara had been by his side. But when Karl died...Clara never recovered. He suspected she blamed him. Not directly, and never verbally. But she didn't have to.

When a woman and man love each other, words are not necessary. He knew. Despite his years at the Pentagon, he couldn't bring back the body of his dead son. Clara loved Peyton, but she didn't forgive him for that.

When she died of cancer, she held his hand. The last squeeze on his finger was accompanied by two words.

I'm sorry.

He knew what she meant. Sorry for being hard on him after Karl died.

Peyton closed his eyes and swallowed the hard knot of emotion in his throat. Then he stared at himself in the mirror. He smiled grimly.

I'm coming sweetheart. I can't wait. I'll see you and Karl soon.

There was a knock on the door. "Come in," Peyton said.

One of his men, dressed in combat fatigues, poked his head inside. His name was Moses, and he was third in command, after Carlyle. He was a former Navy SEAL.

"Sir, it's time to go." He saw the General in uniform and gave a crisp salute.

Peyton nodded. "Any word from Carlyle?"

"He's securing the last of the merchandise, sir. He will meet us inside."

"OK. Let's move."

Peyton went down the stairs of the two-story farm house, followed by the man. The rest of the crew were already in the four gun metal grey Escalade SUV's. Each one of them was armed to the teeth. Peyton got into the first car and the cavalcade rolled on the road.

The nearest town was Waldorf, twenty-three miles southeast of DC. It took them exactly half an hour to get up on the 11th Street South East to cross the Anacostia river. Another fifteen minutes later the procession arrived at the visitor's center of the United States Capitol building. Peyton's SUV was flagged down by a member of the US Capitol Police. The other three cars stopped behind them. Peyton opened the door and got out.

The police officer halted when he saw Peyton. He looked behind at the checkpoint, where a police car waited, with two more of his colleagues leaning against the car. Both were watching him.

Peyton said, "Name and rank officer."

The man swallowed, then pushed his shoulder back. "Tim Cussler, Sargent, USCP Precinct 34."

"Pleased to meet you Sargent Cussler. I am General Peyton Mildred of the US Marine Corps. We have a national emergency in our hands. The Capitol Building is under imminent danger of a terrorist attack. Have you been briefed?"

The surprise on Cussler's face was obvious. "No sir, no one told us."

Peyton frowned deeply and took a deep breath. "Phil Henriques is your Chief, right?"

Mention of his boss' name made the Sargent stammer. "Yes…yes sir he is. Do you kno-

"I need to speak to him at once. I can't believe you guys haven't been told already. How can I contact him?"

"This way, sir," Sargent Cussler pointed towards the check point. Moses appeared behind Mildred. Cussler glanced at him.

Peyton said, "This is Lieutenant Moses. Stay here."

Moses saluted. "Yes, sir."

Peyton approached the checkpoint. The two USCP officers straightened. Peyton was ushered inside the cabin. Cussler and another officer stayed inside, while the other cop stood near the car.

"Phone is this way," Cussler said, leading the way. The cabin was large enough for a small office, ten by twelve feet roughly. A desk in the middle had fax machines printers and laptops. A red phone hung on the wall, and Peyton recognized the type. This pone would only connect to three lines: The White House Situation Room, The ODNI office and the Pentagon War Room.

As soon as Cussler and the other officer had their backs turned, Peyton moved. From each hand he fired a modified electroshock handgun. The bullets had armor piercing tips and at this distance, would penetrate the body armor the men wore. The guns were made by a start up in Silicon Valley, and designed to generate a 750 volt shock in the victims, which rendered them paralyzed for two hours.

The bullets hit both men below the waist line and they slumped forward. Peyton knelt by them quickly, and pulled out two plastic handcuffs. He ignored their twitching bodies and frothing mouths. He pulled on non-conducting propylene gloves so the electricity wouldn't transmit to his body. He cuffed, then turned the men on their front, face down.

He looked behind him. The officer by the car had turned. Peyton saw Moses remove a 12 gauge shotgun, armed with the same electric bullets, and fire. The officers slammed back against his car, twitching and jerking. Then he slid down, unconscious.

Precise, clinical and no killing of service men. Peyton watched as Moses hurried forward to cuff the man. While the electro bullets were useful at close quarter, Peyton had no illusions. A full frontal assault would need the use of lethal weapons. They had plenty of those.

Peyton went to the red phone on the wall. As he had expected, the number for the security office inside the building was clearly marked.

He pressed the button and the phone started ringing.

It was 5.00 am. Regular staff were yet to start, but there would be a duty clerk manning the phones. A tired voice answered.

"Capitol Hill Security. Identify yourself."

"This is Phil Henriques, Chief of USCP. Listen to me very carefully."

CHAPTER

The barrier at the Capitol Hill Visitor's Center lifted and the three SUV's rushed through. Peyton sat stone faced in the front passenger seat. He checked his watch. The Visitor's Center opened at 8.30am, but those with official business could attend from 7.15am. It was 5.05am now.

As the SUV's came to a stop, Peyton saw the three officers standing outside the stairs that led down to the visitor's entrance. It was subterranean, after the customary checks, led into the huge Exhibition Hall, above which the dome soared hundreds of feet into the sky.

Peyton and Moses were the only ones to alight from the SUV. As they did so, the headlights switched off. Three guards approached them, and they didn't stand a chance. Electricity buzzed around their bodies in a blue wave as the high voltage bullets found their mark, and all three bodies slumped to the floor together. Moses bound their hands and pulled them to the near wall. Peyton marched swiftly down the stairs. He went to the Security Office, and a man and woman stood as he approached.

"My name is General Mildred. Have you been informed of the terrorist threat to the Capitol Building this morning?"

The two officers glanced at each other. Peyton feigned impatience. "Who else is here on duty?"

The woman cleared her throat. "Sir, there's a team of three at the Dirksen Senate Building, two at the Russel Office and Rayburn House-

"No," Peyton interrupted. "Here, now."

The two officers looked at each other again. The woman spoke. "We are the night staff. But we are in constant contact with the National Guard."

Peyton pressed fingers to his forehead. "Get me Phil Henriques, right now."

The woman turned. Peyton shot the man first, who was bending to reach for something behind the counter. The woman heard the sound, turned and her eyes widened in shock. Peyton hesitated for an instant. He had never shot at a woman, in any part of the world. Never mind a service woman in his own country.

It gave the female officer time to draw her weapon. Two hard-nosed electro slugs slammed into her torso, thrusting her backwards. Her limbs flailed as the electricity jolted around her body, and she crashed into a pile of computers. They fell on the floor with a loud noise.

Peyton vaulted over the counter, nimble for a 61 year old man. There was a door at the far end, and he opened it, scanning with his weapon. There was a desk, TV and coffe machine. The room was empty. He tapped the bud in his ear and spoke into the dot microphone fixed to his label.

"Bravo one this is Zero. Clear."

Moses replied. "Copy that Zero. We are proceeding as planned."

Peyton went to the circuit board on the wall, and one by one, switched off the alarm systems. He ran out into the foyer, the brilliant whiteness of the floodlight lit dome visible through the steel reinforced glass ceiling. He paid it no heed. He had done his recon several times.

The conveyer belts and metal detector check points were silent. He went through them and into the Exhibition Hall. High above his head, the oculus in the rotunda of the dome held the massive Apotheosis of Washington painting, done by the Italian painter, Constantino Brumidi in 1865. Peyton's eyes were drawn to it, although he had seen it several times. But never in complete isolation, or in almost near darkness. The only light was the faint sunbeams filtering in through the windows beneath the dome.

The fresco seemed to glow with a life of its own, an ethereal, other worldly sight in the half light. Peyton had always regarded the painting as strange. George Washington was a national hero in the ninenteenth century, but he wasn't a saint, and he wasn't being canonized.

But today, the intricate pattern of the walls, leading up to the oculus, and the round yellow orb in the center of the painting, seemed to look down at him like an eye from heaven. Peyton stood transfixed, alone in the seat of power in the USA, overcome by a sudden feeling he was being watched and judged.

He wasn't a religious man. True, Clara took him to church on Sundays, but religion had never been his thing. This was different, somehow frightening.

He felt goosebumps prickle his skin, and the hair stood up on the back of his neck. He breathed heavily and averted his eyes from the painting. His forehead was masked in sweat.

Peyton took a moment to compose himself. He had to make his way to the National Statuary Hall. It was a two story Hall with sculptures and paintings, located immediately south of the Rotunda.

The time was 5.30 now, and he was already late in taking up position.

He grabbed the butt of his real weapon, the Colt M1911, chambering 0.45 ACP slugs. His favorite handgun. He ran to the side of the exhibition hall, and climbed the stairs rapidly.

CHAPTER

As General Mildred made his way to the south of the Rotunda, the three SUV's were tearing round the corner, heading for the Senate Carriage Entrance, open 24 hours. The three security men at the checkpoint stopped them. Moses was the first man out and shot the two guards who came up to him with his 12 gauge shotgun. One of his men fired from behind him, taking out the remaining guard inside the checkpoint. This had to be a long range shot, and it used lethal force. The rounds pumped into the officer, two at mid zone and one that exploded his face.

First casualty, Moses thought as he stepped inside the check point, and pressed the button for the barrier. He checked the bank of CCTV images. Most were in darkness, which meant the General was doing his job. Below the table was a console of switches. The digital locks for the entrance doors were marked. Moses pressed them and came out, nodding at the man who took up position as guard.

Moses jumped on the last SUV, standing on the side, door open. Boots clattered on the stone steps as they went in. The doors were open. Rifles on shoulders, locked and loaded, the men fanned inside. Moses ran down the middle, and three broke formation, running after him. They headed to the National Statuary Hall.

Peyton was inside already, looking at the painting called "The Capture of Narcissi." The men took the painting off the wall. Behind the 150 year old painting stood a rectangular box, as wide as the frame. They unhooked the box from the wall and lowered it on the floor.

Peyton punched in the keycode on the digital pad in the centre of the box. The red numbers flashed three time, then a click was audible. Over 2/3 of the box was taken up by an odd looking machine. It had a central section with a round face, and steel tubing came off it. The tubes reconnected into another boxed section, which fed back into the round face.

The other third of the box contained components of assault rifles. Moses passed the pieces around, and the barrels, magazines and butts were clicked into place. Peyton now had a longer range weapon, and he slung it around his chest.

He glanced at Moses who barked out an order. One of the men put his backpack on the floor and took out a tripod, video camera, and high voltage, battery powered lights.

The camera was set up and the lights flashed on Peyton as he stood with the object on the rectangular box.

The camera man held up five fingers and counted down. Peyton cleared his throat. The camera panned to the object, then up to his face.

"My name is General Peyton Mildred of the US Marine Corps. For too long, this country has suffered the tyranny of the few, directed against our good people. Today, that tyranny comes to an end. Today, we create a new America."

CHAPTER

Joint Base Anacosta Bolling
Virginia

Dan shook hands with the HRT guys and introduced himself. The men started loading their stuff on board the Apache. Dan took Trisha to one side and whispered in her ears.

Trisha walked over to Bellamy, who was on the phone. She tapped him on the shoulder. Bellamy turned and pointed to his cell phone.

Trisha said, "Cut the call. This is important. Only you and me can know about it."

Bellamy excused himself and put the cell phone down. His eyes were inquisitive. "What is it?"

"I have mission critical information on Dan Roy. The Director rang me this morning. Did you know he was an asset for the Chinese?"

Bellamy widened his eyes. "Really?"

Trisha looked over her shoulder where Dan was chatting with the HRT guys. She grabbed Bellamy's arm. "Come this way." They walked towards the dark expanse of an old, unused hangar. Trisha went around the corner, out of sight of Dan. Bellamy leaned against the wall.

Trisha said, "This is serious. I think Dan is a foreign agent. If he comes on this mission, he could jeopardize it."

"Just say no."

"He's here now. If I stop him, he'll become suspicious. Have you noticed anything about him?"

Bellamy's face was shrouded in the near darkness. "Come to think of it, yes I have."

Trisha waited. Bellamy said, "Before you went to Robert Murphy's house, I saw him jog to the park next to the WFO. He came back a few minutes later. Then he did the same after you came back. This time, I saw him speaking on the phone."

A voice spoke from behind them. "Like you were doing just now?"

Bellamy whirled around. Dan was standing behind him. He had the Sig in his hand, pointed at Bellamy. Dan stepped closer. Trisha reached for the weapon in her beltline.

Bellamy glanced from Dan to Trisha. "What the hell is this?"

Dan said, "You just lied about me. But I guess that comes to you naturally, right?"

"I don't know what you're talking about."

With his left hand, Dan took out a device that looked like a phone. He pressed a key and Bellamy's voice came on.

"The car just left for the garage. ETA ten minutes."

Dan switched the phone off. "You made that call just after we left for Kowalski's garage. I told Trisha to tap your phone, because I felt there was a leak from day one. Without a leak, how did the sniper know Kowalski was going to meet the FBI? Just surveillance wouldn't have informed Carlyle and his men about that. Someone from inside told them."

Dan carried on. "When the IED exploded in the garage, and you arrived, you knew already that someone had watched us approaching the place. Before Trisha told you. You put men on the roofs, trying to look efficient. But all you did was give yourself away. Trisha never told you what sort of a device it was. You knew someone rang the phone to trigger the IED. You made sure you came after they got away, right?"

Bellamy slumped against the wall. His voice was hoarse. "You have no proof."

Dan said, "If not you, then who? No one else has access to the investigation. It's you, Trisha and myself."

Dan switched the device on again. Bellamy's voice said, "Murphy's house. Twenty minutes."

A different voice said, "Roger that."

Dan said, "When we got shot inside Murphy's living room, you made sure you stayed outside. In fact, on every occasion, you stayed out of harm's away. This phone tap proves it, Bellamy. How much are they paying you?"

Bellamy straightened and came off the wall. "This is ridiculous." He looked at Trisha. "I'm going to the helicopter."

Trisha pointed her gun at him. "You're not going anywhere, Bellamy. You are under arrest."

He gawked at her. Dan closed the gap between them swiftly and thrust him against the wall, face first. He frisked Bellamy, while Trisha covered. Dan cuffed his hands with plastic ties, then turned him around.

"How much did they pay you, Bellamy?"

Bellamy clenched his jaws and remained silent.

"Fine," Dan said. "You're about to have FBI's finest interrogate you. Good luck."

He grabbed Bellamy and pulled him along. Blue light flashed as an unmarked Escalade pulled up, and two men in suits came out. They flashed their FBI badges and took custody of Bellamy.

He held Trisha's eyes as he went it. She shook her head as the car did a three point turn, then headed back towards the air base gates.

Dan said, "Nice work."

Trisha didn't reply for a while. Then she said, "No, it's not."

A man shouted at from behind. It was the pilot. He was waving at them.

"Time to get going," Dan said.

CHAPTER

Valona felt a blunt pain explode in her lower back and she cried out. Mud smeared her cheek and she felt brackish fluid in her mouth. The man's knee was on her back as he tied her hands. A hand grabbed her collar and pulled her up.

She faced the man with the lopsided, evil looking scar on the left cheek. When she smiled, the scar moved as well, giving his face a ghoulish appearance.

"Miss Kowalski," Carlyle said, "You really have to stop playing hard to get."

Valona spat on the ground. Despite the pain, and her fear, a strong underbelly of rage flowed inside her.

"You bastard. You killed my father."

Carlyle shrugged. "It's old news, right? He couldn't protect himself. You, on the other hand, are a different matter. Where did you learn those survival skills?"

Valona didn't say anything. Carlyle said, "Where is your research?"

"What research?"

"Don't play to hard to get, please. My men here," he indicated behind her, and around him. For the first time, she noticed the men who stepped out from behind the tree trunks. All wore brown camouflage tactical gear. Had they been waiting for her?

Carlyle continued, "I don't wish to be crude, but my men haven't been with a woman for a long time. I can let them loose on you if you want. Or you can tell me what I want."

Valona snarled at him. "Then what? You call me a cab and get me out of here?"

Carlyle looked towards the sky. He remained in that position till Trisha followed his eyes. The canopy of trees above was dense.

A pain suddenly rocked her face as Carlyle slapped her. He backhanded her, flinging her face to the other side. Pain exploded in her face and her cheeks stung. A drool of blood came down her lips.

"You work for Radnet, at the EPA. Your job is to measure radiation. And you just happen to be the daughter of Victor Kowalski. I don't think that's a coincidence."

Valona blinked back the tears of shame and anger. No show of weakness to this animal. She panted and shook her head. "I don't know what you mean."

"You don't? Is that why you came here on your own, to take readings?"

She was surprised. "How did you know that?"

"Ever since we found out what you did, we followed you. Your father told you to come here, didn't he?"

Valona could feel her heart beating like she's run a marathon. She was thinking furiously. *How did this guy know?*

Carlyle narrowed his eyes. "Either you're a good actress, or you really don't know. But it doesn't matter. Where is your research?"

"What research?"

He hit her again, this time harder. It felt like her head was smashed against a stone wall, and her eyes rocked, going out of focus. She sagged, held up by the man behind her. For a while, she couldn't see anything. The pain was like an avalanche pressing on her face, not letting her breathe.

She felt her chin being lifted, then water splashed on her face. A voice came from far away.

"Tie her up against the tree."

Valona felt hands grab and drag her. Hardened bark pierced her clothes and she winced in pain. Her hands were tied to the sides of the trunk. Trying to wriggle only made it worse.

She could see now. A group of men in army fatigues stood in front of her. Carlyle stepped closer.

"I have no more time to waste. You had your chance. Now my men will start on you. Carlos!"

A short, but immensely wide shouldered man stepped forward. His face was small and round and looked strange on his thick neck. The eyes were dark, and very small. They moved up and down her body.

Valona felt a cold sweat break out on her scalp. She turned to Carlyle. "You can do what you want. But you need to know if I don't get back to my office in 48 hours, then my research goes public."

Carlyle gave a short laugh. "Well then, all the more reason for us to get started. Carlos."

With a grunt, Carlos stepped forward.

CHAPTER

The rotor blades spun furiously and the rear cabin of the Apache shook. Dan held on with his outstretched hand to the trembling side of the aircraft, while Trisha leaned against him. All of them wore headphones and were hooked to the same comms channel.

"Where will you land?" Dan asked. Far down below, Dan saw wilderness like he had expected. No clearing in site for the bird to land. But he also saw a yellow line, and the black ribbon of a road curling through the foliage.

"Land on the road if you have to," Dan shouted in the mic. "We can call the State Troopers to block it."

He glanced at Trisha who gave him a thumbs up. Wind whipped in through the sides as the bird did a circle. Trisha was speaking on the external channel, calling the WFO to patch her onto the Virginia Highway Patrol. They got affirmation eventually, but it would still take time for the Troopers to arrive on scene.

"We have no time to waste," Dan said. Trisha nodded. She was the commanding officer.

"Land at the nearest spot. How far are we from Waynesboro?" The pilot said, "I can drop you off in town if you want me to, but the traffic will be more hazardous. But it does beat trying to find a clearing through these trees."

"I think that's the best option," Trisha yelled back. "The traffic will scatter, don't worry. You got a loudspeaker, right?"

"Right."

"Then do it."

The nose of the bird dipped as the rotors spun harder against the wind, and picked up speed. It flew above the trees till Waynesboro became visible, a collection of buildings in the center of a large road junction.

The pilot maneuvered the bird till it was hovering right above the center of town. Dan could see a gas station to his left, and more buildings further up ahead. A couple looked like hotels. He could read the sign of Holiday Inn. The gas station cameras had picked up the license plate of the Honda Valona was driving. With any luck, he thought, the gas station he was looking at was the right one. He couldn't see any others.

He jabbed a finger. "Take us down there."

The pilot nodded and banked to his left. The HRT guys got ready. Their leader Colin grabbed hold of the lanyard on his waist rig, and hooked it up on the metal bar on the ceiling.

"I go first, then you" Colin mouthed at Dan.

Dan nodded and looked at Trisha. "Have you ever rappelled down from a helicopter before?"

"Nope. But there's always a first time," she said. "I should go before you."

"Fine," Dan said. He showed her to hook her legs into the saddle. He didn't need the saddle himself, preferring to use his gloved hands and legs around the rope.

The pilot's voice was blaring on the loudspeaker. "This is the FBI. Clear the space for the aircraft to land. State Troopers are informed."

Trisha made it down safely. Dan hooked his feet around the nylon rope, and skimmed down. A crowd had gathered around them. Cars had stopped and people came out bars and shops. The noise from the bird was ear splitting. When the team were on ground, the bird lifted up higher, sparing everyone's ears.

Dan heard sirens in the distance as he ran inside the gas station. The owner looked at them with wild eyes, but came to his senses quickly when Trisha explained.

"She went that way, into town."

Towards the hotels, Dan thought. She needed to stop for the night.

He turned to Trisha. "Valona stole the doctor's wallet right. Didn't you say we had the credit card data?"

Every transaction of a credit card sent out an electronic signal. Trisha pulled out her cell phone. "Good thinking, Dan. I have it here."

She pulled her emails out, and then downloaded a PDF that had the data. Her eyes lit up. "Last used at the Best Western Hotel of Waynesboro."

Dan ran across the road with Trisha. The lobby of Best Western Hotel was empty, and the reception team looked up in surprise as two sweaty, breathless individuals ran up to them.

Dan showed them Valona's photo. " This is the FBI, and this is a national emergency. Have you seen this woman?"

The two women and one man gathered around. One of the women frowned and leaned closer. Her name badge said Tina.

"She looks familiar, I don't know why."

Trisha asked, "Do you have any camera's that might show her?"

"Sure. Come this way."

Tina went to two TV screens that showed a number of camera angles. She clicked on the keyboard and got up several images. She pressed play. Dan leaned in. One of the showed a dark haired woman with glasses approaching the desk.

"Stop and zoom in," Dan said. He felt Trisha stiffen as the face came into close up.

"That's her! She's in disguise."

Dan turned to Tina. "Do you know where she went."

"As a matter of fact, I do. She wanted to know about the Route 340. I think she's headed up there. Took a map from me."

"Anything else?"

"Yes." Tina tapped her chin. "She seemed in a world of her own when I was telling her about the Shenandoah National Park, which is up the 340, driving north."

CHAPTER

Trisha and Dan came out the revolving doors of the hotel. Trisha started speaking to the two State Troopers who had just arrived with their patrol cars. Dan went to one side and called the pilot, whose name was Andy.

"Andy this is Dan."

Dan could see the bird. It had come to land a couple of hundred meters away where the road was broader.

"Shoot, Dan."

"Do you have a thermal image scanner? One that shows up figures by searching for body heat?2

"Not only that, I also got high precision cameras mounted on the underside of the Apache. Might be better in daylight. You looking for the car, right?"

"More the woman actually, but yes the car would be a good start. We need to head up the 340. It's the road that goes right from the traffic lights."

They were in the helicopter shortly, roaring above the road, heading north. Dan had his eyes glued to the screen, Trisha next to him.

"Stop," she said. "I saw tire marks on the road, veering off to the right. But there's no road there. Did she just go off into the woods?"

Andy did a circle and came back. Dan pointed. "There's a road." He zoomed in with the camera, which could be operated from the screen keyboards. "There, see?"

Within seconds, they could see the log cabins and the river that ran through the clearing. The cluster of trees caught Dan's attention.

"Can you land there? It's clear."

"I'll try," Andy yelled. "But if the grounds too soft, I can only hover. You have to jump out."

"Roger that," Dan said. The HRT guys were busy checking their weapons. The bird started to lose height rapidly.

There was a whine suddenly, and the glass window above Dan's head fragmented. More whines followed, and the sound of dull impacts against metal.

"We're under fire!" Andy screamed from the cockpit, his voice hoarse on the mic.

The bird started to rotate and move away.

"No," Dan shouted. "Get us down, Andy. We need to get there."

"Get ready to jump," Andy said. "No way I'm landing."

A glass panel exploded behind them. Colin pointed his rifle out the window and let loose a long volley of fire. His friend joined in. The bird had turned and now it wobbled in the air, shaking as it lost speed. Trisha slammed into Dan who fell forward from his seat.

The ground rushed up to meet them. Dan judged it to be about six feet away when he let go of Trisha, unhooked the lanyard from his belt and jumped. He rolled over smoothly, old habits kicking in.

He was on his belly, HK 417 locked and loaded onto the clump of trees where the fire was coming from. Set to automatic mode, he sprayed bullets, watching with satisfaction as bark flew off the trees, kicked up dust. Spent cases flew out from the rack, and the muzzle grew hot. His ears were turning deaf.

He spent one magazine, ejected it, reached into his chest rig and slapped another one in. Colin had appeared next to him, and was returning fire.

"The others are headed for cover on the sides," Colin yelled at him between bursts.

"Roger that."

Colin withdrew a grenade, fitted it to the underarm grenade launcher fixed on his rifle, lifted the muzzle and fired. The grenade lobbed up and landed inside the trees. A brilliant yellow flash exploded, rocked the ground around them.

"Cover me," Dan shouted. He got up and raced forward.

CHAPTER

The butt of the rifle was solid on Dan's right shoulder. He scanned it left and right as he ran. Colin kept up the fire to one side, traces of yellow streaking into the trees with lethal force. When he was ten meters away, Dan went to ground. He could see a mound of earth above him, it looked like a hillock. Someone was digging. The fresh smell of earth, mingled now with cordite, reached his nostrils.

The muzzle of a weapon appeared from behind a tree trunk. Dan waited till he could see the hand, then fired twice. There was a scream and the rifle dropped. Dan crawled forward on his belly.

Movement. Three o clock. A running figure, scampering between trees. Dan fired, and missed. But Colin had seen it too, and he didn't miss. With another scream, the figure went down. Dan got closer still and he could now see the hole in the ground. A bullet whined over his head and he rolled over.

A figure stepped out from behind the mound, firing. Dan picked him out with two shots to the midriff, which felled him. Muzzle flash appeared from his right again. The trees were ringing now with the sound of gunfire, echoing in the smoky hills.

Dan saw a figure lose control and fall ten feet away from him. His bullet had found its mark.

Then he heard a voice. It was a woman's and it was loud. "Hold your fire. Hold it!"

It was Trisha. Dan eased his finger off the trigger. He shouted at Colin, who was still firing. When he realized Dan had stopped, and was screaming at him, he stopped too.

The sudden silence was almost unnerving. The air was thick with gunsmoke. Dan took his handgun out, and ran to the nearest tree trunk. He could hear groans.

"Dan, are you there?" It was Trisha's voice.

"Right here. Are you OK?"

"Yes. I think I found her."

CHAPTER

Dan leaned over the tree to glance at the clearing. He saw four bodies lying on the ground. He stepped out gingerly.

Trisha said, "I'm coming out." She appeared from behind a tree trunk. "The HRT guys are patrolling the area. Valona is tied to a tree," she indicated with her hand, "back there."

Dan heard more groans, and he looked downwards. A man was trying to lift his head. Dan walked over quickly and stepped on the hand that was trying to reach for the gun next to him. He kicked the weapon away.

Dan knelt, and turned the guy around. He wore a combat vest and a dark stain was spreading across his midriff. The man's eyes fluttered. Dan could smell death. He took out his kukri and sliced across the vest. The rounds had penetrated just below his chest. There was no exit wound. His aorta was probably ruptured, and he would bleed internally till he died.

He lowered his face to the man's.

"There must be more of you. Where is Carlyle?"

The man mumbled something. Dan couldn't hear what he said, despite his ears being close to his face. Dan put his backpack down and took out a bottle of water. He lifted the man's head and helped him drink.

"Where is Carlyle?" Dan repeated.

The guy looked at Dan with dull grey eyes. "You're dead," he whispered. "We're all dead." His eyes fluttered closed again. Dan shook him, then slapped him across the face, hard.

"Where is Carlyle?"

The man's head lolled to one side. Dan straightened it. The guy's lips were moving. He said one word twice.

"Mildred."

"Who's Mildred?" Dan asked. A bluish hue was spreading across the man's lips. Cyanosis. He opened his mouth and Dan gave him more water. He shook his shoulders.

"Where?"

"D…"

Dan listened closely as the man spoke his last words. "Tell me," he urged.

"DC."

The man's head rolled back, and his eyes stared forward. His chest had stopped inflating. Dan rose, and walked over to where Trisha was sitting next to a woman with short dark hair, a white blanket wrapped around her. They sat on a felled tree trunk, next to another mound of earth, and the hole. Only, this hole was empty.

Dan didn't waste time in preamble. "Valona," he addressed the other woman, "before that guy died he said we're all dead. What did he mean?"

Valona shivered as she met Dan's gaze. "I think he meant the machine. The one behind you."

"What are they?" Trisha asked gently.

Valona shook her head. "I don't know."

"What happened to Carlyle?" Dan asked. When Valona looked at him questioningly, he said, "The leader? As far as I remember, he had a scar on his face."

Valona went stiff and her body shook. She didn't speak. Trisha patted her on the back. "It's OK."

Valona said, "He left. With the other men. They took the rest of these machines with them. The one that's left is set to blow up, any time now. That's what the dead guy meant."

Dan said, "They've taken them to DC."

He swung around and headed for the machine in the ground. Colin came up next to him and shone a torch inside.

Dan shone his light inside. It was a ten by six feet dark chamber. There was a rectangular box on the floor, made of black metal. It was roughly seven feet in length, and four feet wide. The lid was open, and Dan could see inside.

He signalled at the others, and lowered himself into the hole. Mud squelched under his boots. Closer up, he could see the central console better. There were signs in the Cyrilic alphabet. Russian. An array of switches and dials lined the top of the device. Below it there was two round white dials, and then the console. The device was square. He heard the others come in behind him.

Dan flashed his light to the left. He saw a three tubes come out of the side and disappear inside the device. There was glass box where the three tubes inserted, like the glass box showing the pendulum of a clock.

Then he saw it. A timer, ticking down. The numbers glowed red in the darkness:

0.4:10:24:10

The last two digits were moving quicker than anything Dan had seen. A micro second counter. The first digit was not moving, which made it the hour counter.

Dan said, "We got ten minutes before this thing blows. We need to disarm this, and get the hell out of here. If this goes off…" his voice trailed off.

His throat was bone dry. Was this a nuclear weapon? The source of the radiation that Valona had picked up? He had to assume it was. Dan was no stranger to explosives. He had fitted and charged hundreds in his career. But he had never seen an explosive like this. He looked at Colin, who shrugged at him.

Dan was way out of his league here, and he knew it. "Trisha," he called out. She came running. Dan pointed at the machine. "The timer's ticking down. We can't run fast enough, even the bird will get blown out of the sky if this thing goes."

"Wait." Trisha fumbled with her phone. "There's a guy at the Nuclear Regulatory Commission who might help."

Dan reached for his own phone. He called McBride and explained the situation quickly.

McBride breathed in sharply. "Nuclear weapon? You have a nuke down there?"

"Yes and I need to know how to defuse it. Now!"

"Hold on, let me make some calls. How long you got?"

"Ten minutes."

Trisha was outside already, speaking to one of the FBI agents. She came back and told Dan, "Remember Walker's friend, Mile Crais at the Pantex Plant, in Texas. You need to speak to him. If anyone knows how to disarm this thing, it will be him."

Dan was watching the seconds count down. Now there was less than nine minutes left. He felt his palms become moist. He did not mind facing an entire enemy battalion on his own. With nothing but his Heckler and his kukri. He might die, but he would take them with him.

That was how he had lived.
One day, that was how he would die.
But he had never thought he would face what he was facing now.

A nuclear explosion in continental USA.

Silently, he took the phone from Trisha's hand.
The scientist spoke rapidly. "It's Mike Crais. Describe to me what you see in front of you, Dan."
Dan talked as fast as he could. Crais listened in silence. Trisha had a live video feed on, and Crais could see everything.

He said, "Jesus Christ, a tactical nuclear weapon. Any idea of its capability?"
Dan said, "Negative. We just stumbled on this. The letters on it are definitely Russian."
Crais said, "Can you see anything around the main weapon?"
Dan looked. The console, with its dials and switches, was about four feet long. Next to it, connected in parallel, he saw three large black shapes. He saw the wires that made the parallel connection. He informed Crais.
Crais said, "Is the thing connected to a mains AC?"
Dan flashed his torch around. "It's in the hole in the middle of a forest. I doubt it will be."
"But there could be a cable bringing electricity to it, unless its solar battery powered."
Colin said, "I tripped up on a tube. It turned out to be a steel encased wire. It was colored green for camouflage."
Crais asked, "There are cable lines around there, Dan, I can see it on my map here. This is an illegal line, stealing electricity to power these devices."
Dan looked at the rear and found the connection of the wire to the machine. It was a large plug socket, similar to those found behind a printer, but five times the size, easily. The wire snaked in underground, but it wasn't plugged in."

When Crais heard this, he said, "Then they must have disconnected it as they were getting ready to move it. Now listen very carefully, Dan. You see those three large black shapes to the right?"

"Yes."

"Those are the batteries. Disconnect those, and then the anti tamper device is disconnected. Then all you have to do is unscrew the top of the console, and take out the warhead."

Yeah, right. That easy?

Dan wiped the sweat that was now pouring off his head, and tried to quell the rising tide of panic inside him.

"How do I do it?"

Crais asked Dan if he had scissors and a screwdriver. Dan asked Trisha, who got them from one of the FBI guys. They had pliers and cable cutters as well, standard gear for the HRT.

Crais said, "Can you see the different colors of the battery wires?"

"Yes."

"They are colored for a reason. Can you see the blue, orange and black ones?"

"Yes."

"Cut those first."

"Which one?"

"Sorry, the blue one."

Trisha shone the light, and Dan cut the wires. They were steel armoured and he had to use the cable cutters in the end. His fingers were getting stiff again. His body was drenched in sweat. He looked at the timer on the machine.

Seven minutes left.

Crais said "The KGB devised hundreds of these weapons, and it was rumoured that they came into the country by ship and via Mexico. There was a search for them, but nothing was ever found."

Dan said, "Let's spare the history lesson for later. This is no longer an urban myth. Wires are cut, now what?"

Crais said, "Can you see the screws along the edges?"

Dan did, and one of the FBI guys helped him unscrew the top. Crais`s voice was urgent. "Lift that lid very carefully."

They did, and Dan saw why immediately. Packed in the middle of the console was the putty like shape of at least thirty pounds of C4 plastic explosive. He put his hands in and gingerly lifted the explosive out. He put it to one side.

Crais said, "Well done. That was the tamper proof explosive."

Dan asked, "Now what?"

"Can you see the three tubes coming into the machine from below?"

Dan nodded. "Well, that is the switching device. The dials are there to monitor the temperature and humidity inside the machine. We need to isolate the switching device, and then the weapon is disarmed."

Dan looked at the clock. It was slow going.

Six minutes left.

He tried his best to keep his voice steady. "Sir, we don`t have much time left."

Crais said, "OK Dan. Now you need to find how the switching device is connected to the main weapon."

Dan could feel his heart pounding in his ears. "How do I do that?"

"Feel it."

Dan put his fingers where the three steel tubes entered the device from the rear. It was smooth. He lifted the machine up slightly, straining as his left hand took the weight. He felt the rear. Smooth again. The light over his shoulder began to dim. Then it died out completely.

Trisha said, "Shit. Shit."

One of the FBI guys switched his light on. The beam was not as good. Dan could feel the seconds slipping away. He continued to feel along the metallic underside of the weapon. Then he found it. A small recess, like a latch. It was twinned at the top and the bottom, where the three pipes came out from the rear to enter the top.

He pressed them. Nothing happened. He told Crais what was happening.

Crais said, "Those are round nuts. You need to screw into them, and then release them."

The fact that it was on the underside made it harder. One FBI guy held the machine up, while Dan lay on his tummy and did the best he could.

Trisha said, "Five minutes left."

Dan was not getting much purchase on the bolts with the round head screwdriver he had.

He told Crais, "We might have to turn this thing face down to get better access at these bolts."

Crais said, "That might be dangerous. You could dislodge the nuclear material inside. It won`t come out as it is well protected in a lead chamber. But lead cannot absorb all radioactivity. You could be setting yourself up for lead poisoning."

Trisha said, "Dan, we have to do this."

Dan went to the floor again. His fingers were stiff as hell, and his forearm was beginning to burn where he had hit the ground. He panted with the effort.

"Four minutes left," Trisha said. At the last word, her voice broke.

Dan tried to ignore it, and focus on the job. The screwdriver was jammed into the oval shape, and would not move. He grabbed the tool with both hands, and clenched his jaws tight as he turned it with all the strength in his body.

Trisha said, "Three minutes."

The nut moved. Dan applied pressure, and it moved some more.

"Twenty seconds."

Dan finished unscrewing the last bolt. It fell on the floor. Dan pulled the section that was loose. Nothing happened.

"Ten seconds. Dan…"

After another tug, the part came off the machine, and into his hands. As soon as the object came loose in his hand, there was a loud beep and a side of the object thrust outwards. Dan put it down on the floor.

There was silence for a while. Dan scrambled out and leaned against the wall, wiping his forehead with his shirt sleeve.

Trisha shone her light on the dial. It was not glowing any more. No numbers were visible.

Crais spoke for all of them. "Phew, you had me worried there.

Well done. See that bit that kicked out? If that had hit the trigger inside the machine, it was all over."

CHAPTER
Capitol Building
Washington DC

It was a Sunday, and the usual throng of office workers hadn't descended on Capitol Hill. Most of the people who came were visitors. Moses and one of his men were manning the visitor's check point. Moses was six feet five, a giant of a man. A former Navy Seal, he had earned the nickname of Shrapnel among his peers because his large frame had absorbed a fair amount of bullet and grenade fragments. His size made him an automatic target.

He stood by the USCP patrol car and watched as the first visitors began to trickle in. A family car stopped as he held up his hand. He went up to the driver's side as the man opened his window. A dad and mom with two kids in the back. Under his breath, Moses swore to himself. Just what he didn't need. The General's orders had been clear. No ordinary citizens. If a politician presented himself for weekend duty, that was a different matter. If that happened, Moses had express orders to call Peyton immediately.

Moses said, "Sorry, but Capitol Hill is closed today."

The man said, "We just thought we could take a closer look-

"Not today, sir. And there's been a development. A big one. I suggest you keep your family safe and get out of here."

The man's voice dropped to a whisper. "Is it a terrorist attack?"

His wife pulled his sleeve. "John, leave it."

Moses didn't allow any sentiment on his stony face. "Get back now sir. This place has no entry."

He stood with hands on his twin belt holsters as the 4x4 did a K turn, then drove swiftly down, the driver no doubt harried by his wife to drive quickly. She was clearly more sensible than her husband, Moses thought.

He barked some orders to the two men at the check point, then jogged to the Senators Carriage entrance.

He turned another three cars away, but the fourth car caught his attention. It was an armor-plated Lincoln, windows black tinted. The driver stopped and put his window down.

"Senator Archie McHugh wishes to visit the Senate basement. For private reasons."

Moses signaled to the man behind him. He smiled at the driver. "Sorry, new security detail. But the Senator is most welcome. Can I see your ID please?"

The driver hesitated, then lowered his window. Senator McHugh was out of his car and going up the marble steps of the entrance. The driver took his ID out and Moses shot him in the face once. It was point blank range and one shot was enough to make his brains scatter over the upholstery.

The Senator heard the sound and paused to look back. Moses and his colleague ran up and grabbed his elbows.

"This way, Senator," Moses said. "We got a busy day ahead of us."

*****

FBI Headquarter
Between 9th and 10th Street
Northwest DC

Wade Moynihan, the FBI Director had lost most of his hair in his forties. Now in his early sixties, after a lifetime of federal service, lack of hair was the least of his concerns. Especially today. Thirty years in the FBI had given him a god nose for trouble, and the case of Victor Kowalski had bothered him right from the start.

His secretary stood behind him as he gripped the top of an armchair in the conference room, and looked over the mahogany table at the screen. The screen displayed an image from a live feed on Special Agent Trisha Dunne's phone. Trisha was speaking. "This is the machine here. With the help of Mike Crais at the Pentex Plant, we managed to defuse it." Trisha moved her phone closer to the device on the ground. Dan had lifted himself back on ground now, but still stared intently at the device like it would do something any second.

"Is that big guy Dan Roy?" Wade asked. Trisha had her earphones on, so Wade's words were silent to everyone else at the scene.

"Yes. Couldn't have done it without him."

"One hell of a gamble, but I guess it paid off. So, let me get this straight. You chased Kowalski's daughter down. She says these men want to kill her for her research into radiation. By the way, those radiation numbers that Chris Walker left us have been verified by the Nuclear Regulatory Commission."

"They did. Great."

"No. not great. So, this thing I see inside the hole, that was releasing all this radiation?"

"That's our guess, sir. Valona agrees with us. It couldn't be anything else. The naturally occurring radioactive minerals in Virginia are minimal."

"Are there are any more of these things in the ground?"

Trisha pointed her phone away. "Can you see those mounds there? I counted three more. All three are gone."

"Gone where?" Wade frowned.

Trisha switched the phone camera back to her face. Her cheeks were drawn and eyes sunk in their sockets.

"We got one man to speak before he died. Dan?"

Wade saw the big man turn around with agility. He looked at the camera as Trisha asked him the question.

"He said Carlyle and the rest of his men are in DC. With the weapons I presumed. Unless the weapons are somewhere else."

Wade felt a cold sweat break out on his forehead. "Where in DC?"

"I don't know," Dan said.

"Who the hell is Carlyle?"

Trisha explained to Wade. He fumed. "What does this Carlyle want? I mean, this is insane. Why on earth would he want to set off nuclear weapons inside his own country?"

Dan said, "I'm not sure. It seems a step too far even for Carlyle. But I think there are other players involved here."

Wade closed his eyes and shook his head. A migraine was rearing its ugly head.

"What other players?"

Trisha said, "We don't know sir."

Wade leaned on the chair and pressed his forehead. "This is just great."

Dan said, "Kowalski was a colonel in the GRU, Russian military intelligence. Murphy had to be the same. Between them, they knew something that no law enforcement agency in USA does. Not the CIA, NSA, ODNI or the FBI."

"Which is what?" Wade barked.

Dan pointed a finger at the nuclear weapon on the ground. "This. These are small, portable, tactical nuclear weapons. I bet my bottom dollar Kowalski and Murphy brought these into the country, or knew who did."

"But they defected to us. Why didn't they say anything about these weapons?"

Dan shrugged. "Ask the CIA. They must have had a handler. This is going back 30 years, in the 80's. Or maybe they fed the CIA other information, and kept quiet about this."

Another woman appeared on the screen. She was wrapped in a white blanket and her left cheek was swollen and bruised. "This is Valona Kowalski," Trisha said.

Valona looked at the phone. She could see Wade's face. "My dad used to bring me and my Mom here when I was young. He told me once that I might need to come here again one day."

"And he never told you why?"

"Maybe I was too young," Valona said. "But he did ask me test my new scanner around here. When I found the high readings, he told me to drop the research."

Wade frowned and shook his head. He made a decision.

"Right, enough of this. All of you, get back here. If this nutjob Carlyle is in DC with a bunch of tactical nukes, we need to neutralize him without delay."

CHAPTER

National Reconnaisance Office (NRO)
Chantilly, Virginia

The NRO is a sprawling, huge organization that designs and operates most of America's satellites. It is the principal provider of Signal Intelligence (SIGINT) to the five main intelligence bodies in the US. Despite being a giant employer, the NRO employs very few federal employees, relying instead on defense contractors.

Rumors abound that the NRO does this because it spies on government employees and federal law enforcement often use the NRO for domestic investigation, which the NRO does not have a mandate for.

The DNRO, or Director of the NRO Zeb Hammett was running down the hallway outside his office. He opened a door and came into the large, semicircular space that NRO insiders called Watcheye, or the central area where all the US satellites in geo spatial and geo synchronous orbit above the Earth feed their information to.

Row after row of analysts sat staring at screens in the darkened office, each going through the image feeds of a satellite. The images were from every corner of the world, but focused especially on flash points like North Korea, the South China Sea, the Middle East.

Zeb's chest was heaving. He had a paunch that spilled over his belt line, and regardless of his lack of fitness, the news he had just been told was enough to make him breathless with panic.

He almost barged into a desk that overflowed with junk food packets from KFC. A black man in his mid-twenties, adjusted his glasses and frowned at the interruption. His forehead cleared when he realized it was his boss.

"Angus," Zeb breathed. "This is important."

"Shoot boss," said Angus, one of the brightest analysts in the MASINT (Measurement and Signature Intelligence) discipline.

"This is top secret. It comes from the FBI Director. Keep it to yourself."

Angus nodded. Zeb said, "We have a situation in rural north Virginia. Thirty miles south of the Shenandoah National Park. There could be a nuclear device there, planted by foreign forces."

Angus' eyes were round like the round framed glasses he wore. "Shit."

"That's what I said. But it gets worse. Some of these weapons could be on their way, or already in, DC."

"What?"

"I know it sounds crazy. But this ain't some film. This is happening."

Angus looked at his screen and his fingers flew over the keyboard. Despite his young age, Angus was one of the few analysts in the NRO who conducted ultra-secret, domestic eavesdropping.

Angus spoke as he typed. "Boss, you want me to get SAR images of Virginia, including DC?" SAR stood for synthetic aperture radar, the modern way satellites covered the earth's terrain. SAR could penetrate clouds and see under water up to a depth of 500 meters.

"Yes. And also, any satellite based communication originating from mainland USA."

Angus stopped and turned around. "Whoa, that's a lot. Never mind the military, all those little sat phones that the public loves to use-

"Just do it, OK. And Angus?"

Angus stopped moving his fingers and turned to face his boss. Zeb's lips were stretched in a grim line.

Zeb said, "This is urgent. We need info on these machines now."

Angus said, "Do you have their GPS location?"

"Yes." Zeb removed a black card from his pocket. A golden line ran through the middle of the card. He touched it to Angus' screen and there was a series of beeps, then a cursor began to flash. Zeb removed his card and a new site opened, asking for username and password. Zeb pressed his card again.

"You are into the ID-300 and MYSTIC supercomputers of the NSA now," Zeb said. "Do not leave this terminal till you have the data I request."

"And when I do I turn the terminal off," Angus said.

"Attaboy."

Zeb sped off to attend a teleconference with the FBI, DNI and NSA directors. Angus pulled the location of the tactical nuclear weapons in Virginia. Then he accessed the data feeds of all five Lacrosse, or terrestrial radar imaging reconnaissance satellites currently in orbit. Each satellite spacecraft had malware built into it to infect satellites of other nations, which in practice meant Russian satellites.

Angus accessed this hacked data as well. Unknown to NATO forces, the Lacrosse satellites also hacked into UK, French and German satellites. Angus compiled all the space based radar data, as well as terrestrial feeds and put them on a graph.

Next, Angus collected all the electric and digital signals originating from the GPS locations of the nuclear weapons, as well as the surrounding twenty mile radius. As he suspected, there wasn't a great deal of signal volume, as this was the foothills Applachian mountain range.

When he had all the information, land and space based, he put them all into one screen, and ran a search. He didn't know what he was looking for. Anything unusual.

It took almost five minutes, time he spent doing a cross word. Employee mobile phones were not allowed inside the NRO offices. Access to social media was also forbidden while on duty.

When the screen beeped, Angus looked up. He had programmed the software to divide the signals into high and low bandwidth and frequency.

One signal stood out like a bell-shaped curve. It was wide in amplitude and higher in frequency than anything else on the screen.

"Gotcha" he whispered. He focused on the signal, tracing it back to the origin, and destination. The origin was in mainland USA, but frustratingly, the signal wasn't more precise. The destination was the nuclear weapon. But in between, the signal had been to another satellite.

Angus's mouth went slack. Fear spread cold tentacles into his limbs. "Oh no."

CHAPTER

Waleed Al-Falaj was pacing the room of his mansion in Alexandria. From the window he had a view of the back garden, which opened into a jetty at the river just beyond the house. The house had been chosen for a reason. The Potomac allowed easy access from Alexandria into DC via boat. Waleed was getting impatient. His life's greatest achievement was about to happen, but he could not be on the field himself. He knew that as the leader, he had to keep himself alive. At the same time, he longed to be close by, watching as the events unfolded.

He had received the code for one of the weapons from Evanovich. Promptly, he had put it to use. He opened up his laptop again, and logged into the software that allowed him access to the weapons database via the satellite.

The five weapons had their distinct entry codes. The codes originated from programmers in the old KGB, and only Evanovich knew of them. The others were either dead, or didn't have access to the code book. But so far, Waleed had only got one, which irritated him. He swore in Arabic. He was too careful. He had agreed to pay Evanovich in instalments. $250 million per nuclear weapon, each with a payload of ten megatons. One of them was enough to incinerate a city of a million people. Reduce it to rubble and ash, and the resulting nuclear radiation that would last for decades. A wasteland. Waleed had agreed to pay in instalments only because he didn't know if the weapons would work. They had been hidden in the Virginia mountains for decades.

Hence, he had paid Evanovich for one weapon and got the code for it. He now checked the weapon's database again. It was still green which meant the weapon was armed. It would go red if the code was wrong and after three attempts, bar him from accessing the weapon entirely.

Waleed was happy that he was in, and the weapon was activated. He glanced at the TV in the corner. CNN and Fox News was on, but there was no mention of a huge explosion near Shenandoah National Park. He returned to his laptop screen. The weapon was still active. What was going on?

He called Carlyle for the third time and left a message. Carlyle would leave one weapon in the Virginia mountains with Valona Kowalski. This explosion would be the test and also get rid of Valona for good. Carlyle had stayed till the weapon was activated, then he took the remaining weapons and left for DC.

Waleed's phone buzzed and he snatched it up from the desk. It was Carlyle.

"Where have you been?"

"I am in position," Carlyle said. "It's all under control."

"Is it? What about the explosion in Virginia?"

Carlyle spoke slowly. "It hasn't happened yet?"

"You fool! You should have made sure the weapon was working before you left."

"It was," Carlyle said in an unruffled voice. "Don't panic."

"I set it on a time of ten minutes. It's been more than an hour. What does that tell you?"

A flashing on the laptop screen caught Waleed's attention. He cut the call and focused. Next to the weapon, the green bar had started to flash. Letters in Russian appeared – words Waleed didn't understand. Then all of a sudden, the entire line went red.

Waleed rang Evanovich, who answered on the first ring.

"Have you heard any news?" the Russian asked.

"No. The explosion didn't happen. What does a red line across the weapon control bar mean?"

Evanovich paused. "Tell me exactly what you see."

When Waleed did, and Evanovich asked more questions, there was complete silence on the other end.

Waleed raised his voice. "What the hell is going on?"

Evanovich said, "Someone has tampered with the machine. If you saw the green bar, then signal definitely got through and activated the weapon. It should have fired. But someone managed to deactivate it. How, I don't know."

"It's not possible. It's-

Waleed suddenly stopped speaking. His head felt like it would burst open through his skull.

Valona and her research.

And that big, tough guy that Carlyle had told him to eliminate. The one who escaped from the safe house upstate. *Dan Roy.*

Who else could it be? Unless Carlyle double crossed him, which he doubted. Carlyle was as much in this as him.

Waleed clutched his head and pulled at his hair. They knew. The great *shaitan,* the devil Americans, they knew.

His great gamble was falling apart. Which meant there was no time to lose.

He called Evanovich back. Waleed was panting like he'd run ten miles. "I'm sending you the rest of the money to the account in Geneva. All of it. I want all the codes, right now."

"Are you sure?"

"Don't question me!" Waleed screamed. "This is God's will. A billion US dollars will be in your account now. Send me the codes as soon as you receive the money."

Waleed clicked on his keyboard and got access to his Swiss account. Evanovich's account was on his contacts list. He hit transfer and watched the transaction go through.

CHAPTER

Bethesda
Virginia

The White House Chief of Staff is one of the busiest men in Washington DC. Aligning the Presidential agenda with the rest of the government isn't the easiest of tasks. Negotiating hard with each one of the government's myriad bureaucracy is paramount, or no work would ever get done in the White House.

Besides, the COS has the President's ear, and can push an agenda right under the President's nose. This makes him the target of every single power broker in the capital of the world's most powerful democracy.

When Matt Durkin took the job, he knew his years as partner in a civil law, and then as the Washington DA, was poor prep for the role. But he had managed the campaign of Derek Auster, his one-time law school friend who went on to become the President. That kind of helped.

He didn't want the job, and only relentless pressure from the President had persuaded him. Now, as he stared at his cell phone screen on a Sunday morning while he spent time with the family, he reminded himself that a resignation wouldn't be a bad idea.

His three-year-old son, John, tried valiantly to get hold of the cell phone. Matt stood, balancing his son on one arm while staring at the phone in irritation. Caller ID was withheld.

No one called the White House Chief of Staff with caller ID withheld.

Matt put his son down and John pulled his father's pants down, almost succeeding. John squealed in delight as his father grabbed the belt.

"Velma!" Matt shouted for his wife. "I gotta take this call."

He answered. "Who is this?"

"Open the TV." A deep voice, distorted by a machine. *What the hell?*

"What? Who are you?"

"Matt Durkin, open the TV now."

"Hey, how do you know - no hang on, how did you get this number?"

"Open the TV and you'll find out. Turn on CNN." The line went dead.

Matt swore under his breath and picked up the remote. The massive flat screen TV on the wall came to life.

A blonde news anchor was staring intently at the camera and speaking.

"In the early hours of this morning, a package was left outside the CNN Washington DC office. Inside it, there was a recorded video tape of a man, a General of the US Army, no less, who claims to have occupied the Capitol Hill Building. He says he is armed, has hostages, and also a lethal weapon that he says can incinerate the entire capital city. Here is the video."

Matt watched open mouthed as General Peyton Mildred came on the screen, standing in the National Statuary Room of the Capital Building.

The remote fell from Matt's hand.

*****

Pentagon
Chief of Staff's Office

At almost exactly the same time, Joint Chief of Army Staff, Steven Harding, answered a similar call from a caller ID withheld number. He too, turned on the TV, and thumbed for CNN.

Harding stared at the screen as his colleague of many years, Peyton Mildred started his speech. The camera showed the rectangular object at the feet of his friend. Harding stepped backwards, tripped over a chair leg, and banged his elbow on the side of the table, sending waves of pain up his arm.

Peyton was speaking. "The blood of our traitors will wash our land clean. Unfortunately, many of these traitors live among us, and proclaim to be the very opposite…

Harding reached for the red land line phone on his desk. When the operator answered, he said, "Nine-oh-nine-oh-three-one."

There was a series of buzz and clicks, then the direct line to the White House Situation Room connected. The duty clerk answered.

Harding had to clear his throat three time before he could speak. "Call the President. We have a situation."

CHAPTER

Dan was first off the helicopter when it landed at Joint Base Anacostia-Bolling, and he helped Trisha out. They ran for the SUV that was waiting at the gates. Colin and the three HRT men followed.

Traffic was light on a Sunday, and the vehicle tore through the streets, headed for the FBI HQ. An agent sat in the front passenger seat and brought them up to date. General Mildred had occupied the Capitol Building. No one seemed to know the real reason why, but Wade Moynihan wanted them in the HQ immediately.

The HRT men rested while Trisha and Dan were shown into the Director's room. Wade was pacing his large office with hands behind his back. A TV was showing CNN's coverage of the breaking news. Three other men that Dan didn't know either stood or sat around a table facing the TV. Wade stopped pacing as they walked in.

"Good job," he told Trisha. "Where's Kowalski's daughter?"

"Valona had mild hypothermia. She's been checked out at George Washington University Hospital."

No one had asked them to sit down, but Dan grabbed a chair and passed it to Trisha. He sat down too.

Wade's eyes softened. "Guess you guys had a rough time."

Dan said, "It wasn't too bad. But some coffee would be nice."

Wade pointed to the corner of the room where a machine sat with a half filled pot of black coffee. "Help yourself. You're Dan Roy, right?"

They shook hands. Wade introduced Dan to the three Divisional Chiefs of the FBI, men whose names and titles Dan listened to with half an ear. He went to the coffee machine, filled two cups with coffee and brought them back to the table.

"Thanks," said Trisha, sipping gratefully.

"Watch this," Wade said, putting the TV on. As Mildred's face and voice filled the scene, Dan forgot to sip his coffee. Then his eyes fell on the device at Mildred's feet.

"Stop!" Trisha spoke before Dan could.

"What?" Wade asked.

Dan said, "That weapon is the same as the one we just disabled."

Wade paused and scrolled back. "Are you sure?"

Dan nodded. "Positive. Same dial in the middle, and the steel tubes coming off it into that lead box. When the machine's activated, the enriched plutonium atoms fire down those steel tubes and crash together in the lead box. The unstable plutonium breaks up and causes the explosion."

Wade asked, "Do you think it's going to work?"

"I'm not the expert. Get hold of Mike Crais at the Pantex Plant. But I wouldn't take any chances."

The fixed line phone on Wade's desk started to ring. He dashed for it, and listened without speaking. When he turned, there was urgency in his voice.

"I have been summoned to the White House Situation Room. They're trying to establish a two way link with General Mildred in the Capitol Building. Dan, Trisha, is there anything else you can tell me?"

Dan said, "The two Arabs who tried to kill me. Did you get anything out of the one who survived?"

Wade grimaced. "He asked for a lawyer and he got a hotshot one too. Can you believe it? Somehow, he has access to a lot of money."

"I know how," Dan said. "His boss is a man called Waleed Al-Falaj. I got to their safe house and they tried to torture me. But I managed to escape. Waleed gave me his name because he thought I was as good as dead. I figure he's the one bankrolling this whole thing."

One of the FBI Director's said, "Let's put out an All Points Bulletin out with his name and description at every American border zone. Can you describe him to me, Dan?"

Dan reeled off what he remembered.

"Have you two got cell phones?" Wade asked. Dan and Trisha nodded.

"Keep them switched on. I might want your help. But the White House was very clear about one thing. Do not attempt to get inside the Capitol Building. Do you understand?"

Dan said. "Sir, I think we can negotiate with General Mildred. That will take time. But Waleed is a loose cannon. Finding him is critical."

Wade said, "I still don't get how he's connected."

"Neither do I. But we have to assume the worst. He knows Carlyle, he admitted as much."

"And by the worst you mean…"

Dan nodded. "He has access to the nuclear weapons."

CHAPTER

White House Situation Room
West Wing Basement
White House

The 5,250 square-foot conference room that is the White House's intelligence nerve center, was slowly getting filled. White House insiders describe the room as the Fusion Place, where hundreds of intelligence documents are daily analyzed and briefed for the National Security Council and the President.

Derek Auster, the President, was the last one to come down the steps of the basement. Like everyone else, he placed his cell phone in the lead lined cabinet of the reception desk. The others stood as he entered, but he waved them down. He walked past the two rows of seats, and took his place at the head of the table. Behind him, and directly opposite him, the wall held six rows of TV screens with videoconferencing capabilities.

From the ceiling, sensors monitored the unauthorized use of personal digital devices. Cameras under the table watched the hands and feet of every occupant, including the President.

"Do we have a two-way connection yet?" the President asked.

Matt Durkin said, "Yes, sir."

"Before we call him. Give me the latest, in case I missed something."

Wade Moynihan spoke. "Two of my agents, with the help of a nuclear weapons expert, just defused one of the weapons in Virgina. We think the same weapon, or weapons are inside Capitol Building."

"What strength are these warheads? And are we sure they work?"

"Mike Crais, the scientist briefed me on the way, Sir. They are about ten kilotons each."

Steven Harding from the Pentagon took over. "Ten kiloton weapons are small fry. They are old, and were designed for tactical use in battlefield. They can be fired from a Howitzer, or a field artillery weapon. Most of the modern nuclear warheads in our submarines are fifty or seventy megatons."

Matt Durkin said, "Sir, I have Mike Crais on the line. Shall I put him on the screen."

"Yes," the President said.

Mike Crais face flickered on the screen banks behind and facing the President. Crais had balding hair, rising up in a quaff at the back. He wore tortoise shell glasses and a crumpled linen coat. His thin face and bushy eyebrows completed the nutty professor look.

"Mr. Crais can you hear us?" Mattt asked.

"Call me Mike and yes I can."

"Tell us about these weapons, Mike."

"As you just heard, these weapons are small fry. But I would remind you, the weapon that demolished Nagasaki was only twenty kilotons and killed one hundred thousand people. A ten kiloton weapon will easily kill half as many, and if more than one is deployed, the destruction is magnified."

"And how do you know about these weapons?"

Steven Harding raised his hand and Mike Crais stopped speaking.

Steven said, "Well, the US Army developed these weapons first. It was in the wake of the Cuban nuclear crisis. If the Soviets landed in Cuba, then we had to be prepared for a ground troop assault. Using tactical nuclear weapons on the battlefield gave us an advantage back then, as the Russians didn't have any. They did enough damage to kill entire Army divisions, without harming civilians outside the battle zone."

Crais said, "Yes, but the Russians learnt of it soon when we tested them. Ten kilotons explosion is still huge and cant be hidden. They developed theirs soon. I would add that these weapons are much lighter, and can fit in a suitcase. Hence the name suitcase nukes was developed for them. Two men could easily carry one. Transport was never an issue."

The President said slowly, "And you say the weapon in Virginia had Cyrillic numbers on them?"

"Not only the serial numbers. The instructions on the side of the weapon are all in Cyrillic, or Russian. The make and look of the weapons fit exactly what we have on our weapons intelligence files. I looked them up last night."

Silence fell like a shroud on the table. The most powerful nexus of men on earth suddenly seemed to be lost for words. Derek Auster was the first to utter what was on everyone's minds. "How did the Russian weapons get here?"

Derek looked at the faces of his colleagues and one by one, each looked down. It was Harding who spoke.

"There was a myth that did the rounds in the late eighties and early nineties."

"Go on," Derek urged.

Dick Lombard, the CIA Director was looking closely at Steven. Steven looked back at him. Both men seemed to know what Steven was going to say next.

"Apparently, some senior members of the KGB and GRU hatched a plan after they devised these tactical weapons. They would smuggle them into mainland USA via Mexico and Canada, two borders where security was lax. Numbering in the hundreds, these suitcase nukes would be strategically placed at areas of national importance."

Steven paused and Dick Lombard took over. "Since this is intelligence from the CIA, I should tell you the rest. These nukes would be controlled by satellite from anywhere in the world. All they needed was a satellite receiver, like a Sky dish on top of any building. Remember this was the eighties, and satellite dishes weren't common place. Neither were computers. Regardless, the Russians thought they could paralyze our country by simultaneously exploding the devices."

Derek leaned forward. "And how did the CIA or the Pentagon come across this information?"

Dick said, "I looked back in our classified documents. It was about the time a spy called Victor Kowalski, a GRU colonel defected to us."

Derek frowned. "The same Kowalski who was killed?"

"Yes, sir."

"Wait. If you knew about this, why didn't you act on it?"

Dick said, "We did, sir." He indicated Wade, who nodded in agreement. "Again, from our classified's files, I learnt that we turned our military installments, airports, harbors, submarines all upside down in 1991. Just after the first Gulf War. But no cache of small yield tactical nuclear weapons was found."

Derek leaned back in his chair. "Instead, they were hidden in the wilderness of our vast country. Clever."

Wade asked, "So, was it Kowalski who told us this? How did the myth start?"

Everyone looked at Harding and Dick. No one had an answer.

CHAPTER

It was the NRO Director Zeb Hammett who spoke up. "There is another important thing to note."

Head swiveled towards him. Zeb said, "We know that the satellite that is communicating with the weapons now is a Russian one. A Zemlya satellite, to be precise. They were launched in the 1980's. But more worryingly, the computer that is communicating with the satellite is within USA."

"Must be one of Mildred's men, right?" Wade asked.

Zeb shook his head. "We don't know. It's possible. They're managing to mask their GPS location, which is frustrating. We breaking down the encryption as we speak. But the danger is obviously they manage to activate a weapon before we get to them."

Derek said, "Has to be Mildred. Get him on the line now."

Wade said, "One last thing. There is an Arab in the mix. We don't know how he links up." Wade told them about Waleed.

"Right, that concerns me greatly. I trust you have your best men on it."

Wade nodded. "Yes sir."

Derek said, "But first we need to find out what Mildred wants."

Matt Durkin was clicking on his laptop. He left the room for a minute to speak to one of the analysts at the reception. Then he came back.

"The line is ready. If he answers, he should be on screen any minute."

*****

Peyton Mildred was staring out the window of the west front of the Capitol Building. Green lawns stretched out in front of him. There was a knock on the door and Carlyle poked his head in.

"Sir, we have a call from the White House. It's them."

Peyton put his uniform jacket on, buttoned it, and fixed the hat on his head. He walked to the corner of the National Statuary Gallery they had set up as a make shift studio.

"Bring Walsh," Peyton said, referring to the Speaker of the House of Representatives. Peyton stood in front of the camera, one of the weapons at his feet. The cameraman made some adjustments with the mic attached to his lapel.

James Walsh was dragged in. His eyes were blood shot red, hair tousled, hands tied behind his back. He was forced into a chair, and Peyton stood behind it.

The cameraman held up four fingers, then one. A TV screen on the floor, next to the cameraman, showed the White House Situation Room.

Peyton cleared his throat. "Gentlemen, as you can see I have a guest."

There was a gasp of surprise as the Speaker, a well known figure amongst politicians, was recognized.

Walsh mumbled something, but the duct tape over his face prevented him from speaking.

Peyton said, "James Walsh is not the only one. I have Senator Archie McHugh as well, and Walsh's secretary, Sam Porter."

The President's voice cut through. "What do you want, Peyton?"

"What I want? I want all of you to resign from your posts and admit you have wronged the people. Admit that you have filled your own pockets and those of your friends. While the real Americans suffer. Will you do that, Mr President?"

Derek said, "You know that's not possible."

Harding spoke up. His voice was beseeching. "Peyton, it's me. Please. This has gone far enough. Come back. We can sort this out, I'm sure."

"No. There's no going back and you know it well enough."
Derek said, "Do you have any other demands?"
"Yes, I do. I want the US Government to acknowledge all the
deniable missions it has undertaken in every corner of the
world. I'm talking south America, the Middle East, China,
everywhere. I want the families of the service men who took
part in these missions to be paid ten million dollars each."
Silence followed his statement. Then there was a buzz of
conversation. Dick, the CIA Director said, "Do you know what
that will do to our intelligence networks? To our assets
overseas? We will betray all of them in one stroke. They'll be
killed, Peyton."
"You put them there, now get them out, Dick."
Matt said, "And our position in the international community
will be tarnished. The setbacks will be serious. Russia and
China will be furious. I'm talking about trade wars and our
diplomats being kicked out. It might even start a war. Think
about what you're saying, Peyton."
"You're fighting a war right now, Matt. All of you. A war that
no one wants or needs. Why don't you fight a real war for a
change?"
Derek leaned forward, his voice suddenly harsh. "Peyton,
enough of this. Surrender now. I can guarantee you will not be
harmed."
"I have three weapons, each of ten kiloton yield. I will
detonate all three at the same time. DC will vanish, and so will
all of Arlington, Bethesda, Alexandria, even Joint Base
Andrews in the southwest."
"Where are the weapons, Peyton?" Harding asked.
Peyton smiled thinly. "There's only one here. The other two
are hidden nearby. You'll never find them so don't even
bother looking."
There was silence again. Eventually Derek asked, "What if we
cannot give you what you want?"
Peyton took out his Colt M1911 and pressed it against Walsh's
head. Walsh whimpered.

"Then I start killing by killing the Speaker. Then Senator McHugh. When they're dead, I detonate the nuclear weapons."

CHAPTER

Waleed Al-Falaj put his AK-47 and hand grenades inside his duffel bag. Fakhar, one of his right hand men, knocked on the door.

"You wanted to speak to me, *Sayidi?*"

"Yes. Gather the men downstairs. I need to speak to them." He walked forward and put both hands on Fakhar's broad shoulders. Fakhar was a former Saudi special forces soldier. He was tall and rangy, and one of the best fighters in Waleed's unit.

"Fakhar, the infidels know what we are planning. They are onto us."

Fakhar narrowed his eyes. "Are you sure, *Sayidi?*"

"The explosion in Virginia didn't happen. The signal did go through and the machine was activated. But someone tampered with it. They got there just in time."

"*Harami.*" Fakhar swore.

"So, there is not one second to lose now. There is another weapon left in Virginia now, and I will activate that. If that doesn't work, then I will have to fire up the others and hope for the best." Waleed's face was contorted, anguished.

"Don't worry Sayidi," Fakhar said. "I'm sure this will work."

"Me too."

Fakhar left to instruct the men. Waleed opened his laptop and looked at the screen. The one billion dollars was still going through. He kicked the chair in impatience. What was the point of having a private swiss bank account if it took so long for the money to transfer?

He focused his rage on the last bomb that remained buried in Virginia. He hadn't told Carlyle about this. Evanovich had given Waleed all the information, for the promise of 1.25 billion dollars.

The KGB plan, hatched in the 1970's had failed. Only a handful of the weapons came across Mexico. The ship bound for Canada sunk. The weapons that made it across were all buried in Virginia, so they could be transported to DC if needed, but remote enough that no one would find them easily.

Only Kowalski and Murphy knew. Both were now dead. Waleed and Evanovich were the only ones with the knowledge, now.

Waleed had the entry codes for the last weapons left in Shadow Valley in Virginia. While he waited for the other codes, he would blow this weapon up.

He didn't know if the Americans were there to defuse this one as well. There was only one way to find out. Waleed didn't care about giving his own position away. The server he was using connected to a line in London, then bounced across Germany, Turkey, a few cities in China before hitting the satellite. It would take a while for anyone to get his GPS location.

Waleed found the weapon, and clicked on it. The usual Cyrillic letters and numbers came up, that he didn't understand. But the blank row started flashing.

Waleed logged into the fake industrial materials website and accessed the email account where Evanovich left the codes. He wrote the thirty-six digit down on paper. Then, with great care, he started to enter the code on the blank row.

CHAPTER

Shadow Valley
North Virginia

The satellite dish that was hidden in the trees had gone unnoticed by Trisha, Dan and the FBI HRT guys. The helicopter pilot hadn't seen it either and he was the best positioned. The fact that the aircraft was being strafed with bullets while he was trying to land had distracted him. Because without a satellite receiver dish, the signal from a satellite, sent as a radio wave thousands of feet high up in the atmosphere, cannot be received. It's the same way that a commercial Sky dish gets its signals.

This dish was put into position by Carlyle and his men. Satellite dishes can come as a collapsible metallic umbrella, and one man slung it on his back, and laboriously climbed a tall fern tree. On the top branch, he had used a drill to hammer nails into the base of the frame, and another man helped him to open the arms of the dish. The dish connected remotely to the weapons, but to be on the safe side, a coaxial cable ran from the tree into the weapon buried underground. When Waleed had entered all thirty six digits of the code and pressed Return, the bar began to flash green. He waited warily. No red bar appeared this time. Instead, the bar stopped flashing and a line appeared in Russian. Waleed thumbed the page on the code book to see if it was written in English. It was.

Weapon activated. Hold on.

Within seconds, the high frequency radio wave from the satellite had hit the receiver dish. The signal travelled to the weapon, and the electric generator started to hum. The fissile uranium molecules, bulky and unstable were whirled around till they gathered critical speed. Then they shot out from the steel tubes at the speed of light.

In the lead chamber they came together at that manic speed and the atoms disintegrated with the most powerful force known to mankind.

The entire clearing, and the log cabins, vanished in an instant. Within one second, every animal within a radius of four square miles died. Hills were flattened, rocks turned to liquid mush. Another second later, the ground temperature rose to eleven million degrees at the site of the explosion. Wildfires broke out spontaneously, and a gigantic fireball rose from the ground and expanded at thousands of miles per hour in a circular pattern.

One second after that, and three seconds after the initial explosion, the shockwave started. This was a wall of pressure, released by the heat, and it expanded outwards with unbelievable force, pulverizing anything that stood to the ground. But nothing stood in its way, which wasn't a good thing, because the shockwave kept propagating till it spent itself, lasting for almost ten square miles.

When the pressure was spent, it sucked in air all around it, hoovering dust, rocks, trees into the epicenter by intense convection currents. This rose higher and higher, above the clouds, and visible to anyone hundreds of miles away as the mushroom cloud that strikes fear into the hearts of all humanity.

No life was possible in the radius of the carnage, but any creature left alive would die from the fallout of the highly ionizing gamma rays, and the radioactive pollutants like Plutonium-239 and Americum-31 that would persist in the atmosphere for decades.

One corner of beautiful Virginia was forever tarnished.

CHAPTER

North American Aerospace Defense Command (NORAD) Cheyenne Mountains

NORAD monitors all flights, terrestrial and atmospheric over American skies and globally. The entire complex is built deep in the heart of the Cheyenne Mountains, built to withstand a nuclear explosion. After the long road tunnel, five feet thick steel doors block every entrance.

The ten thousand open plan floor where all the action happens rests on aluminum springs. In the event of an explosion the whole building will oscillate, without actually breaking.

In the immediate aftermath of the Shadow Valley explosion, a claxon alarm bell started to ring inside the normally quiet hum of the floor. Red alarms started flashing on every screen. Analysts scrambled to their computers.

Above the huge floor rests a glass walled office from where the commanding officers monitor acitivity and watch the giant screens opposite.

General JC Mullins had almost dozed off, reading a paper on the latest satellite research. He shot to his feet and ran to the edge of the glass wall. Pandemonium had ensued on the floor. Hundreds of people spoke at the same time, gesticulated and shouted.

Sargent Bethany Willows, his underling, appeared next to him. She was breathless. "Sir, the seismographs and nuclear sensors have all gone berserk."

"What is it? A missile? Where?"

"In North Virginia, sir."

"Get it up on the map, hurry. Get me the joint chiefs of army, navy and air force. If they haven't told me about a practice explosion, there's gonna be hell to pay." Even as he said the words, the General's heart was sinking. He knew this was no practice run.

"Nothing that we found, sir. And from the amplitude, it looks like a nuclear explosion."

"Oh Jesus. Get me the War Room in Pentagon. And the White House. Right now!"

A moment later, the door slammed open. A man in uniform burst in, panting. "We got an eye witness sir. One of our pilots flying back from Dulles. He says it's a mushroom fireball."

*****

White House Situation Room
West Wing Basement
White House

Derek Auster looked at the rest of his team. "Shall we call his bluff? How do we know these weapons actually work? They've been under ground for years."

Matt Durkin shook his head. "It's a big risk to take, Derek. If they do work we have a huge problem."

"Yes, but what if we could send in a SEAL team inside for a snatch and grab operation? Before Mildred gets a chance to do anything."

"We don't know how many men he has inside."

"Let's find out."

All the phones in the room suddenly started to ring at the same time. The men looked at the desk, then at each other. Matt was the first one to pick up the phone in front of him. His face went white as a sheet as he listened. "Are you sure?" he croaked. The room was deathly still as Matt put the phone down on its cradle gently, like it would explode if put down too quick.

Matt licked his lips and looked around the room, his eyes wide.

"Gentlemen, we have an unauthorized nuclear explosion in Virginia."

*****

FBI HQ
Washington DC

Dan was pacing the floor of the canteen where Trisha and himself had come for some lunch.

"We're wasting time," he said.

Trisha said, "You said that Mildred would negotiate."

"Mildred is not the issue. It's Waleed. But Mildred or Carlyle will know where Waleed is."

Trisha had looked him up on the database already. He had no criminal record, but the Al-Falaj family was well known. Each one of their addresses in USA was being raided as they spoke. So far, there was no sign of Waleed and his men.

Dan said, "Notice how Mildred chose a Sunday to storm the Capitol Building. That tells me two things. He doesn't want to risk civilian lives, and he doesn't have that many men. He won't cause a bloodbath, either way."

"So we should call his bluff?"

Dan stopped and wheeled around to face Trisha. "No. He's still unhinged and dangerous. Crazy even. If he triggers those weapons…"

Dan frowned, then his face cleared. An idea had suddenly struck him. He said, "Hey, you remember how the basement of the WFO connects to the building next door?"

Trisha looked at him warily. "Yeah, and?"

"I know for a fact that the Capitol Building and the surrounding offices are connected by subterranean tunnels. What if we could get into one of those tunnels and reach the Capitol?"

"No, Dan. You heard what Wade said."

Dan slapped his thighs. "Don't you get it? This will get worse from here on. While we waste time talking, Waleed is plotting something."

He walked away from the room. Trisha ran after him. "Wait," she shouted. "Where are you going?"

CHAPTER

Dan ran down the stairs, heading for the lockers where he, with the HRT guys, had stored his duffel bag. He took the bag out and started checking his weapons. He took the Sigs out, ejected their magazines, slapped them in and racked the slides. He checked the HK 416 rifle and finally his kukri. The blade glinted in the light as he thrust the eleven inch knife back into its scabbard and thrust it down the side of his waist. Trisha walked into the locker room, followed by the HRT guys. Trisha's face was pale. Before she could speak, Dan's phone rang. He answered, it was McBride.

"Get your skates on son, we just had a nuke explode in Virginia."

The bag fell from Dan's hands. "What?"

"There was a weapon you didn't get to. Maybe it was unmarked and kept apart from the others. It's not important any more. But someone activated it, and the damn thing destroyed everything in a twelve mile radius."

Dan didn't have to ask McBride how he knew. NORAD had direct links to Pentagon and White House. The entire country would be buzzing now.

Dan leaned against locker for a few seconds. His head felt light, a dizziness came over him. "It's my fault. I was there. I shoul-

"No, its not. You stopped a nuke from blowing up, remember? The problem now is, no one knows. There could be a hundred fucking nukes planted everywhere. How do we get to all of them?"

"Mildred might know. After he all, he was close to Kowalski, right? Was he the handler?"

McBride was silent for a few seconds. "Yes. He was. He got to know Kowalski well. Kowalski was sick, Dan. He was dying anyway. He had lung cancer. Before he died, he told Mildred about it."

"What the hell? Why did you never tell me this?"

"It wouldn't have made a difference, would it? I never knew what Mildred was planning. I wish I did. I was never close to Mildred, only met him at the odd meeting."

Dan digested this in silence. "Still, you don't know how much Mildred knows, right? He could know the location of every single nuke."

"Or he might not. Either way, we need to get hold of him."

"I'm on my way."

"I'm counting on you, Dan. Hell, we're *all* counting on you."

Trisha was staring at him as Dan hung up. She said, "You heard, right?"

Dan's jaws were clamped tight, and his nostrils flared. "I'm going. Alone. Move, Trisha."

She stepped forward. "Please-

"Don't you get it?" Dan said harshly. "We are facing an attack like none before. We have no defense. We can't fight back till we know where they are."

"I was going to say, I'm coming with you."

Dan shook his head. "No. I might not be back, Trisha." He held her eyes and saw a raw emotion flicker through them. She blinked and swallowed.

Colin, the leader of the HRT guys, said, "Dan, we're coming with you." His two colleagues nodded.

Dan said, "Guys, you have orders. I know how it works. I don't want you to get into trouble."

He picked up his duffle bag and made for the door. The others followed.

Trisha said, "I know where the tunnels are, Dan."

He stopped. "I looked at a map of the tunnels as well. It's all online. But Carlyle and his men will guard the tunnels, I know that."

Trisha walked up to face him. "There's something you don't know. The tunnels that run underneath the Capitol Building, Library of Congress and the surrounding offices, aren't the only tunnels."

This was news to Dan. "Really?"

"Yes, really."

CHAPTER

White House Situation Room
West Wing Basement
White House

Derek Auster stood, his face like thunder. On the screen opposite him, JC Mullins was speaking. It was clear the words came out with difficulty.

"Mr President, this is definitely a nuclear explosion. No other bomb would have this sort of impact. We have a Poseidon 700 surveillance aircraft up there now and the images should be with us any minute." Mullins looked off screen as someone spoke to him. He nodded.

His face was replaced by the screen going totally black. Then it cleared abruptly, and a buzzing sound of an aircraft's engine accompanied an image. All they could see was dust in the center of the screen, and in the distance the blue ridges of the Appalachian mountain range.

The dust cleared slowly and the true extent of the devastation became apparent. The gasps from the senior lawmakers was loud and anguished. Matt Durkin collapsed back on his seat, mouth open. He averted his eyes after a while.

All they could see, for miles on end was brown, bare bone earth with a central crater the size of a volcano pit. It seemed like an ulcer had suddenly appeared in the picturesque Blue Ridge Mountains, a massive wound that seemed completely out of place in the surrounding greenery.

Dust and debris flew in the air, with bits of vegetation.

Mullins face came back on screen. His voice was slow, heavy. "I regret to say, there has been some loss of human life. A group of ten hikers were five miles from ground zero. They died almost instantly." Mullins looked down, visibly upset. He composed himself and said, "However sir, we are very lucky. If this bomb had exploded in an urban area, the loss of life would have been at least one hundred thousand. And that's a minimum, sir."

Harding said what was on everyone's mind. "What is there are others?"

Silence followed his question. Derek was still standing. His face was mottled red and a vein was dancing in the middle of his forehead.

Derek said, "General Mullins, increase our crisis level to DEFCON 1."

Mullins raised his eyebrows, "Sir that means-

"I know what it means. We just had the first enemy nuclear explosion in USA. If we're not going to be ready for a full-on nuclear assault now, then when?"

Harding said, "I'm calling Air Force One. You need to be air borne, Mr President, with the Gold Codes." The Gold Codes referred to the encrypted codes that activated the nuclear weapons carried by USN submarines patrolling the Atlantic.

Derek looked at Harding, then at everyone else. "No. I stay here." He waved down their protestations.

To Matt he said, "Get me the Russian Premier on the hot line, now."

Matt reached for the phone. Derek left the Situation Room and entered one of the offices that are adjacent to it. He went in, locked the door, then fogged the window to ensure privacy.

He picked up the phone when it rang.

Matt's voice came on the line. "I got him, Derek. Patching you through."

Derek waited, then a crisp voice came on the line. The Russian Premier spoke excellent English, a fact he took considerable pains to hide from his countrymen in order to appear more patriotic. But a call on the hot line was highly confidential, and connected directly to his office in the Kremlin.

"Pavlov Grigenko speaking."

"Hello Pavlov, this is Derek Auster."

"Mr. President. To what do I owe this pleasure?"

The two men had spoken together before. Despite the renewal of the Cold War, the two men saw eye to eye on several matters. Derek thought he had a good handle on the man. Pavlov wanted the old Russia to rise up as a global superpower, but he didn't want a nuclear showdown. Which was sensible and fine with Derek.

He told the Russian Premier what just happened. In conclusion, Derek asked, "What do you know about this, Pavlov?"

There was a stony silence at the other end. Pavlov said, "If this is your idea of a joke-

"I'm done joking, Pavlov. A Russian tactical nuclear weapon of roughly ten kiloton yield has just exploded in my backyard. I want to know if you guys did this."

"What? No, of course not!" Pavlov wasn't easily flustered, and Derek could sense the man's deep unease. Still, he couldn't be sure it wasn't an act.

"I have raised our defense systems to DEFCON 1. That means we are ready to launch the entire nuclear missile load we have. The first strike will be your missile silos, then Moscow, followed by the rest of Russia. In roughly half an hour, Russia will cease to exist."

"What?" Rage had replaced confusion in Pavlov's voice. "You dare threaten me?"

"No, I'm not. I'm doing it. I promise you Pavlov, we are attacking you. Because you or the KGB planted nuclear weapons on our soil."

"This is lunacy. It's madness. I know nothing about this, I promise."

Both men paused, breathing heavily. Derek said, "Call your cabinet. I'm giving you three hours. Then the Atlantic Strike Force of nuclear submarines will launch their hundred megaton weapons towards Moscow. You want a war, Pavlov? You got one. Three hours. The clock starts now."

Derek Auster put the phone down. His breath came in rasps, and his hands shook.

CHAPTER

Dan was running, with Trisha along side him. Trisha had several calls on her phone. The US Army, Navy and Airforce were at DEFCON 1. Dan didn't know the last time this had happened, but he knew what was coming next. Death and destruction on a scale never seen before. Only the President could raise DEFCON to the highest level, and Dan didn't blame him. First blood had been drawn.

"Which way?" Dan panted. Trisha had parked on the street as it was a Sunday. They got to her car and they piled in, the three HRT guys at the back.

Trisha put her siren on, and several cars honked in protest as she pulled out in front of them. Traffic was minimal compared to weekdays, but DC never slept.

Dan lurched against the side as Trisha did a U turn and headed for Union Station on 2nd street NE.

She said, "The normal tunnels under Capitol Building are used by politicians on daily basis, so they don't have to go in and out of offices. But the steam tunnels are different. They were built a hundred years ago to take hot water and electricity to the Capitol Power Station, situated just under the Exhibition Hall."

"How do you know this? Whoa, slow down!"

Trisha swerved, narrowly missing a pick up truck on the opposite lane, as she overtook a slower car.

"From an old janitor who worked at the WFO for years. These tunnels are smaller and there's asbestos on the pipes, so some people got sick. He was one of them. It was a big deal. He even showed me where the tunnel entrance is, at the station."

"Be grateful for the little things in life," Dan muttered.

The HRT guys were checking their weapons at the back. Dan turned to them. Scott and Leo, Colin's two men were looking inside their bags.

Dan said, "Do you have grenades and flashbangs?"

Scott said, "We also have bolt cutters and NVG's."

"Great," Dan said, relieved. He knew there wouldn't be a spare NVG for him, but he had a flash light.

Trisha said, "The videos so far have come from the Statuary Hall, which is located south of the Rotunda."

Dan had his phone open, looking at an online map of the Capitol. The car screeched to a stop and they jumped out. Trisha's phone rang. She listened without speaking then hung up. She turned to face the four men.

"The President just spoke to the Russian Premier. We have three hours before the first missiles are fired."

*****

NRO Headquarters
Chantilly, Virginia

Angus scratched his head and stared at the screen. He had a live feed monitoring the Zemlya satellite from which the radio signal were coming. He had seen a red line spike up on the graph moments before what he now knew was the nuclear explosion.

His hands flew feverishly over the keyboard. He had already hacked into the access control module of the satellite. From there he could trace the origin of the signal. He saw hundreds of signal, but they all had time stamps. He located the most recent one. He followed it down, and frowned.

The signal fed to an IP address in Stuttgart, Germany. That could pose a serious problem. If the weapons were being activated by this computer, then the operator was in Germany. He located the GPS, and brought up the place on a satellite image.

He paused. The building was a warehouse. He could access images from CCTV inside the building. All he could see was row upon row of mainframe computers. All the computers were on, but not a single human being was present manning them.

It was a click farm.

He used the satellite signal to hack into the IP address. As he thought, the computer had several connections. But the signal Angus was interested in travelled to an IP address in Seville, Spain. Angus went to it, and a sign came up saying he wasn't allowed entry.

Angus opened up the secret folder of malwares and worms that he had devised in his days off. It was his way of relaxing. He let loose all of them at the same time, directed at the Spanish IP address.

"Come on," he breathed as the screen was reflected in his glasses. His fists were clenched. "Come on."

CHAPTER

Colin gripped hold of the metal fork that attached to the rings on the manhole cover and twisted. With a groan, the cover separated from the tarmac. Dan switched on his flashlight and saw the steps to one side, descending downwards. His flashlight beam didn't reach the bottom.

Dan had his chest rig on and carried all his weapons. He started to descend the steps and the others followed. He had tried to make Trisha stay, but she wouldn't listen. She went in after Dan, and Scott was last. He dragged the manhole cover back and pitch-black darkness overcame them till they switched their flash lights on.

Heat was the first thing Dan started to feel. Sweat poured down his forehead and his vest clung to his body. Several times, he had stop to wipe sweat, and Trisha accidentally stepped on his hand.

He was glad to reach the bottom. A slick of water lay on the floor. They were in a roughly ten by twelve foot wide tunnel. Slabs of concrete hung loose from the ceiling. Rusty iron beams were exposed, and water dripped from them. Two sets of pipes ran along the ceiling, these, Dan could tell, were the sources of heat. Hot water for the Senators and Congressmen. Some sections of the pipe were encased in a white material. Trisha had edged close to him as he aimed his flashlight upwards.

"Asbestos," She whispered.

"Let's get moving. We got miles to travel." He wiped sweat on his sleeve and they walked fast in single file.

After ten minutes all of them were panting. The extreme heat and cramped conditions made movement arduous. Dan passed his bottle of water down the line, and it came back empty. They had slowed down without realizing.

Dan wanted to rip his clothes off and walk naked but that would be no help when he got to the other side. He reached behind and grasped Trisha's hand. Her palms were moist.

"You OK?" Dan gasped.

Trisha breathed heavily. "No," she whispered.

They all stopped for a break. Dan checked the time. It was 13.15. Fifteen minutes since they had entered the tunnel.

"How much further?" Scott asked from the rear.

Dan looked at his phone to realize the signal had gone. He swore. "Well, this tunnel only goes to one place guys. Let's get there before it's too late."

With groans of exhaustion, they continued. Dan could feel the heat radiating from his face, burning his skin. His feet were made of lead as somehow, he willed them forward.

Trisha stopped again. Her face was red. "I can't." she gasped. "Go without me."

Dan shook his head. "It's hard for all of us. You can do it."
Trisha covered her face with her hands and leaned against the
damp wall. Her body trembled. Dan hugged her. Then he bent
his knees and lifted Trisha on his shoulders in a fireman's lift.
He walked on, the HRT guys following. He put Trisha down
after a while. She was stronger after the short rest, and she led
them. Colin, Scott and Leo walked after. Dan was slower,
carrying Trisha had taken its toll.
They were leaning against each other as they got to the end of
the five mile tunnel. Their bodies were like sponges, squeezed
of all moisture. A bottle of water was passed around.
Somehow, Dan managed to stand up. He shook his head to
clear the dizziness. The heat was like a malicious cloud
covering his senses, breathing fire into his nose and eyes.
The sooner I get out of this hell, the better.
He grabbed the first rung of the steps and started to climb.
Colin focused a light beam to the top, where, very faintly, a
round cover was visible.

CHAPTER

Waleed screamed in delight. CNN was on, and the views from
the helicopter showed a post-apocalyptic landscape. He
bunched his fists and sank to his knees. He looked towards
heaven and closed his eyes. He rose to his feet swiftly and
checked his laptop once again. The money was still in the
process of being transferred.
Waleed shook his head in impatience. He went downstairs to
the spacious lounge hall where his men were gathered and
ready.
"We have an explosion!" Waleed said and clapped his hands.
His men cheered.
"OK. Let's file out. Fakhar, put two teams in SUV's and
moved down south. We're heading to the Texas safehouse in
Laredo. From there we cross the border into Mexico."

Fakhar said, "*Sayidi*, do you think they now know we are here? Since you fired the weapon?"

"I doubt it, *saadi*. The data from my laptop bounces across four continents and seven computers. If they search my IP address they go on a wild goose chase." Waleed raised a finger. "But, they got to the weapons. Remember that. So, get moving now."

He went back upstairs and checked the laptop again. It was 13.45. When he opened the screen of his online bank account he clapped his hands in glee. One billion dollars had been deposited in Evanovich's account, finally.

He rang immediately. Evanovich answered. "Yes?"

"The money is in your account. Now send me the codes."
*****

Exhibition Hall
Capitol Building

Dan's arms felt so heavy he couldn't lift them. He leaned his body against the narrow iron steps. The cavernous hole beneath his feet seemed to stretch down forever, the darkness only broken by the intermittent flash light. Soon, the batteries of the lights would be dead. He had to get them out of here. But he had barely any strength left. It took all his resolve just to cling on, defying gravity. Somehow, he had climbed to the top and now he had open the trap door. But his arms wouldn't listen to his brain. The heat was less here, thankfully. He felt guilty immediately when he thought of the hell hole the others were stuck in, slowly rotting.

Dan grimaced and put the flat of his palm against the trap door and pushed. Nothing. It was heavy and wouldn't budge. Dan panted. He had come this far and he had to get through. He climbed up till his neck and shoulders were underneath the door. His hands, instead of pushing, now gripped the rungs on the wall. He heaved upwards with every ounce of strength in his body. Veins bulged in his neck, his eyes screwed shut and he bellowed like an animal in mortal pain. There was a sharp crack and the century old trap door moved. But it didn't move enough. It fell back on him. Dan moved down a fraction, then slammed his neck and shoulders into the door again, pushing himself to the limit. The door lifted more this time, and before it could come down, Dan stuck an arm out. He bent his elbow to act as a lever. It was just as well, because the door slammed back, bruising his elbow.
The pain made him see stars and nausea spread in a wave through his body. His feet slipped. He felt himself sliding back down the hole.

CHAPTER

Walnut Room
Adjacent to Meeting Room
Kremlin
Red Square, Moscow

Kremlin is a three walled fortress on the banks of the Moskva river. In the western corner of the Kremlin, overlooking the well sculpted Alexandrovsky Gardens, stands the Armoury Chamber or Arsenal.
Originally the most heavily fortified position in the Kremlin, it is now the designated Meeting Room of the Politburo. Next to the Meeting Room stands a bullet and bomb proof chamber called the Walnut Room. The smaller, urgent meetings were held in this room.

The Russian Premier, a short, stocky man with a bald head looked up at his cabinet. Pavlov Grigenko's voice was quiet. "Well? The Pechora warning center has confirmed what the American President has told me. The US Navy and Air Force are at maximum alert. I have no doubt that nuclear subs are headed to the North Sea as we speak."

The Information Minister, who shared a first name with the Premier, looked up. "All our assets are being contacted in USA and Europe. We need some proof."

The Chief of KGB, a beefy man called Pushkin thumped the table. "Yes. We need proof. It's absolute garbage that this is a Russian weapon. The Americans are looking for an excuse to start a war."

The Interior Minister said, "I agree with Pushkin. If they can threaten us without any proof, maybe you should tell them Pavlov, that we know how to fire missiles too."

Silence. The Premier got up from his chair, and went to the window. He looked down at the beautiful array of topiary shapes in the Alexandrovsky garden, which many said rivalled the Lourve`s. He kept his eyes on the garden and spoke softly.

"I know the US President. He's angry. Very angry. I could feel that. I think he means what he says."

Nobody spoke. Pavlov continued. "He also needs to do something. So would we, if an American weapons had exploded in our country."

Pavlov came off the window and paced the room slowly. His eyes took in the eight members of the Politburo and his cabinet members.

"Where is the War Minister?"

"He's on his way," a minister said. "You said we had three hours. What happens when that time is up?"

"We all die." Pavlov said plainly. He nodded at a Navy Admiral. "Sergei, how many submarines do we have in the Atlantic?"

"The second and third High Seas Fleet are operational, sir. One hundred miles off the coast of Ireland."

"Alert them. If we are hit, then they are to strike back."

"Very well, sir."

Pavlov sat down heavily and stared at the worn oak table. "If these weapons are ours, someone has to know about it." He glanced at Pushkin, who met his gaze, then looked away. Before Pavlov could say anything, the door behind him opened and the stopped figure of the War Minister, Ilyich Gennady, was ushered in.

"I came as soon as I heard," Gennady said breathlessly. "Is it true? A nuclear weapon has exploded in USA?"

"Yes, and they think its ours," Pavlov said. He watched as Gennady frowned, then exchanged a look with Pushkin. Gennady sat down next to the KGB chief.

Pavlov stood. "In two hours time, Mother Russia will receive a blow from which it may never recover. We will fire back and the world will come to an end. If you know anything, tell me now."

He looked pointedly at Gennady, whose face was ashen.

"Gennady?" Pavlov raised his voice. "Pushkin?"

Gennady's hand shook as he ran it through his white hair. *"Troyanskiy loshad."*

"What?"

"A plan called the Trojan Horse. We shipped small yield, tactical nuclear weapons into the USA. We packed them inside bed mattresses and smuggled them across the Mexico border. They could be activated via satellite. In the event of a war, we could annihilate America."

Pavlov banged his fist against the table. "And you never told me this?!" he screamed.

"It was way before your time. It happened in the eighties. To be honest, only a handful of people knew. The agents themselves and me. Most of the agents are now dead. Two defected, and recently they were killed in America. Kowalski and Murphy."

Gennady raised his old, rheumy eyes to Pavlov. "A colonel called Timoshenko was killed recently. I think I know why. Because the only other man who knows and has the code book to activate the satellites, is missing."

"Who is he?" Pavlov snarled.

"Colonel Grigori Evanovich of the GRU."

"You said he has the code book for all the weapons?"

"Yes."

"How many weapons are there, Gennady?"

The old man squeezed his eyes shut, then rubbed them. "Hundreds. The Trojan Horse operation went on for over a decade. We planted weapons all over America."

The gasp of surprise around the table was audible. Pavlov's face was beetroot red. He walked around the table, shoved Pushkin aside, gripped Gennady's coat lapel and hauled him to his feet. For a short man, Pavlov was remarkably strong. He shook the taller, older Gennady.

"Listen to me, you old fool, find Evanovich and kill him, now. Or you and your whole family will die. Slowly."

Gennady gasped. "I'm sorry comrade. He's not at home, and he doesn't answer his cell phone. He never married and has no friends. I don't know where he is."

CHAPTER

Exhibition Hall
Capitol Building

Dan's foot slipped, but his hand, stuck outside, grabbed onto something. It was hard and it creaked on the stone floor as he pulled on it. But it didn't give way. Dan heaved himself up, then sprawled on the floor. The stone cooled his chest as he panted. He took the rifle off his back and lay down, staring up. The trap door was now open, and he knew the others would climb up.

It felt like heaven, being out of the hellish, heat filled tunnel. He could see the top of the rotunda and the massive painting of the Emancipation of Washington. Dan checked his watch. Almost 14.00. Forty minutes had passed since they entered the tunnel. There was no time to lose.

He sat up and did a quick sit rep. It was very lucky the Exhibition Hall was deserted. He would've been a sitting duck for one of Carlyle's men. He took the rifle in his hands and scanned around him. Doors were visible in all directions and stairs wound upstairs from behind him.

"Dan!"

It was Trisha's voice, coming from the tunnel. Dan scooted over, and helped her up. She collapsed against his chest. Dan gave her a bottle of water and gave a hand to Colin who was struggling to raise himself through the opening.

Dan asked Trisha, "Where is the Statuary Hall?"

"That way," Trisha pointed up the stairs. "It's a double story Hall. Better to go up for visibility."

Dan nodded. "You guys rest then catch up with me." He tapped the earbud on his left ear and they did a quick comms check.

Dan stole up the stairs. He stayed low and ran across a hallway, that gave way to another staircase. An arrow with the name National Statuary Hall pointed upwards. The staircase had a narrow entrance. Dan went to ground and shuffled forward on his elbows. He peeked around the corner. The stairs curved upwards and he couldn't see the top.

He listened for ten seconds, then took his suppressed Sig out. He scanned with the weapon and went up. There was a door at the top but it was open. Dan could hear muffled voices. A man stood framed on the doorway, his back to Dan. He held a rifle.

Dan knew the man's job was to guard the doorway. But his attention was distracted, perhaps listening to the voices in the Hall below. Dan put the Sig down and extracted his kukri. Silent as a ghost, he padded up the last stairs till he was close enough to touch the man.

The guy sensed something and turned. Dan's left arm hooked around his mouth and in the same motion, the kukri found the exposed neck. Dan thrust the kukri down savagely, ripping through the muscle and carotid artery. The man kicked with his leg, and Dan, standing on the step, lost his balance. But he didn't lose his kill target. He held the man tight against his chest as he bounced against the wall, pushing the kukri down to the hilt. Keeping fierce pressure on the mouth, Dan tumbled down the stairs.

He collapsed at the landing, jarring his back. The man was dead and Dan cast the limp body aside. The fall had made a noise and it wasn't good. He ran up the stairs swiftly, both ankles hurting from the fall. When he got to the top, he shrank back immediately. There was a balcony, and below, he could see a uniformed man, speaking loudly to another man he recognized as Nick Carlyle.
*****

Peyton Mildred was staring at the TV screen. The reports from CNN was verified by every other channel he flicked on. The image of a giant mushroom cloud, visible from hundreds of miles away was unmistakable. It looked weird, unnatural over the peaceful Blue Ridge Mountains.

He turned to Carlyle, his jaws clenched tight. "Who did that?" Carlyle was watching the TV too. He didn't answer for a few seconds. Then he turned towards Peyton slowly. "It had to happen, General. It shows our intent."

Peyton frowned deeply. "I didn't give the order, Carlyle. Who did?"

Before he could answer, one of the men came forward and saluted. "Sir, it's the White House. The President wants to speak."

Peyton glared at Carlyle. "We haven't finished this yet, Nick." He took the phone and walked a few paces away. "Mr. President."

"General Mildred. I have heard back from the Russians. I know about the Trojan Horse Operation. Kowalski told you everything, didn't he?"

Peyton gripped his forehead. The President was speaking again. "You need to tell us how many weapons there are, General. And if you have the codes for them."

Peyton bared his teeth, then snapped them shut. "I don't think you hold the bargaining chips here, Mr. President. You have to do what I want, first. I want full disclosure to the media about every deniable military operation the US has carried out to this day."

"You know I cannot do that." The President's voice was firm.

"And I'm done talking."

"What do you mean?"

"You want to blow up Capitol Hill? Go ahead. The Army is in the process of removing all civilians out of their homes within a fifty-mile radius. By the time you detonate, the loss of human life will be minimal."

"You're bluffing."

"Go to the top of the Rotunda, or ask your men on the ground. It's happening. I have authorized a mass evacuation of the DC area."

Peyton breathed heavily. The President said, "Bottom line, I am done negotiating. We're coming for you, Peyton. I've ordered a drone strike."

Peyton shook his head. "You've done what?"

The President dropped his voice. "You know what the Capitol Building is, General? It's an idea. An affirmation of our belief in democracy and the rule of law. It's not merely a building." He paused.

"That idea is now under attack. It's not just you, General. There are many others. And by God, my job is to defend that idea. I will do whatever is necessary to protect it. That's why the people of this country elected me." He paused again.

"I'm giving you half an hour, General. If I don't hear from you, the drone strikes are authorized."

With a click the phone went dead.

CHAPTER

Peyton removed the phone slowly from his ear. He stared outside the tall windows at the green lawns. The tall fountain in the middle rose like a finger to the sky.

Carlyle stepped in front of him, blocking the view. His tone was hard. "What did the President say?"

Peyton gazed at him. Like so many things in his life, his choice of commander for this mission had also been a disappointment. Anger flashed inside him, with the bitterness of failure. But with it, also came a calm acceptance. He had done what he had to. He would not go quietly. In fact, he would raise hell.

He said, "It's over."

Carlyle frowned deeply. "What do you mean, it's over?"

"They called our bluff. In half an hour, if I don't surrender, then they bomb us. Therefore, we surrender."

"Surrender? What about the weapons? We could pulverize DC into rubble."

Peyton glared at him. "Have you lost your mind? Did you even think I was going to do that? Kill all the people in DC? I might be a revolutionary, but I'm not a psychopath!"

He continued. "The weapons were a ploy to negotiate with them. They won't listen, or talk. Therefore, we surrender." Peyton lifted the cell phone in his hand. Carlyle reached forward and snatched it off his hand.

Peyton gasped and fought with him. Carlyle was younger, and in better shape. He threw Peyton backwards. Moses grabbed Peyton, with another man. Moses forced Peyton to his knees.

Peyton stared at Carlyle, appalled. "What are you doing, Nick?"

"You are weak, General. Feeble. You disgust me. It's a good job I found someone with more guts than you."

"What are you talking about?"

Carlyle knelt till he was level with Peyton. "The codes. Where are they?"

"Who fired that weapon in Virginia?"

"The man I told you about."

Peyton gasped. "You sold me out? To who?"

Carlyle didn't answer. "Give me the codes. But my contact will have them already. He's getting them from Russia. He's an Arab. I only had to tell him about the plan. He knew who to contact. The Arabs are close to the KGB, as you know."

Peyton was aghast. "What have you done? You fool!"

Carlyle said, "It's you who's the fool. We could have made millions from this, and now we get nothing. One last time. Where are the codes?"

Peyton moved quickly. He leaned against Moses, and grabbed the gun at Moses belt. It came free and Peyton cocked and fired it at Carlyle. He missed. Carlyle fired back and a blinding flash of pain burned suddenly in Peyton's chest. He fell backwards but still managed to squeeze off two more shots. They the hit the glass and the window shattered. Moses pointed his gun to fire as well. But his head splintered into a hundred pieces of blood and bone fragments as the 7.62mm slug from Dan's rifle found its target.

CHAPTER

Angus's feet were on the table and his head was leaning back. His mouth was open and his eyes were closed. He was fast asleep.

The four graphs on his terminal were still plotting data actively. Line after line of programming code, in his favorite language of C+, ran down the screen. All of them were his personal malwares, directed at the computer in Seville, Spain. The lines halted suddenly, and there was a loud ping. The ping kept on, and Angus woke up. He moved fast, and almost fell off the chair. He put his feet on the floor, dropping sheafs of paper, discs and old packets of fast food.

He adjusted his glasses and stared at the screen. White letters beeped on a black screen.

Access Granted.

"Yes, baby," Angus whispered. He pulled up his chair and his fingers flew over the keyboard.

*****

At precisely the same time, Waleed Al-Falaj stared at the screen of his laptop. The email from Evanovich had an encrypted folder, which he opened with his software. Row upon row of data appeared. Every row had a thirty-six-digit code, with the location of the weapons next to it.

For Los Angeles, California, he could see three codes, which meant three weapons were placed either inside, or close to LA. It was likely they were clustered together, because the weapons needed access to a satellite receiver dish. Waleed didn't know if all the weapons were operational, but his men had been to the major cities up and down the Eastern Seaboard over the last year. They had made sure that a satellite dish was connected to the weapons. No one suspected two men setting up a satellite receiver dish outside an office building.

It would take a long time to make sure all the weapons were working. Waleed didn't have that much time. The Americans were on to him.

Let them come, he thought with a smile.

He packed up his laptop, and the extra battery pack. He connected the portable Wifi to the laptop. There was an unlocked sim card inside the Wifi, and it was brand new, untraceable. Waleed would destroy both the laptop and the sim card after the job.

He went downstairs, carrying the laptop and wifi inside an armor plated bag. Fakhar was waiting for him. The others had left already. They went to the back door from where the grey waters of the Potomac were visible.

Together they marched down the garden to the rigid inflatable boat or RIB that was waiting at the jetty. Fakhar helped Waleed on board. The twin 500L engines of the RIB rumbled, the nose lifted, and the boat took off at speed. It was heading down the Potomac for Chesapeake Bay.

*****

National Statuary Hall
Capitol

As soon as Moses dropped, Dan fired at the others. He was behind one of the bannisters in the upper hall, and the men below had no chance. The bodies jerked and shook as lead pumped into them. But Dan had one disadvantage. He was on his own. He didn't get all of them. He counted seven that he could see, and got five, but the other two, including Carlyle, took cover. All three fired back at Dan. Bullets whistled over his head, and picked out chunks of famous statues.

Dan knew he had to move. A grenade lobbed at him would be the end. He fired a long burst, then dived backwards into the stair case. A shadow appeared, weapon pointed. Dan gave it a second to see if it was any of the HRT guys, then he fired twice, rapidly. The man tumbled down the stairs. Dan followed, weapon raised.

He fired at the shape that appeared around the bend, but missed. Dan stopped at the curve and looked over. Bullets splattered plaster over his face. He dropped and fired back. The bullets stopped suddenly and he heard footsteps running away.

Dan moved. He didn't expect the figure that barged into him. The gun was pulled, but he held on. The figure pushed him back and they tumbled on the stairs. A blinding blow rocked Dan's head. His eyes swam and dimmed. Fingers grasped his throat and he gagged.

A voice close to his ear said, "Well well, if it isn't Dan Roy." Dan grabbed the hand at his throat. The pressure was increasing, he was being throttled to death. The gun had fallen from his hand. He reached for his belt line and his fingers circled around the butt of the kukri. He pulled it out and stabbed the figure choking him. The knife pierced the lower ribs at the side. The man screamed and the pressure on Dan's neck eased.

Dan rose up, smashing his body into the man, then both of them against the wall. He withdrew the kukri and plunged it in again, in the soft of the belly.

Then he saw the face and the scar on the left cheek. Carlyle.

Carlyle had a gun in his hand but Dan had the advantage now. He slapped it away, and punched Carlyle across the face. He made sure Carlyle had no access to weapons, then got his face close to his.

"Where are the weapons? Where is Waleed?"

Carlyle grinned, his face deathly pale now from the loss of blood. "You'll never find out."

Dan pulled the knife out of Carlyle's belly, pushed his head back on the floor and with the tip of the kukri, cut under the left eye. Carlyle screamed, squirmed, but Dan held him down.

"Where are the weapons? Where is Waleed?"

Carlyle screamed as the kukri moved into the eye socket. The eye ball lifted, a ghastly white, bloodstained orb.

"Get ready to lose your eye, Carlyle," Dan said.

"Fuck you."

Dan pushed the tip in deeper, turned and sliced it down. Carlyle screamed louder and thrashed but Dan was stronger. His teeth were clenched tight, his left elbow was rammed against Carlyle's neck. Behind him, gunshots echoed and the blast of a grenade made him flinch.

"Where are the weapons? Where is Waleed?"

Dan moved the knife to the right eye, and knicked blood at the base.

"Wait," Carlyle said. "The weapons are in the Exhibition Hall."

"How many?

"Two. And there's another two in the Senate Chamber."

"Where is Waleed?"

"He has a house in Alexandria. That's all I know. He got the codes from Grigori Evanovich in the GRU."

Dan stood. He took out his Sig and fired twice in Carlyle's chest, then once in the head.

CHAPTER

White House Situation Room
West Wing Basement

Wade Moynihan spoke on the phone, then stood abruptly. The faces around the table glanced at him. Wade cupped a hand on the receiver. He pressed a button on the phone to make it loudspeaker mode.

Gunshots and the sound of screaming suddenly filled the room. Everybody hunched forward.

Wade said, "This is a team of FBI operatives who are in the Capitol now."

Derek looked stunned. "Under whose authority?"

"I don't know, sir. I told my agent not to go in. But I think they disobeyed my order."

Harding said, "Do you know what's happening in there?"

"Yes, just hold on. Trisha, can you hear me?"

The sounds of gunshot were louder and then there was a scream. Footsteps ran, then the sounds became muffled. Trisha's voice came on the line.

"Sir, is that you?"

"Yes. Give us a sit rep."

"Mildred is dead. He was killed by his own men, led by Carlyle." Trisha told them the story. "We came up behind Dan, and killed the rest in the Hall. But there might be others around, we don't know."

"Who's Dan?" Harding asked.

Wade said, "A Black Ops guy who's been helping us. He worked for Intercept."

Harding's brow cleared. "McBride," he whispered under his breath. No one picked up on what he said.

Trisha continued. "There's two weapons in the Exhibition Hall, which we are still looking for. And another two in the Senate Chamber."

Wade asked, "Can they be activated?"

"It depends on who has the codes to fire the weapons. Hold on." There was a delay, then Dan's voice came on the line. "This is Dan Roy. Peyton Mildred and Nick Carlyle are both dead. I found the code book in Mildred's pant pocket, sewn to the inside. The letters are in Russian with handwritten English translation."

Derek said, "Dan, this is the President. If you have the code book, that is great news. What the hell happened in there?"

"Mildred was bluffing, sir. He was never going to fire those weapons. But Carlyle sold out to the Arabs. A guy called Waleed Al-Falaj. He is the main threat now, because he has the codes. And he can fire the weapons from anywhere in the world, if we don't get to him."

The temperature dropped several degrees inside the room.

Dan said, "Carlyle said Waleed is in Alexandria. I don't know if that-

Another phone rang, cutting Dan off. Zeb Hammett the RNO Director reached over and snatched the phone off its receiver. He listened intently, then looked up.

"I got news. My analyst has got the IP address of the computer used to fire the Virginia weapon. He also has a location on it now."

Dan could hear the exchange. He raised his voice on the line. "Where is it? That has to be Waleed's computer. It was him who fired the nuke."

Zeb said, "If this is Waleed, he has at a riverside mansion in Alexandria."

Dan said, "I'm heading down there now. I need transport. Can a bird pick me up from the East Lawn of Capitol?"

Derek said, "I'm dispatching Air Force One's helicopter to you, Dan."

CHAPTER

Marine One, the US Marine Corps VH-60N "White Hawk" helicopter, hovered over the East Lawns of the Capitol. The distinctive, white liveried aircraft is one of the most well-equipped birds on the planet. Its defensive capabilities include a radar jamming and deception system to ward off anti-aircraft missiles, and an array of electronics against nuclear electromagnetic pulse.

The staccato, rhythmic beats of its rotors flattened the grass as Dan watched from behind a portico. Trisha was standing next to him.

"I'm coming with you," she said.

"No," said Dan. "The HRT guys need your help."

All four of the weapons had now been located. They were identical to the one Dan had defused in Virginia. Each one was connected by a cable to a circuit board. The boards in turn, connected to the satellite receivers in the Capitol. Colin, Scott and Leo were still chasing the cables down, hunting for the circuit board. It was a time intensive task, and Dan had directed them to the satellite receivers.

Dan said, "The satellite dishes in the Capitol Building need their connections broken. If they are intact, the weapons could still fire. Stay here and help them."

"An entire company is on its way from Fort McNair. So are military architects who have detailed plans of the building. What good will I do?"

Marine One had landed, and the sound was loud even at this distance. Dan said, "Waleed won't be alone. He knows his game's up. This will get messy."

"Are you trying to scare me or imply I'm not good enough?"

Dan shook his head and looked away. He glanced at his watch. It was past 14.30. The clock was ticking, and any second, the weapons could blow up if they didn't get to Waleed. He had access to hundreds of these bombs across the USA. Dan didn't know how many of them had satellite links, but he did know one thing – even one more nuclear explosion would drive America and Russia to nuclear Armageddon.

"Let's do this."

Bent at the waist, Trisha and him ran for the white bird. Two Marines helped them on board. Within seconds the powerful, compact bird was airborne. Dan was hooked on to the comms system, and he asked the pilot to connect him to the Situation Room.

Matt Durkin answered. "Marine One?"

Dan introduced himself. "Am I on the loudspeaker?"

"Yes you are. Go ahead, Dan."

"Even if we find Waleed before he activates any of the weapons, we haven't dealt with Evanovich. He sold the code book to Waleed. Mildred got his from Kowalski. I have Mildred's code book on me, right now. I'm leaving it with the pilot for safekeeping. But we need to lean on the Russians to find Evanovich. He can start firing the weapons himself, or sell it to someone else."

"Roger that, Dan." Matt said.

*****

Stafford
South of Alexandria, Virginia.

The RIB was bobbing up and down in the water. An armed man sat at the wheel of the moored boat. He kept his AK-47 out of sight but kept a close look around him. Fakhar and the rest of Waleed's men had taken up position outside the disused warehouse. Stafford was on old harbor town, and the harbor was last used a hundred years ago. The ruins provided a good hiding place on the Potomac's banks. They had stopped to buy food and supplies, and two men had hired a car into town for that purpose.

Waleed wanted to use the time for a different purpose.

His men took up station at every entrance of the warehouse. Inside, Waleed sat down cross legged on the floor. He charged up the laptop and connected it to the portable WiFi. He waited for the signal to connect. He smiled when the green signal came on. He was online.

Waleed accessed the software on his laptop that contained the weapon control module. He tested a signal to the Zemlya satellite, it worked. Waleed opened the file that contained the codes. He chose the weapon for New York. Five weapons were planted in New York, and he chose the one planted in an office in the Lower East Side, one he knew was connected to a satellite dish.

The destruction this weapon would cause, and the loss of human life, would garner global attention. Waleed's name would become famous, at par, or above Bin Laden himself. Waleed bent over his laptop and with great care, started inserting the thirty-six-digit code.

*****

National Reconnaissance Office
Chantilly, Virginia

Angus stood, stretching, but his eyes were fixed on the screen. He had used a program called Sky Crawler to get the geolocation hook on the IP address of Waleed's laptop. He found another WiFi address at the same location. But instead of a fixed line, this WiFi was operated by a SIM card. Immediately, Angus had used SkyCrawler to latch on to the SIM card. It had proved a wise move. Because the IP address started using the using the SIM card to access cellular data networks via the new WiFi. Angus didn't understand why Waleed switched his router, but he could guess. The SIM card meant the WiFi was now mobile. Waleed was on the move.

Every WiFi has an identifying number called MAC. Whenever the WiFi is turned on, the MAC number can be accessed without the user knowing. The MAC numbers are unique, and no WiFi on earth has the same MAC. Once Angus got the MAC number, he could now track Waleed's movement via the WiFi.

Angus had also reverse engineered his way into the IP address, which he could follow even if the connection was closed. It was open currently, and Angus had found his way into the email box. He looked at the recent emails, and one in particular caught his attention.

Emails from a ball bearings manufacturing company, located in Vladivostok, the far eastern corner of Russia, near China. Waleed had accessed an email inbox at this company's website on a regular basis. He never received any emails from the company, but visited this inbox regularly. Angus clicked on one of the messages that Waleed had downloaded to find the message encrypted. Suspicions aroused, Angus unleashed his decryption software at the message.

At first, he didn't know what he was looking at. Endless rows of numbers. He scrolled to the right of the page and saw names next to every row. They were in Russian, but he translated the page quickly.

The names were in alphabetical order. It started with Anaheim, South California. As he looked down, a chill spread down his spine. The numbers looked like codes, and this could only be one thing. A list of the weapons planted in mainland USA.

Angus knew what he had to do. He had to stop the WiFi connection from working. That would prevent Waleed accessing the weapons software control module. But stopping a WiFi from working was easier said than done. The only way to do it was to destroy all cellular data networks close by. If all the masts were destroyed, then the SIM card wouldn't be able to get data.

But neither would all the phone lines and WiFi routers in that area. Working quickly, Angus brought up a list of cellular data masts in the area. His heart sank. There was more than 300. He didn't know which ones needed to be destroyed – and neither did he have the means. Taking down 300 data masts would cause a major outage. This was way above his pay grade. Shooting down telephone masts was an act of war, and with the collateral damage it would case, virtually impossible. Angus reached for the phone. He had direct access to the phone in front of Zeb Hammett in the Situation Room. Zeb answered immediately. Angus explained the situation about the WiFi.

"Waleed's on the move." Angus peered at the map with the flashing green dot on his screen. "He's stopped at a riverside town called Stafford, ten miles south of Alexandria."

"Well done. But I don't know if we can cut the connection. Hold on," Zeb said. "I'll call you back."

He came back on line after five minutes. "No can do, Angus. Shooting down those masts can cause casualties, not to mention the communication disruption which could adversely affect our own operation."

"So what can we do? I think this guy is getting locked and loaded."

"We've sent a man down there. Dan Roy. He better succeed, that's all I can say."

CHAPTER

The rotors of helicopters are notoriously noisy, making them unsuitable for a stealth approach. But new modified rotors, made with lighter material, and rapid absorption of the air disturbed by the rotors, has achieved just that. Modern birds are lighter, and make far less sound. Like the birds that attacked Bin Laden's compound, their exterior shapes are different, designed to deflect radar signals.

Marine One was one such bird. In addition to being stealthy, it is also enabled with Hellfire missiles and Gatling machine guns. Trisha held a tablet device in his hands, and it was giving them the real time GPS location of Waleed's WiFi. They were almost at Stafford. The green dot had stopped moving, and Dan found that ominous. Waleed was stationary which meant he was doing something on the laptop. Like activating another weapon.

He checked his watch. 14.30. Trisha was staring down at the river and land below her. She looked up and he read the tension etched in her face.

Dan said, "I'm rappelling down when we get there. These guys can provide covering fire."

Trisha nodded. Dan noticed she had her weapon out. Their headphones buzzed.

"Team this is Marine One." It was the co-pilot. "We will be visible from Stafford in five minutes. What do you want me to do?"

"The GPS shows he's very close to the river. He moved down the river as well, so he must've used a boat. Is this area populated?"

"No, sir. It's an industrial area, and its not been used for many years. The civilian town is ten miles inland from the river."

Dan thought to himself. Although the place was unused, there was a chance of innocent casualties if a Hellfire missile was deployed.

"Use the Gatling's to fire at the target as soon as we are within range. Keep up firing as I rappel down."

"Roger that."

Dan hooked his lanyard to the chain above the door and put his leather gloves on. He did a quick weapon check.

"Let me get a satellite image up," Trisha said. The pulsing green dot was now inside a low, flat roofed building. Similar buildings lay around what seemed like a large yard.

Trisha said, "Could be a warehouse." She pointed further up the map. "There's a road connecting this area to the town."

"One minute," said the co-pilot.

"Could be a warehouse, or some other abandoned building. We fire as soon as we can, just to buy some time if nothing else."

"Thirty seconds."

The bird tilted to the right and they saw the river meandering in the same direction. The old harbor came into view. Rusting buildings and the carcass of two trawler boats were clearly visible. So was a black RIB that looked brand new.

Dan saw men running out from a warehouse, and they were armed. He saw them lift their weapons and fire at the bird, but the bullets didn't reach. A man knelt on one knee, a rectangular object at his shoulder.

"Ten o clock, RPG!" Dan shouted.

There was a whining sound, and the Gatling machine guns started chattering, their round barrels spouting fire. The figures shook and fell on the ground, bullets strafing the ground, raising dust marks.

"Aim for the GPS signal," Dan shouted, as the bird lost altitude rapidly.

*****

Waleed was halfway through entering the code when he saw a red alarm button pop up at the bottom of the screen. It was his malware detection software. Waleed frowned and clicked on it. His eyes widened. A system had accessed his WiFi MAC code, and placed a tracker app on it. Waleed deleted the tracker app instantly. Almost at the same time, he heard a thumping sound coming above his head. It took him three seconds to realize it was a helicopter. He put the laptop down and ran to the window with his AK-47. His worst fears were confirmed. A white bird was bearing down on the warehouse. He didn't understand why he hadn't heard it till now. His men were running out into the yard, and the RIB driver was firing already.

"Shoot it down!" Waleed screamed at his men. "Use the RPG."

Waleed picked up the laptop, portable WiFi, battery charger pack and shoved them into his backpack. The yard echoed with the rattling of heavy ordnance, and the rusty warehouse walls shook. Waleed ran out the back where a path led to the road. The two hired cars were parked there, keys in ignition. One of his men was guarding the cars.

"Get in and drive," Waleed shouted as he got in and slammed the door shut.

*****

Wind whipped around Dan's face as he rappelled down to ground. The firing kept up from the bird, and he ran for the nearest cover he could find. It was a shed, and he dived behind the door, sliding to the floor. Bullets pinged against the iron surface, shaking it. Dan spotted two men behind the warehouse, firing at the helicopter. He aimed and took them down with his HK 417.

His earbud chirped. The co-pilot's voice said, "Figure ran out of back. A blue Honda Civic is driving off."

"Stop them. By any means necessary."

Dan flattened himself on the floor and switched to automatic mode. The bird veered off above his head, the bullets from the powerful Gatling gun stopping suddenly. They were replaced by the 7.62x51mm rounds from Dan's weapon, and the remaining bodies jerked as the bullets pumped into them.

Two weapons were still firing from behind cover. Dan unhooked two fragmentation grenades and lobbed them one after the other. He ran backwards and took cover. The ground trembled with the impact of the grenades as they exploded. Dust and debris rained down on him.

When Dan lifted his head, he heard nothing but the drone of the bird above him, fading. He did a quick 360 degree sit rep, then ran as fast as he could towards the road. He was just in time to see bullets rain down from the bird again. There was a loud bang as the tires exploded and the car jolted to the left, then stopped. The rear door opened and a figure ran out. A backpack bobbed on his back. It was Waleed.

"Take him down," Dan said on the microphone. The Gatling fired but Waleed ducked and weaved, then ran inside an abandoned wooden building that looked like a deserted shack. Dan moved forward. The shack had a porch, wooden steps, and windows without glass. Waleed had shut the door. The bird hovered overhead, the rotors deafening.

Dan looked inside the car – the driver was slumped in one corner, bleeding from the head. He shot him once for good measure, then approached the shack. The time for stealth had long gone. If he had to take a bullet to the chest, so be it.

Dan jumped on the porch and crouched below a window. He raised his head and looked inside. He expected bullets but saw Waleed sat against a wall, fingers moving briskly on the laptop keyboard.

Fear gripped Dan in a vice like grip. He knew exactly what Waleed was doing. "Waleed," he screamed and pointed the muzzle of his rifle.

Waleed looked up, and their eyes met. To Dan's horror, a slow smile spread across his lips.

Too late, Waleed mouthed.

He lifted a finger in the air, poised above the keyboard. Dan knew he was going to press Enter. He fired immediately. The round destroyed Waleed's head, reducing it to a bloody pulp. Waleed slammed back, but his finger had already descended on the keyboard.

CHAPTER

Vladivostok

Far Eastern Russia

Vladivostok is so close to the Chinese border in the north east of China, it might as well be a Chinese city. But emphatically, it is not. For strategic reasons, it is one of Russia's most important ports, and where the Russian Navy has one of its largest bases. To the left, lie the islands of Japan.

It is also beautiful and a major tourist spot and getaway. For this reason, Colonel Grigori Evanovich had chosen Vladivostok as his last refuge in Russia. In his small apartment overlooking the large harbor, he hunched down in front of his laptop. He could see the money in his Swiss account. 1.25 Billion US dollars took time to transfer, even by Swiss standards.

When it had, and he had verified the online transfer by speaking directly to the bank, he hadn't hesitated to transfer the codes to Waleed Al-Falaj. Waleed could do whatever he desired with them.

But Grigori wasn't a fool. He didn't underestimate the Americans. He also knew the KGB never forgave those who betrayed the Motherland. Waleed might succeed, but that increased the chances of the Americans finding out and blaming Russia for it.

He had to escape. The one-way ticket to Tokyo was resting next to his laptop, and the ship was waiting in the harbor. Tourists travelled frequently between Vladivostok and Japan. Grigori would disguise himself as an older man, and melt into the tourist district of Tokyo.

Grigori checked the email box of the industrial ball bearing company he had based here. There was no company, the IP address was merely his computer, fixed to the landline. It was safer to open an email account here than in Moscow. He could see that Waleed had accessed the inbox and downloaded the PDF with the codes in it.

Grigori sighed. He turned the news on. What he saw took his breath away. The explosion in Virginia was in every channel he flicked through. CNN, BBC, Al-Jazeera.

Grigori stood up, excitement running like fire through him. This was what they had wanted in the old days. They – the KGB. He knew he had sold out to the Arabs, but if the old guys were around today, they would be applauding him. Finally, someone had the guts to bring America to its knees. Feverishly, he sat down and accessed the software that housed the satellite control module. Any minute now, he knew, the Americans would get hold of this site and shut it down. Or corrupt it somehow. Was it not his duty to help Waleed? After all, he had the codes as well.

Grigori grinned to himself. If Waleed was activating the weapons in the Eastern Seaboard, he would try in California. He opened up the software, logged in and selected the weapon for Los Angeles. He rubbed his hands together, then started to enter the code.

A knock came on the door. Grigori frowned and looked up. He wasn't expecting anyone. He reached for the Makarov handgun and flicked the safety switch off. He pointed the gun at the door and didn't answer.

"Colonel Grigori Evanovich, we know you are in there. Please open the door." A voice said in Russian.

Sweat broke out over Grigori's forehead. The SVR had found him. How, he didn't know. He stared at the laptop. Could it have been this IP address in Vladivostok? Had the Americans found the email inbox he shared with Waleed?

"Colonel, open the door now!"

Grigori remained silent. He heard the sound of weapons being cocked. At that instant, Grigori knew he was as good as dead. His eyes fell on the blinking cursor, in the code box for the weapon.

Before he died, he would give the world a gift they would never forget.

He picked up the laptop and moved away from the door to one corner of the room. His fingers moved swiftly. He started to enter the code.

Bullets pounded against the door and the rattle destroyed the lock. There was an explosion, and the door burst free from its hinges, falling on the floor. Dressed in black combat gear, three Spetznaz soldiers burst in, brandishing their weapons in every direction.

Grigori concentrated. He was up to the twentieth digit.

"Stop!" one of the soldiers said.

Grigori didn't pay any heed. He grit his teeth and carried on. He was at the twenty fifth digit when the first bullet struck his elbow. With a cry his hand fell off. The second bullet pierced the lower neck, destroyed the trachea and almost cleaved his cervical spine in two.

Grigori Evanovich was dead before he hit the floor.

CHAPTER

Dan saw Waleed's hand drop on the keyboard.

"No!" Dan screamed. He jumped headfirst through the window of the deserted shack. Rolling over, he was by Waleed's lifeless body within seconds. He picked up the laptop, ripping his gloves off. The screen showed a program a lot like a spreadsheet page. Each row had a number, then a box. The box on the top row was filled and next to it there was a green and red button.

With a thumping heart, Dan realized that every box was empty, save the top one. He could tell that Waleed had just filled the box in. But had he pressed the green button? The writing on the buttons were in Russian. The green button said Go while the red button said Abort.

Dan took a deep breath, then pressed the red button. The button started to flash and a red line appeared, travelling through the code. Dan got his phone out and called the Situation Room. He asked Zeb Hammett to put him through to Angus. Dan flicked to video mode, and Angus could see Waleed's laptop.

Angus said, "I think you disabled the weapon. But to be on the safe side, go to Settings."

"How do I do that?" Dan asked.

Angus talked Dan through. The software was soon shut down and blocked from further entry. Dan shut the laptop down and carried it carefully. He checked Waleed once. Definitely dead.

Marine One had landed in the field opposite. Dan took his weary legs down the steps of the shack. Trisha came running up to him.

"Is he dead?" She asked.

Dan nodded. "I think we got here just in the nick of time. Do me a favor. Ring New York to find out there hasn't been an explosion. Waleed armed that weapon. I shot him before he could fire it."

While Trisha rang, and the co-pilot went inside the shack, Dan sat down and leaned against the woodwork. He suddenly felt bone tired, like his body couldn't carry him anymore. He looked up as Trisha stepped closer.

"It's OK," she said. "No explosion in New York, or anywhere."

CHAPTER

Valona Kowalski was dressed in black. The Russian Orthodox priest read the hymns as the coffin was lowered into the grave. Valona watched with a stony face. It was best to keep her mind blank, emotions at bay.

She now understood everything. It was ironic that her chosen career had led to her father's murder. She didn't want to think of it that way. But it was the truth. It was also true that Victor Kowalski hadn't pushed his daughter to test her radiation sensors in Virginia, the weapons would always remain hidden.

It was her father's actions that started this ball rolling down the hill. She wiped a tear drop as it ran down her cheek. So much for keeping emotions on hold.

The thought she couldn't bear to live with was her father's guilt. She had seen it in his eyes when he came to warn her to keep her research secret.

I am so sorry, he had whispered.

Now she knew he was doing the right thing. He wanted the world to know, and she wondered often if he would come out one day and admit his role in it. Now, she would never know. He confided in Peyton Mildred, who went off to do something no one could have imagined. Valona thought that Mildred and her father were similar in many ways. Maybe that's why the two men were friends. Both tortured, twisted, broken. She hoped they now found their peace.

The priest beckoned at her and Valona walked forward. She dropped some flowers on the grave and the one next to it, her mother's.

She stood for a while, then walked back with the priest. Dan Roy was standing near the trees with Trisha Dunn. With them was an old man she hadn't seen before.

Dan introduced him. "This is Jim McBride. He used to be my boss." Valona shook hands with McBride, feeling the iron grip in the old man's hand. His slate grey eyes were sharp.

"Sorry about your loss. I never knew your father, but knew General Mildred."

Valona nodded, not knowing what else to say. She was grateful when Trisha stepped forward and held her hand.

"Let's walk," Trisha suggested. Valona nodded and they walked off towards the parking lot.

*****

Dan and McBride followed slowly behind. Dan said, "Did you know all along it was Peyton?"

McBride shook his head. "No. But he did tell me to contact Kowalski."

Dan sighed. "So, he wanted you to know as a fail safe. He never had a plan to blow it all sky high. If anything, he dropped you a clue so we could find out what Kowalski knew."

"Yes."

"In a way, he sabotaged his own operation. All he wanted was the attention so he could expose the deniable missions."

"And to atone for his son. I think that drove him till the end."

Dan said, "Crazy."

McBride stopped and looked up at him. "No. Not crazy. When you stand in someone's shoes and try to understand what they're going through, you see it. It made sense for Peyton."

"Well, what I had to go through was crazy."

"You're still here."

"So are you," Dan said. McBride smiled and walked off. Dan watched the old man for a while, then shook his head and walked in the opposite direction. Ahead, he could see Valona and Trisha waiting for him by the car.

THE END

Made in the USA
Coppell, TX
02 July 2020